ENGLISH TRANSFER-PRINTED POTTERY AND PORCELAIN

THE FABER MONOGRAPHS ON POTTERY AND PORCELAIN

Present Editors: R. J. CHARLESTON *and* MARGARET MEDLEY
Former Editors: W. B. HONEY, ARTHUR LANE
and SIR HARRY GARNER

other books by the author
STAFFORDSHIRE POT LIDS AND THEIR POTTERS

ENGLISH TRANSFER-PRINTED POTTERY AND PORCELAIN

A History of Over-Glaze Printing

BY

CYRIL WILLIAMS-WOOD

FABER AND FABER

London   Boston

First published in 1981
by Faber and Faber Limited
3 Queen Square London WC1
Printed in Great Britain by
BAS Printers Limited, Over Wallop, Hampshire
All rights reserved

British Library Cataloguing in Publication Data

Williams-Wood, Cyril
    English transfer-printed pottery and porcelain. –
    (Faber monograph on pottery and porcelain)
    1. Pottery, English – Collectors and collecting
    2. Porcelain, English – Collectors and collecting
    I. Title
    738.2   NK4085

    ISBN 0-571-11694-9

for
THE THREE GRACES
Eleanor, my wife
Marie, my mother
Hermione, my daughter

FOREWORD

The ceramic industry of eighteenth-century England can lay claim to a number of original inventions—bone china, creamware, Wedgwood's 'dry bodies'—but none was more far-reaching in its effects than the development of transfer printing, which allowed two operators in 1756 to decorate in six hours (in their own words) 'more [tiles] in number, and better, and neater than one hundred skilful pot painters'. This technique was destined to play an essential part in the economic success of the British industry in the nineteenth century. The wares of this epoch, however, were mostly transfer-printed underglaze in blue, black and a number of other high-temperature colours. This type of decoration was preceded by on-glaze printing, where it was not necessary for the pigments used to be resistant to the high temperatures required for glaze-firing. The first tentative steps were taken in the enamel industry in the middle years of the eighteenth century, but the process had been transposed to porcelain within a matter of five years, and to various types of pottery—delftware, salt-glazed stoneware and creamware—almost as quickly. Its economic benefits were soon realized, and its expansion was rapid. Underglaze printing, almost exclusively in blue, was introduced on porcelain before 1760, and on pottery became the potent force referred to above. The present book, however, confines itself to the use of on-glaze printing in the earlier phase.

It is surprising that a subject so intimately connected with the rise of the British ceramic industry should have had to wait so long for a book to be devoted to it. The last general survey was William Turner's *Transfer Printing on Enamels, Porcelain and Pottery*, published so long ago as 1907. Mr. Williams-Wood's book should repair this gap.

Mr. Williams-Wood has had practical experience of graphic techniques as an amateur etcher and engraver; and thirty years' close association with the printing and ceramic industries has concentrated his attention on the application of printing methods to the decoration of pottery and porcelain.

R.J.C.

CONTENTS

CONTENTS

ILLUSTRATIONS

*Where no locations are given for pieces in the captions to the plates, they are in private
collections.*

ACKNOWLEDGEMENTS

When engaged in research into ceramic history it is impossible not to be impressed by, and deeply grateful for, the help tendered by fellow collectors, directors of museums and keepers of ceramics and applied arts. Today these are mostly very busy people, but nevertheless invariably they are courteous and helpful and give unstintingly of their time. This book could not have been written without their aid, which varied from the exchange of a few letters to many hours devoted to the unlocking of show-cases, and examination and discussion of specimens; to say nothing of delving into those caverns beneath so many of our museums which seem to hold tenfold more treasures than those displayed in the limited spaces for public exhibition. The assistants and staff have been found always to mirror the amiability of those for whom they work.

To try and weigh the help of one against another would be invidious, so suffice it for the author's sincere appreciation to be recorded to the following, in alphabetical order; and those towards the bottom of the list have his twofold sympathy.

G. F. Arnold

J. S. Ash

J. C. Baker, Keeper of Glass and Ceramics, Sunderland Museum

Lionel A. Burman, Keeper of Ceramics and Applied Art, City of Liverpool Museums

D. W. Cross, Town Clerk, St. Austell with Fowey

Miss M. Mellanay Delhom, Curator of Delhom Gallery, Mint Museum, Charlotte, North Carolina

Miss A. V. Gill, one-time Deputy Director and Keeper of Applied Art, Laing Museum, Newcastle-upon-Tyne

Peter Hughes, one-time Assistant Keeper, Amgueddfa Genedlaethol Cymru, Caerdydd (National Museum of Wales, Cardiff)

Ernest W. Kirtley, one-time Acting Director, Sunderland Museum

A. T. Lucas, Director, Ard-Mhúsaem Na hÉireann (National Museum of Ireland, Dublin)

The late Professor Giuseppe Liverani, Il Direttore, Museo Internazionale delle Ceramiche, Faenza

J. V. G. Mallet, Keeper of Ceramics, Victoria and Albert Museum

Miss Dinah Mitchell, Research Assistant, The British Museum

Arnold Mountford, Director, Stoke-on-Trent City Museum and Art Gallery

R. Oddy, Keeper, The Royal Scottish Museum

Miss Jessica Rutherford, Keeper of Applied Art, Brighton Museum

Henry Sandon, Curator, Worcester Royal Porcelain Museum

John T. Shaw, one-time Director, County Museum, Sunderland

Alan Smith, one-time Director, City of Liverpool Museums

Norman Stretton

John Teahan, Keeper of Art Division, Ard-Mhúsaem Na hÉireann (National Museum of Ireland, Dublin)

Miss Cleo Witt, Curator of Applied Arts, Bristol City Museum and Art Gallery

However, to one friend, without any special interest in ceramics or antiques, is owed an especial debt. This is the late Neville Brooks, Chartered Patent Agent, who some twenty years ago carried out for the author searches at the Public Record Office and Patent Registry, and supplied him with records and copies of many scores of patent applications and specifications, relative to transfer printing and ceramics. These have proved to be of quite inestimable value.

Appreciation must be expressed to Edward G. Hodgkins for his customary diligence when taking the excellent photographs that form the basis of the illustrations, and thanks are also due to those helpful private persons and institutions who have supplied other photographs. Lastly acknowledgement must be made to the publishers, and particularly to Giles de la Mare for his great patience and understanding; to Robert J. Charleston for his ever watchful surveillance; and to Charlotte Roberts for her painstaking and clever interpretation of a complex manuscript when preparing this for the press.

Chapter 1

INTRODUCTION

Although the art of ceramic transfer printing has been practised now for well over two centuries only one book has been exclusively devoted to the subject. This was written as long ago as 1907 by William Turner of Cheltenham.[1] Much that was then accepted as factual is now known to be wrong. In varying degree the same applies to all past works on ceramics, and it is daunting for any author to realize that no matter how much care he has exercised, or how thorough his researches, he will in the not very distant future be proved on many counts to have been in error. There is small comfort to be gained from the words of the late Sir Mortimer Wheeler, who speaking of his early theories on his discoveries at Camulodunum said, 'If it is right for more than half a century, then it must be wrong.' All that can be done is to minimize the possibility of mistakes, and beg the indulgence of those who follow, at the same time seeking comfort in the words of Oliver Goldsmith, 'A book may be amusing with numerous errors, or it may be dull without a single absurdity'.

To deal adequately with the whole history of transfer printing is beyond the capacity of one book. Because of this, underglaze printing has had to be omitted, as also has what is generally referred to as 'bat printing'. The latter is an unhappy phrase used to describe a specialized type of on-glaze transfer printing, from very fine stipple-etched or engraved plates. It was introduced about 1795, and in actual fact was sometimes tissue-transferred, whereas much ordinary line etching and engraving was transferred by gelatine bat. It is, however, a subject that justifies a volume on its own.

In the preparation of the present volume an endeavour has been made as far as is practicable to trace back information to its source. On general matters of ceramic history it is surprising how much of our present knowledge is derived from the writings of Simeon Shaw and Joseph Mayer.[2] Shaw was probably one

---

[1] *Transfer Printing on Enamels, Porcelain and Pottery*, London.
[2] Shaw, *History of the Staffordshire Potteries*, Hanley, 1829; Mayer, *The Art of Pottery*, Liverpool, 1855; and *History of the Progress of Pottery in Liverpool*, Liverpool, 1871.

of the most obsequious, parochial and irritating authors of all time; nevertheless an enormous debt is due to him for an incredible amount of information which cannot be obtained from other sources. Many of his facts and dates are now known to be erroneous, but for a vast volume of the information he has recorded there is no alternative to accepting his word. Even with the risk of some inaccuracy, our knowledge is abundantly richer through his writings. Joseph Mayer was no different in his great enthusiasm over local affairs and reputations, and his statements need to be accepted with caution; this is particularly necessary when considering his observations about transfer printing in Liverpool.

Until the close of the nineteenth century the industrial revolution had little effect on transfer printing or on the ceramic industry generally, and a workman of 1770 would have been at home in a pottery of 1870, noticing only that power was supplied by steam, instead of by wind, water, horses and small boys. The process of transfer printing remained largely unaltered for at least a hundred and thirty years after its invention in 1753, so that the frequently applied and arbitrary division into craftsmanship up to 1830, and mechanization thenceforth, is quite invalid.

Because wages were so pitiful, it is not generally realized how very expensive in real terms were fine-quality pottery and porcelain in the eighteenth century. As a rough guide, the prices of 1750 must be multiplied by one hundred to obtain some idea of the 1980 equivalent in real terms. Pottery and porcelain in themselves were comparatively cheap, but anything other than simple decoration was beyond the reach of all except the affluent. Transfer printing changed this, and made pleasantly ornamented wares available to the rapidly expanding middle classes. Josiah Wedgwood in 1774 charged the Empress of Russia £3,000 for a dinner service of 952 pieces, but it is remarkable that the average factory-cost of the creamware pieces was five and a half old pence each, whereas the decoration involved him in an expenditure exceeding two pounds per article.[3] Later, in 1816, when the value of money was less, the Worcester Porcelain Company charged the Prince Regent three guineas each for plates, and three and a half guineas for soup plates.[4] By comparison the price Sadler and Green charged Josiah Wedgwood in 1783 for printing a service of 250 pieces for David Garrick was £8 6s 1½d, or an average of sixpence per piece, roughly equal to the cost of the creamware articles.[5] The price of modern china shows that proportionately little has changed.

[3] William Chaffers, *Marks and Monograms on Pottery and Porcelain*, London, 1874, 15th ed. 1965, Vol. II, pp. 31–2.
[4] R. H. Binns, *Worcester Pottery and Porcelain 1751–1851*, 1877, p. 242.
[5] Llewllynn Jewitt, *The Ceramic Art of Great Britain*, London, 1878, Vol. II, p. 31.

FOREIGN CLAIMANTS TO THE INVENTION OF
TRANSFER PRINTING

It is sometimes a problem even for the experienced to decide whether an early piece is transfer-printed, or hand pencilled.[6] If the picture is underglaze the assessment is a much more formidable one. This is because the cobalt used in both pencilling and printing became circumfused with the surrounding glaze. That difficulty has led to wrong judgements followed by much speculation and error.

The marriage of printing and ceramics occurred in the middle of the eighteenth century, and has always been considered a British achievement. It has been the subject of considerable research over the last seventy years, and although there is argument over detail, its history is well documented and confirmed by surviving marked, and often dated, pieces. It comes as a shock to our accepted beliefs that in 1971 a claim was advanced that the invention of transfer printing under glaze preceded that on the glaze, and was of Italian origin. Roberto Bondi is the author of a published paper advancing the theory that the first underglaze blue printing took place at Doccia.[7] This factory near Florence was founded in 1735 by the Marchese Carlo Ginori, and is famous for its high quality porcelain. Its products were invariably unmarked until very late in the eighteenth century. Bondi illustrated a number of examples chiefly from tea-sets, but also a porcelain snuff-box, two large bowls and a dish. One of these pieces is a teapot in the Victoria and Albert Museum with an underglaze blue picture (Plate 11). This is a genre subject of children, after an engraving, *Les Jeux et Plaisirs de L'Enfance*, Paris, 1673. It and some of the bowls and saucers are attributed by Bondi as having been made between 1740 and 1755.

Because the decoration is entirely underglaze the pieces do present an unusually difficult problem, but it is the opinion of the present author that there is no transfer printing on them and that they are entirely hand pencilled. It is remarkable that of the twenty-eight examples illustrated in the paper, as well as twenty-one others to which reference is made, none has precisely the same picture. Furthermore, arguments advanced to prove that the designs were transfer printed are technically unsound. Many ceramic experts seem to be of the opinion that if the decoration on a piece is in fine line, and has hatching and stipple, then it must have been transferred from an intaglio plate. This is quite wrong. A pen-and-ink artist working on paper can only show shading by hatching and stipple, in the same manner as an etcher or engraver. (That is ignoring washes of different strength, which are not relevant.) It has to be proved that the Doccia pieces do not carry carefully pencilled pictures

[6] 'Pencil' is used throughout, in its eighteenth-century and correct meaning of painting with a small fine brush, usually of sable.
[7] 'La Decorazione a Riporto Nella Produzione Primitiva di Doccia', *Faenza*, 1971, Florence, Vol. 57, p. 38 et seq.

executed on the bisque, in the same way as a pen-and-ink sketch, except that a very fine brush would have been used. An engraved line must start at a point where the graver touches the metal, and widens as the requisite pressure and forward motion is applied. Similarly, as the pressure is released at the end, and the graver lifted, the line narrows to zero. As a result, each end, under magnification, will be seen to be of lanceolate shape. A line made with a brush is quite different, for both ends tend to be half-rounded, or even clavate. Unless the artist is careful, and never has his brush fully charged, this tends to be worse at the end that the brush is lifted, because due to gravity and molecular adhesion the pigment tries to form a blob. In the case of the Doccia teapot, it will be seen that all lines have very rounded ends.

Of the forty-nine examples to which reference is made, no less than thirty-four are stated to have the figures printed, and the backgrounds pencilled. A distinction in style which could lead to this belief is clearly visible on the teapot in the Victoria and Albert Museum. However, the suggestion that in so many pieces parts of single pictures are printed and parts pencilled is difficult to accept in view of the fact that the *raison d'être* of transfer printing is that it permits serial production without the need for additional hand work. Such a combination of different techniques would seem to stultify the whole purpose of transfer printing. Of the illustrations accompanying the paper three have designs which comprise somewhat similar groups to those in three other designs, but with different backgrounds. Nevertheless, the figures themselves differ in detail. A possible explanation is that the Doccia factory employed an artist who was a talented and faithful copyist, as were many Chinese artists who decorated Jesuit ware, and that he pencilled the figures. In conformity with the centuries-old custom of Florentine and other artists, it is conceivable that these porcelain pieces were then handed over to less talented painters to pencil in various backgrounds.

This difficulty of discrimination between carefully hand-pencilled work and transfer printing, even if on-glaze, can be a trap for the expert. An example that well illustrates the danger is a Worcester Porcelain Company's saucer of 1757, with the familiar portrait of the King of Prussia. It figured as recently as the autumn of 1973 in the catalogue of a firm of most reputable auctioneers, described as follows: 'A RARE WORCESTER SAUCER, printed in black and washed with coloured enamels with a portrait of the King of Prussia.' This piece is illustrated because in actual fact there is not a printed line or dot on it (Plate 12). The outline is hand pencilled in a variety of shades from grey and grey-brown to drab, and the delicate polychrome washes are obviously by the same artist. It was purchased by one of the most renowned dealers in early Worcester porcelain who, also thinking it was printed, sold and invoiced it as such. A comparison with the Robert Hancock print of the same subject on a Worcester mug will emphasize the difference in techniques (Plate 24). The print is monochrome in a deep brown-black.

IMPRINTS

Great confusion exists over the meaning of names and initials found on ceramic transfer prints, and it is essential to appreciate the alternatives that these can signify. With ordinary publishing there are four types of imprint, any one, two, three or all of which may appear at the foot of a print. When acknowledgement was made of the artist or painter his name was succeeded by any one of the following, *pinxit, pictor, pinx., delineavit, delineator, delin., invenit, inventor, inv.,* or *figuravit.* The name of the engraver of a copper plate was followed by *sculpsit, sculptor, sculpt., sc., incidit, incisor, incid., inc., caelavit,* or *caelator*, and that of an etcher by *fecit, fec.,* or *f.* The distinction is somewhat blurred when a plate is both etched and engraved, as so often happened with transfer printing, and the term used then shows the method employed considered by the artist as predominant. The publisher was often described as such, or by *pub.,* or *divulgavit.* Finally the printer's name, if not described as such, was followed by *formis, excudit, excud.,* or *exc.*

With transfer printing it is unfortunate that the imprint was often confined to a single name or rebus, and it can refer to artist, engraver or etcher, printer or publisher. Lack of appreciation of the possible implication of an imprint has led to much erroneous conjecture as to who were engravers or transfer printers. Therefore it is necessary to be clear on the possible references. A single name or rebus may be that of:

(1) The artist from whose picture or engraving on paper the transfer-printing plate was copied, such as Murillo, Teniers, etc. This is infrequent.
(2) The etcher or engraver of the copper plate used for the transfer printing, like Hancock, Rothwell or Abbey.
(3) The transfer printer who could also be the engraver, as Abbey or Radford, or a separate person like Sadler, Johnson or Holdship.
(4) The publisher, who could be either the printer, such as Sadler or Fletcher, the potter, such as Christian or Greatbatch, or the potter's customer like Mortlock or Jackson.

It was customary when the potter or his customer paid for the copper printing-plate for him to have his name added as an imprint. That had the advantage of deterring the transfer printer from using the plate for the decoration of his own or a competitor's wares. These imprints have caused much confusion, for potters like William Greatbatch, Philip Christian and John Aynsley, to name but a few, almost certainly never engraved or transfer printed in their lives. If a factory opened its own transfer-printing department, as did those at Worcester and Derby, it automatically became the publisher, and often had its name as such in the form of an imprint. Towards the end of the eighteenth century these imprints were engraved or etched on the copper plates separated from the designs. After printing they were snipped from the tissues, and transferred to the backs of the ceramic pieces, where they also served as back-marks.

It is noticeable that when a potter plagiarized a competitor's design he usually omitted any imprint. Furthermore, many retailers refused to handle marked pieces for fear that customers might buy directly from the potter. Some, like Mortlock, insisted on having their own marks, which often described them as manufacturers.

METHODS OF PICTORIAL PRINTING

The arts of the graphic printer and of the potter are quite distinct in their origins, and up to the mid-eighteenth century in their histories. Printing is a comparatively recent accomplishment of man, having been invented by the Chinese in the sixth century AD, while potting goes back to prehistory; certainly to more than a hundred centuries BC. Transfer printing is popularly divided into three categories known as on-glaze, underglaze and 'bat printing', as we have seen. None of these terms is descriptive in any way of the type of printing involved. Without some knowledge of the various printing methods that have been used for transfer work, it is impossible to appreciate the skills and efforts that have contributed to the decoration of a ceramic piece.

Block and plate printing have been used as a mode of expression by the most famous artists, including such masters as Albrecht Dürer and Rembrandt van Rijn, and in this country by William Hogarth and J. M. W. Turner. Each printing technique, and there are many, has its own idiosyncrasies of expression, its own characteristics and singularities; and each of these its own nuances in the hands of different artists. When prints are transferred to ceramics it is inevitable that some of these qualities are lost: nevertheless, enough remain to interest and fascinate.

All printing falls into three broad categories: surface, intaglio and planographic. For graphic printing the first two use blocks or plates where parts of the surface are lowered, leaving the unworked portions at the original level. In surface printing the original or highest parts of a block or plate are inked and supply the printed impression. It comprises all woodcuts, line and half-tone blocks and all printing type, and is the process used for the vast majority of cheap popular printing, including newspapers, magazines and books. By contrast, intaglio printing is a system where the design is sunk in a metal surface and the cavities are filled with ink. After the untouched highest parts are cleaned, the hollows then give the printed impression. All engraving, etching, mezzotinting, and aquatinting fall into this category. Planographic printing, as the name suggests, is when the printing surface remains perfectly flat. Known as lithography, it was not invented until the turn of the nineteenth century, and does not concern this volume.

The earliest known woodcuts are Chinese, dating from AD 594. It took almost six hundred years for the art to spread to Europe. The *St. Christopher* woodcut, considered to be of English origin, is dated 1423, but it was not until the end of the eighteenth century that we find a really outstanding British-born woodcut artist. He was Thomas Bewick (1753–1828), a countryman, born and bred in Northumberland (Plate 47). He had an amazing power of observation and talent for carving in the minutest detail miniature woodcuts, sometimes as small as two centimetres square; and he may at one time have been associated with the St. Anthony's Pottery of Newcastle-upon-Tyne.

In the early days a piece was cut from a plank of comparatively soft wood, such as sycamore, beech or fruit-wood, and upon this a drawing was made in black ink. From the surface of the block were carved away to a depth of about a quarter of a centimetre all those portions of the picture which were to remain white on the finished print, leaving the drawing standing proud (Plate 1). Towards the end of the eighteenth century, boxwood came into use, and this was prepared so that the working surface showed a section across the grain. Such blocks could be worked in any direction without risk of splintering up the grain. They accepted much finer detail, and had a very much longer working life.

The block was inked by means of a roller, or a pad of soft leather called a dabber, charged with thick printing ink. A suitable dampened piece of paper was then placed on the face of the block, and the two subjected to vertical pressure, usually in a simple press (Plate 2).

Until the last quarter of the nineteenth century the overwhelming proportion of the printing of ceramics was based on the use of intaglio plates. The plate, usually of copper, could be worked in a number of ways, but no matter what method was used the manner of printing was the same. The plate was heated until just bearable to the touch, and the ink similarly. This made the latter more fluent, and when the entire surface of the plate was covered the ink was forced into every recess however fine, by means of a dabber or dolly covered in leather and charged with ink. The plate was then cleaned on the surface by means firstly of a flexible spatula, then a soft muslin rag, and sometimes finally by the ball of the thumb. Still hot, the plate was placed face upwards on the bed of a plate printing-press, and a suitable piece of dampened paper was placed on top. Over this were laid blankets for padding. By means of a spoked wheel the whole bed then moved between rollers, rather like an old-time domestic mangle, which forced the paper into the recesses where it picked up the ink. The pressure could be as much as three tonnes, depending on the width of the plate, for at any time it was concentrated on a thin line immediately between the rollers (Plate 3).

The reason that dampened paper is almost invariably used in intaglio printing is twofold. Firstly, it softens the fibres and enables the paper to be forced into the recesses of the plate, and secondly, because of the antipathy between oil and water, it prevents the oleaginous pigment, while warm and in its most fluid state, from being absorbed by the paper.

Engraving was at one time the most popular method of preparing the printing plate. Its origin is lost in antiquity, but the idea of printing from engraved metal is reputed to be attributable to the goldsmiths of Florence in the fifteenth century. The design is cut in the plate with a tool called a graver. This is a diminutive chisel with an inclined diamond-shaped cutting edge, and a rounded handle which fits the palm of the hand. Mostly it is pushed forward by the artist, and makes an incised line with a curved sliver of metal on one side, much as a plough makes a furrow and a ridge. The expelled metal is removed by another tool called a scraper. Usually the plate is held by one hand on a small, hard, sand-filled pillow of kid leather. By dextrously rotating the plate, and always pressing the graver straight forward with the other hand, free curving lines are obtainable in any direction. Nevertheless, engraving is a long and arduous process, and it is very troublesome to correct a mistake. Because it is such an exacting art, today it is all but moribund.

By far the most popular form of intaglio printing, and one used extensively in ceramic decoration, is etching. It is a method of preparing a plate, not by cutting, engraving or punching, but by biting or eating the lines into the metal with acid. Armourers first used the process for the decoration of weapons in feudal times. The craft was developed and popularized by Jacques Callot (1592–1635), who devised the method of biting lines of differing depths by the use of multiple acid baths.

Until the mid-nineteenth century etching was nearly always a preliminary to the preparation of plates used for transfer printing on pottery and porcelain, so it is as well that the process should be thoroughly understood. A copper plate of between one and a half and three millimetres thick, after being scrupulously cleaned with whiting and ammonia, is covered on one surface with an etching ground, which is a preparation to resist acid. This has to be soft enough to be removed easily by an etching needle, with a minimum of pressure; it must not flake or crack; and it must be tenacious enough to cling to the metal in the minutest quantities which may be left between lines or stipple. Usually it is based on beeswax or white wax. It is either laid in powder form on a heated plate, or in solution with chloroform, ether or spike of lavender, which evaporate in seconds to leave a thin skin. Then most etchers smoke the surface so that the design will show up brightly during the course of the work. That is simply done by holding the plate inverted over a candle or taper, but not so close as to melt the wax (Plate 4).

The artist draws on the wax with an etching needle, as if using a pencil, held almost at right angles to the surface. No great pressure is required, for it is undesirable to score the metal. An etching needle, which may be of various thicknesses, is a simple tool, like a pencil with a steel needle instead of graphite. Should an error be made it can easily be corrected by painting over the area with liquid ground, and re-drawing. The facility of etching compared with engraving is illustrated, probably unconsciously, by Abraham Bosse in a picture of an art gallery, with artists at work, back to back, with a light reflector

1 *The Woodcutter*: WOODCUT by Jost Amman, in H. Schopper's *Panoplia Omnium Artium*, Frankfurt, 1586. *See page 29*
British Museum

2 *The Printers*: WOODCUT by Jost Amman, in H. Schopper's *Panoplia Omnium Artium*, Frankfurt, 1586. *See page 29*
British Museum

3 *Intaglio Printers at Work*: ENGRAVING by Abraham Bosse in *Lislle du Palais*, Paris (sic), 1642. *See page 29*
British Museum

between them. The etcher is smiling and in a relaxed posture, in marked contrast to the intent concentration and awkward attitude of the engraver (Plate 5).

When finished the edges and back of the plate are protected with Brunswick black, and the plate lowered into an acid bath. Etching mordants vary like etching grounds, but most are based on hydrochloric acid, nitric acid, or a combination of both. By Jacques Callot's method, when the finest lines are bitten sufficiently deeply the plate is removed from the bath, washed, and these lines are painted over with an acid-resistant stopping-out varnish. The plate is then immersed again in the acid until the next finest lines are adequately bitten. The process can be repeated *ad infinitum*; four or five times are customary. After cleaning with methylated spirits and turpentine to remove all traces of ground, stopping and backing, the plate is ready for printing.

Many artists strengthen an etched plate by engraving over the etching for the deepest shadows and strongest lines. While this is frowned upon by purists, it was introduced by no less a person than Albrecht Dürer. From the earliest days a combination of etching and engraving has been employed on plates for ceramic transfer printing. Firstly, the design was etched, which allowed for fluid lines and free draughtsmanship, and if necessary was easy to alter. After biting, the plate was then over-engraved to strengthen the shadows and foreground, thereby providing perspective. It is lack of appreciation of such a dual method of preparation of plates for transfer printing that leads so many ceramic experts to the belief that transfer-printed designs have often been over-pencilled by hand to give emphasis or correct faulty printing. The re-engraving of worn plates also inspires the same mistake.

When coloured prints were required for pictures, playing-cards or maps, it was customary well into the nineteenth century for the colour to be added by hand painting to monochrome impressions from woodcuts, engravings, etchings, mezzotints and aquatints (Plate 6). It is true that over the centuries desultory attempts had been made to print from multiple blocks or plates—one for each colour, sometimes as many as thirty—and to register these on the paper, but the processes were so difficult, exacting and fallible that they never prospered. It was not until George Baxter (1804–67) perfected his process in 1835, which employed a combination of an intaglio plate and wood-blocks, that any commercially viable method was achieved.[8]

The difficulty with multiple blocks was to obtain impressions in perfect register, and the method used by Baxter and all before him was known as 'pricking'. This entailed piercing the paper with a number of pins. Obviously this could not be done to ceramic pieces, which is the reason that transfer printing, until a method of registration of transfers was invented in the 1840s, was coloured by overpainting with ceramic enamels.

Mention should perhaps be made of a little used means of obtaining prints in

[8] Patent specification No. 6916/1835. Inrolled 23 April 1836.

4 *The Making of an Etching*: ENGRAVING by Abraham Bosse in *De la Manière de Graver*, Paris, 1658. *See page 30*
British Museum

5 *The Etcher and the Engraver*: ENGRAVING by Abraham Bosse in *Lisle du Palais*, Paris, 1643. *See page 32*
British Museum

two or three colours from a single printing plate, by painting fairly large areas with different coloured inks. It was very difficult, and time consuming, to prevent the colours fouling each other. As far as is known, it was used once only for a 'bat print' on Herculaneum pottery, and by John Davenport for some underglaze printing, both in the nineteenth century. The 'Liverpool' floral plates sometimes referred to as colour printed, are, in the opinion of the author, hand-enamelled prints.

IDENTIFICATION OF TRANSFER PRINTS

The tiro at print collecting either on paper or ceramics, as a matter of course, asks how to distinguish the method by which a particular print has been produced. This is as difficult to explain to a beginner as how to attribute to an individual factory a piece of unmarked pottery or porcelain by paste and glaze. The artist's practice of combining two or more methods of producing intaglio plates is sometimes confusing enough when executed on paper, but it is much more so with transfer printing on ceramics.

The woodcut has its limitations; intaglio printing permits finer detail and strength of line. It is because the thickness of ink carried by a plate is considerably greater than that picked up by a wood-block. The difference is easily felt by running the tip of a finger over an engraved visiting-card or letter-heading. It is this amplitude of ink that makes the process so suitable for transfer a second time to a ceramic surface. With woodcuts, as with lithographs, it is possible to show solid areas of print. That is impossible with intaglio plates, because in such a solid area the ink would be wiped out when the plate was cleaned. The artist overcomes this by hatching and cross-hatching. However, a watch must always be kept for hand washes in the same colour as the print, and with underglaze blue circumfusion often produces solid areas from fine cross-hatching.

A preponderance of white lines on black usually denotes a woodcut made since 1770, and these lines often taper to a point at the ends. Before that date the black lines were usually thicker than those made by intaglio plates, and much less free. They tended frequently to branch from other lines. When lines cross, as for example when delineating a fishing net or shading by means of cross-hatching, the wood-carver has to painstakingly cut away numbers of little diamonds and other shapes representing the white spaces. Seldom is this so skilfully done that under a glass the residual black lines look perfectly straight. The engraver or etcher has no more difficulty in making lines across than does a draughtsman with a pen or pencil on paper.

Line engraving and etching are confusing because of the frequency with which they were used in combination. By engraving it is easier to make deep, sharp-edged lines, but in etching much freer lines are possible. With on-glaze transfer printing it is often possible to detect under a glass the difference

6 *The Print Colourer*: WOODCUT by Jost Amman, in H. Schopper's *Panoplia Omnium Artium*, Frankfurt, 1586. *See page 32*
British Museum

between etched and engraved lines by examination of their ends. Engraved lines tend to terminate in a lance shape, whereas acid rounds the ends of etched lines. Perhaps the most important distinction is the fact that an engraved line can be thick or thin according to the depth and width of the incision in the metal due to the pressure placed on the graver; but an etched line, although it can be of varying thickness according to the size of the needle used, is of much the same breadth throughout its length, having been made by the needle passing only through the wax. Much the same distinction is apparent in stipple-work. The flick of a graver or a dry-point needle makes a sharp irregular spot often of triangular or polygonal shape, which contrasts with the more rounded dot of an etching needle, further rounded by the action of the acid. When both processes have been used they can be detected by the underlying evenly etched dotting, beneath the engraved coarser stipple of the darker tones.

COLOUR

Colour is the hardest of all qualities to convey in words. It is however of the greatest importance in transfer printing, and in describing the glaze and paste of ceramic articles. Attempts have been made to classify and describe colours:

in America by the Munsell system, and in this country by the British Standards
Institution. Only the Munsell system is comprehensive enough to cover all
hues and shades met with in the study of ceramics, but if the serious collector
has not this for reference, it is recommended that the three standards published
by the British Standards Institution be obtained.[9]

The problem is that all colours are met with in a variety of tints and shades,
and complication is increased by a multiplicity of names for the same colour,
and the common use of the same names for different colours. Throughout this
book care has been taken to use the same terminology for any single colour, and
at the end is a glossary of terms showing the Munsell references, as well as the
equivalent British Standards reference number, where such a standard
exists.[10] This applies to the colours of transfer prints as well as to the colours of
ceramic bodies and glazes. When assessing a colour, as solid a piece of printing,
or as thick an area of glaze, as possible should be selected, for other areas will
show a lighter tint.

A large proportion of on-glaze printing occurs on creamware, and colour can
be very helpful in both attribution and dating. First to consider is the overall
surface colouring, and then the colour of the actual glaze where it is thickest.
That is often in the angles formed by footrims, spouts and handles. The
following approximate tables may be helpful, although it must be borne in
mind that they are by no means comprehensive, and that vagaries in materials
and firing conditions often caused variations from the normal. Some firms like
that of Josiah Wedgwood made a steady progression from a dark tint to a light,
while others like the Leeds Pottery produced many different hues
concurrently.

Transfer-printed Creamware

	Factories	*Approxi-mate dates*	
Surface colours			
Pale biscuit	Leeds Pottery	1820–	
Cane	Wedgwood, Josiah	1761–1763	
	Leeds Pottery	1761–1765	
Pale manilla	Wedgwood, Josiah	1762–1765	
	Leeds Pottery	1765–1775	
Very pale lime	Derby Pot Works	1764–	Very smooth paste

[9] BS 381C: 1964; BS 4800: 1972; and BS 2660: 1955.
[10] See p. 00.

Pale reseda	Melbourne Pottery	1775–	
	Neale and Co.	1776–	Very smooth paste
	Leeds Pottery	1795–	
	Castleford Pottery	1795–	Sandy body
Pale cream	Wedgwood, Josiah	1765–1768	
	Leeds Pottery	1775–1780	Creamy or chalky
Ivory	Wedgwood, Josiah	1768–1785	
	Leeds Pottery	1775–	
	Swansea Pottery	1790–	Sandy body
	Low Ford Pottery	1795–	Very smooth paste
	Herculaneum Pottery	1796–	
	Ring, Bristol	1800–	
	Wear Pottery	1803–	Very smooth paste
	Garrison Pottery	1807–	Very smooth paste
Off-white	Wedgwood, Josiah	1785–	

Glazes

Buttercup	Leeds Pottery	1761–1775	Mostly uncrazed
Primrose	Wedgwood, Josiah	1762–1768	Crazing rare
	Leeds Pottery	1775–1787	Mostly uncrazed
	John Turner	1775–	
	Ring, Bristol	1786–	
Pale canary	Leeds Pottery	1760–1775	Mostly uncrazed
Pale straw	Wedgwood, Josiah	1761–	Often crazed
	Leeds Pottery	1820–1825	Mostly uncrazed
Reseda	Neale and Co.	1775–1785	
	Herculaneum Pottery	1796–	Often crazed

Pale reseda	Wedgwood, Josiah	1768–1775	Crazing rare
Pale lime	Derby Pot Works	1765–1779	Linear crazing
Lime tinted	Swansea Pottery	1790–	
Very pale eau-de-Nil	Wedgwood, Josiah	1775–1785	Crazing rare
	Melbourne Pottery	1775–	
	Leeds Pottery	1775–1780	
	Low Ford Pottery	1797–	
	Garrison Pottery	1810–1820	
Pale grass-green	Leeds Pottery	1795–1815	
	Castleford Pottery	1795–1815	
French grey	Leeds Pottery	1785–1825	
	Castleford Pottery	1790–	Sandy body
Pale olive	Leeds Pottery	1765–1780	
Colourless	Wedgwood, Josiah	1785–	Thin and even
	Leeds Pottery	1785–	
	Swansea Pottery	1790–	
	Low Ford Pottery	1795–	
	Wear Pottery	1803–	

CERAMIC KILNS

To understand the early development of transfer printing and its progression from japanned wares to enamels, and finally to ceramics, it is necessary to have knowledge of the completely different firing conditions requisite for ceramics, which made it impossible for those engaged in either of the other trades with their existing equipment to fire pottery or porcelain. The kilns, temperatures and methods of firing, virtually prohibited even experimental work on materials other than those for which the stoves and diminutive kilns had been constructed.

Ceramic kilns had to be gargantuan, and the temperatures required in glost kilns (that is, those used for glazing) ranged from 1,000°C for earthenware to 1,400°C for hard-paste porcelain. The most fundamental difference, however, was that until the present century all pottery and porcelain had to be fired in what are known as intermittent kilns. These were loaded in a cold state, fired, held at maximum temperature for some hours—a period known as soaking—and allowed slowly to cool. That took up to four and a half days for porcelain, and perhaps a day less for earthenware. The reason it took so long was that contemporary earthenware and particularly porcelain were extremely sensitive to thermal shock, and therefore had to be heated slowly and evenly, and cooled still more carefully. Only ovens of great capacity were in any way economic because, after loading was complete, the body of the kiln and all the kiln furniture had to be heated from air temperature, and at the finish cooled again, before the contents could be removed. The kiln furniture included the great mass of the saggars and muffles described below.

By fluxing the ceramic pigments the hardening-on of on-glaze transfer prints could be done at slightly lower temperatures, 700°C up to 1,000°C, but the underlying glaze still had to be brought to a viscous state for proper fusion to take place. Much porcelain of the eighteenth century would not stand boiling water, so that even after manufacture and glazing the hardening-on of transfer prints at eight times or more that temperature was of necessity a very slow process. As one would expect, most firing-on of prints on glazed porcelain and pottery was originally carried out in the ceramic enamelling ovens. If the prints were hand coloured, one firing sufficed for both prints and enamels. In the mid-eighteenth century bottle ovens were used for this, and it was necessary to protect the contents from flames, flying ash and fumes which would stain. This was achieved by the ceramic pieces being placed in saggars, which were refractory boxes made of fire clay and 'grog' (broken pieces of old fired saggars), which minimized the cracking of the saggars themselves. Later, muffle kilns were introduced, which were kilns with inner refractory shells to protect the contents from all direct contact with the source of heat. A great economy of labour and space (therefore fuel) resulted. In the next chapter is explained how completely different were the firing requirements of japanned wares and enamels.

Chapter 2

INVENTION OF
TRANSFER PRINTING

There is a story of the inspiration for printing on pottery which, as so often with ceramic inventions, is no doubt apocryphal. John Sadler, a Liverpool printer, is said to have come out of his works and found children, to whom he had given some spoiled prints to play with, sticking them on pieces of broken pottery for the ornamentation of their doll's houses.[1] This, it is averred, gave him the idea of decorating pottery with printed pictures. In any case, Sadler was not the originator, for his success came four years after the process had been invented and well publicized. Another widely accepted theory rests on the fact that for the use of the many scores of priests at the Catholic mission at Macao, the Chinese pottery at Ching-tê-chên produced in the seventeenth and eighteenth centuries white porcelain tableware, which was decorated with hand-painted copies of Dutch, Italian and Portugese engravings, and known as Jesuit ware. These were so skilfully executed as to look exactly like original engravings, and the examples that reached Europe were supposed to have set men thinking of the possibilities of printing on pottery and porcelain. That theory was probably no more correct than the first.

In the mid-eighteenth century, it had become a fashionable craze to cut out engravings and, after sticking these on japanned trays and other domestic articles, to colour them and paint over the whole with transparent lacquers. When the hobby had become popular enough to justify it, there began to be published both in loose sheets and in bound parts a sort of do-it-yourself kit which included special instructions. The bound publications by Robert Sayer (1725–94) of Fleet Street in the City of London are believed to have been issued in three successive editions. They were given the title *The Ladies' Amusement or Whole Art of Japanning Made Easy*. As the title implies they were essentially intended for amateurs, and the japanning process described

[1] First recorded by Joseph Mayer in a paper read to the Historical Society of Lancashire and Cheshire, 1871, p. 55.

did not in any way resemble the commercial craft. It is thought that each subsequent edition embodied the original designs with further engravings added. Robert Sayer from about 1751 had a prosperous business as a print seller and artist's sundriesman on the south side of Fleet Street at the corner of Mitre Alley. In 1755 he entered into partnership with J. Bennett. Many of the prints carry no publisher's imprint, but more than half have his sole name as such, so it is a reasonable assumption that these sheets were first published prior to 1755. An edition of *The Gentleman's Magazine* in 1760 contained an advertisement for *The Ladies' Amusement* under the classification 'Miscellaneous New Books'.[2] This must have referred to one of the reissues. The only extant copies are thought to be of the second edition which comprised two hundred sheets with nearly fifteen hundred designs. Any additional illustrations embodied in the third issue are today unknown. Although it does not appear to have been the intention of the publisher, the pictures later proved to be a great source of inspiration for commercial artists in a number of trades—not least that of ceramic transfer printing.

Sayer made use of five artists whose initials or names figured in imprints. They were Charles Fenn, Roësel, Jean Pillement (1727–1808), E. Walker and A.B.[3] The works of these artists were engraved by eight engravers, Peter Paul Benazech (d. 1783), Kenton Couse (1721–90), William Elliot (1727–66), C. H. Hemmerich, Robert Hancock,[4] J. June (fl. 1740–70), James Roberts and K. Stevens. The designs comprise all types of floral specimens, sprigs, bouquets and arrangements, insects and birds of every sort, shells, domestic and wild animal studies, street scenes, rural views, genre subjects, Chinese architecture and figures, sailing vessels, amorous and sporting studies, extravaganzas, festoons and borders.

Some designs were copied without alteration for transfer printing. An example is *The Salutation* found printed by Sadler and Green on delftware tiles (Plate 49). It is a reproduction of the vignette in the top right-hand corner of plate 28 of the guide (Plate 7). Other transfer-printed designs were made up of a combination of smaller items. Examples are the famous *Liverpool Birds* designs used also by Sadler and Green for Josiah Wedgwood and other customers (Plates 71–4). These were almost certainly inspired by birds featured on a number of different plates by Charles Fenn.

The volume commenced with the instructions, 'The Art of Japanning Made Easy'. Here are formulae for making transparent varnishes of various colours by mixing pigments with diluted gum arabic (acacia gum), or with a medium made from 'Quince-Kernals'. After hand colouring the designs on the paper,

'The several Objects you intend to Use must be neatly cut round with
Scisars or the small Point of a Knife; these Figures must be brush'd over on

[2] February 1760, Vol. XXX, p. 96.
[3] These initials are confined to six floral studies, and the drawings could be the work of the famous botanist Anna Blackburne (d. 1794).
[4] See p. 58 et seq.

7 *The Salutation* and other prints: ENGRAVINGS by William Elliot, after E. Walker, from *The Ladies' Amusement or Whole Art of Japanning Made Easy*, pub. Robert Sayer, London, c. 1755. *See page 41*

the Back with strong Gum-water, or thin Paste, made by boiling Flour in Water: then take the Objects singly, and with a Pair of small Pliers, fix them on the Place intended, being careful to let no Figure seem tumbling, and let the Buildings preserve an exact upright . . . and when properly plac'd, lay over your Prints a Piece of clean Paper, and with your Hand gently press them even.'[5]

There then follow instructions for the application of between seven and twelve coats of varnish, which after hardening for several days is polished with tripoli (decomposed silica) on a piece of cork, and finally with rottenstone (decomposed limestone). No stoving was required.

The hobby would naturally have inspired the idea of printing straight on to the japanned wares. In the event just such a method was devised by John Brooks in Birmingham in the 1750s, and there is a direct chain of development

[5]P. 5.

8 *The Draw Well* (in mirror image): Pull on potter's tissue from copper plate engraved by Robert Hancock for transfer printing. 138 mm (5.4 in) high. *See pages 44, 84 Worcester Royal Porcelain Company Limited*

from this decoration of japanned ware, through the ornamentation of enamels, to ceramic transfer printing. The method devised required the preparation of an intaglio printing-plate, or a woodcut, from a selected picture or drawing. Copper plates could be either etched or engraved, or in a high proportion of cases produced by a combination of both methods. Because two successive impressions take place in transfer printing, first on a transfer medium and then on the ceramic or other article, reversal of the picture on the printing plate is unnecessary. In this respect the artist's work was simpler than that of an engraver or etcher preparing a plate in mirror image for printing on paper.

Because of this difference, we know conclusively that in the early days plates made for printing on paper were often used for the decoration of enamels and ceramics, and vice versa. A well-known example is an engraving of Maria Gunning, Countess of Coventry (1733–60), thought to have been the work of John Brooks about 1755, found on enamel plaques, which it is believed was subsequently used for printing on paper.[6] Even more striking are ceramic pieces decorated with prints signed in reverse — that is in mirror image. A number of early pieces made by the Worcester Porcelain Company are like this, and these are considered in the section dealing with that factory (see pages 70–91).

For most transfer printing the vehicle of transfer employed was a piece of tissue paper. This was dampened in a solution of soapy water. It was wetted, as for conventional intaglio printing, to make it soft, but soap was added to prevent too much absorption of the oil in the ink by the thin tissue, and to act as a parting medium after the impression was transferred to the ceramic piece (Plate 8). It was most important that both the ink and the printing plate should be kept heated, for ceramic ink even more than printing ink, if cold, would have been too thick to be workable. The plate had still to be hot when passed through the press, otherwise the ink would have stuck to it, as would the tissue. A perfectly normal plate printing-press without modification was employed (Plate 9).

All smooth-surfaced articles, including glazed ceramic pieces, needed to be prepared for receiving the transfers by being painted with a size, varnish or some other resinous material. When dry this provided a tooth which facilitated the adhesion of the impression, but in the case of ceramics later volatilized and vanished in the kiln. The omission of this simple practice, which with hindsight is so obvious, was the cause of many early failures of would-be pioneers of the process.

With underglaze transfer printing such sizing was unnecessary, because of the more receptive texture of the bisque, but when on-glaze it was an absolute essential if proper adhesion of the transferred ink was to be obtained. It is of interest that Jean Rouquet, giving a somewhat sketchy account of transfer printing as practised in London in 1755, stated it was necessary to have 'first

[6] Bernard Watney, 'Petitions for Patents', E.C.C. Transactions, Vol. 6, Part 2, 1966, p. 69 and pl. 65.

9 'Printing on thin paper, impressions transferred to the fired ware, and paper washed off':
ETCHING, over-engraved, from *A Representation of the Manufacturing of Earthen-
ware*, 1827. See page 44
Robert Copeland Esquire

rubbed it (the part of the porcelain to be decorated) with thick oil or turpentine'
(see page 58). It is extremely doubtful whether these substances, even if
thoroughly dried, would have sufficed to give the requisite key, and it is
probable that he saw size in use, and mistakenly thought it was oil or
turpentine. It is possible that this information contributed to the failure of
some would-be transfer printers. What is clear is that it was necessary to
prepare the ceramic surface to receive the transfer.

For many years this part of the process was a most closely guarded trade
secret, but by the beginning of the nineteenth century it had become more or
less general knowledge. By mid-century a patent granted to Frederick Collins
and Alfred Reynolds in respect of 'Improvements in the Art of Ornamenting
China, Earthenware, and Glass' stated:[7]

'But if it be required to transfer this same pattern, subject, device, or design
while the colors are wet from the prepared tissue paper *on to glazed china or
earthenware*, or on to glass, the surface of these articles over which the
pattern is to extend *must be coated with ordinary varnish in the usual way*, and
when this coating is dry the tissue paper turned over upon it, and when the

[7] Specification No. 12097/1848. Inrolled 13 September 1848.

colours become dry the tissue paper is removed by damping . . .' (italics are the author's).

Immediately on coming from the press, and while the ink was still warm and viscid the tissue was placed printed side down on the ceramic surface. It was firmly rubbed by a very hard flannel boss until the tissue was free of wrinkles, and in complete unbroken contact with the surface of the article. In place of a flannel boss a smooth wooden spatula was occasionally used. From the earliest days it was customary to employ the labour-saving device of having a number of designs engraved on a single copper plate, and the tissue was cut up after coming from the press. With shaped wares, and the rims of plates and bowls, it was often necessary to snip the edge of the tissue so that small overlaps could be made to allow the paper to follow the contour of the article. These cuts frequently show up as small interruptions in the detail of the pattern. The tissue was removed either by sponging with water, or briefly immersing the article in a water vat. After preliminary drying the print was fired in a muffle kiln at 800–900°C, to fuse it to the glaze.

To transfer print it was essential for the press and stock of ceramic articles to be in juxtaposition, and for more than a century and a half, if the press was not at the pottery, the wares had to go to the printers.[8] Furthermore, unfired prints were very vulnerable to damage by the slightest rubbing, and it was impossible to pack and transport printed wares before they were fired. The only solution was for there to be a muffle kiln at the works of the specialist transfer printers.

By the mid-eighteenth century it had been the tradition for generations of engravers and etchers that they should do their own printing, or if they did not do it themselves, it was carried out in their studios under their direct supervision. Only posthumously, or in other exceptional circumstances, did this not occur, the reason being that it had always been a process which was not finished with the preparation of the printing plate. So much depended upon the composition of the inks, how the plate was wiped, the degree of dampness of the paper, its texture, and the pressure used in the press, that printing could not be left to others. The belief that eighteenth-century engravers and etchers sold their plates to publishers and print sellers who then printed from them is incorrect. The same distinction between publishers and printers prevailed then as today. In *The Ladies' Amusement* Robert Sayer, as publisher, made plain on each sheet that it was printed *for* him, and not by him. A similar distinction was made by John Bowles, another London publisher, who is considered in the next chapter under the Worcester Porcelain Company. That the various engravers themselves printed the sheets on Sayer's or Bowles's premises is unlikely, and it is more probable that they did so in their own studios, and sent the folios to them for binding and distribution. However, although it is unfortunate that with transfer printing subtleties of texture, shade and depth

[8] Since the 1880s, because of the invention of dry ceramic transfers, these can now be printed and sent in bulk to the potteries for application.

were partially lost, old habits die hard, and for many years after its invention the engravers mostly worked either at the pottery, or for the specialist transfer printer. The later development of underglaze printing changed all this, and created a category of free-lance engravers and etchers who sold their printing plates to the potters, who did the printing and subsequent glazing.

Until the turn of the nineteenth century, it is always safer to assume that, where an engraver's imprint occurs on a piece of pottery or porcelain, the printing was carried out by, or under the supervision of, that engraver. Even when a pottery closed, it is most doubtful if printing plates were sold and subsequently used by different engravers, or other potters. When Robert Hancock retired from the ceramic industry, he was working as selling agent for Thomas Turner, his one-time pupil, then manager of the Salopian China Manufactory, Caughley. It seems that he must have left with Turner some of his original printing-plates, one at least of which was signed. These were discovered in the mid-nineteenth century by Llewellynn Jewitt, at the Coalport China Manufactory, the successors to Turner.[9] It is remarkable that none of these Hancock engraved plates appears ever to have been used on Caughley or Coalport wares, or indeed at all after they left Hancock's possession.

The keystone in the discovery of the method of printing ceramics was without question the transference of the wet impression from paper to the pottery or porcelain article, but the hardest problem which delayed the application of the process, and when once solved caused so much trouble to would-be imitators, was not a physical but a chemical one. Ordinary printing-inks on a ceramic base rubbed off in a trice, and if such a print had been fired it would have burnt away. The coloured glazes and enamels, long used for painting on pottery and porcelain, were quite unsuitable for charging intaglio printing-plates with their fine hair lines. Such material could not be forced into the interstices, and even if it could would have been dragged out when the plate was wiped. The desideratum was a substance with quite complex characteristics.

(1) It had to be suitable for charging an intaglio plate; of a consistency which would allow its being forced into engraved or etched lines, and with sufficient adhesion to remain there while the surface of the plate was wiped clean.

(2) In the printing press it needed to part from the copper plate and cling to the dampened tissue.

(3) With appropriate pressure it was necessary for it to part from the paper and adhere to the prepared glazed surface of pottery or porcelain.

(4) When subjected to sufficient heat it had to fuse to the underlying glaze to give a print of the colour desired.

(5) Lastly, and of great importance, its constituent materials had to be such

---

[9] Op. cit., p. 234.

that they did not abrade the copper printing-plate to such an extent as to reduce its life, so that it ceased to be commercially viable.

The problem was such that it could only be solved by the pooled knowledge and experience of both printers and potters. The latter, familiar with ceramic enamels, would have suggested the inclusion of finely powdered flint glass in the printing medium. This was in fact a solution, but there was an unexpected side effect.

Constituents to assist in the printing were unknown proportions of boiled and raw linseed oil, sweet oil of almonds, oil of amber, resin and turpentine. These vanished in the firing. The pulverized vitreous element, which was powdered glass, caused inordinate wear of the finely engraved and etched plates, and proved the downfall of many of the pioneers at transfer printing. Every time the printing plate was inked and wiped the effect would have been similar to rubbing it with fine glass-paper. The large number of prints from similar but different plates suggests that at Battersea, Bow and Worcester this was a major problem.

POUNCING

There is fortunately documentary evidence as to how the Liverpool printers overcame the problem of excessive printing-plate wear. John Sadler kept a notebook in which he recorded all manner of things, including medicines, his own formulae and those of his customers.[10] One entry details a receipt for black printing which shows clearly his method. It is headed 'The Old Black', so possibly was his original formula. He printed with one part raw manganese (a black metallic oxide) and two parts white lead, presumably mixed in an oily medium, and this was transferred by tissue to the ceramic article. It resulted in a sticky impression of the desired picture, which was then dusted with a sable brush or swansdown charged with a pounce which adhered only to the sticky medium. The article was then cleaned by insufflation, and gently wiped with cotton wool, which cleared all the powder from the unprinted parts. It was fired in the normal manner. The pounce was composed of:

2 Bl. U. Highly Colr. [Black umber]
2 Calx Zaffre [Calcined oxide of cobalt]
1 Burnt Manganese
1 Best Flint Glass
1 Bismouth
$2\frac{3}{4}$ Blue Flux.

[10] The remains of John Sadler's notebook are in the Merseyside County Museums and Library. Extracts most easily referred to in E. Stanley Price, *John Sadler, Liverpool Pottery Printer*, privately printed, 1948.

The last ingredient, the blue flux, was composed of:

6 Best Flint Glass
2 Red Lead
2 Calcined Borax
1 Calx Zaffre
Well vitrified together.

It will be seen that by this contrivance all abrasive ingredients were kept from the printing plate, which would therefore have as long a life as one used for printing with ordinary printer's ink. Before the days of steel facing, even with careful handling, this could have been little more than a few thousand impressions. All Sadler's receipts for no matter what colour were based on the same principle of printing the pigment with white lead, and later pouncing the vitreous ingredients.

Sadler did not in fact record with what he mixed his pigments and white lead. That was doubtless due to the fact that he was an experienced printer, and he probably used the compound with which he was familiar, which would have been a preparation based on linseed oil. William Evans recorded in the middle of the nineteenth century a formula which consisted of a compound of cold-drawn linseed oil, turpentine and Barbadoes tar.[11] Alan Smith quotes some recipes in the personal papers of Joseph Tompkinson (1784–1836), a one-time employee at the Herculaneum Pottery.[12] These included:

Oils for printing
1 qt Linseed Oil
$\frac{1}{2}$ pt Oil sweet almonds
1 teaspoonful Red Lead.

Before the turn of the nineteenth century the experiment was tried of printing only in the sticky medium without any colour, and mixing the pigment only with the vitreous ingredients to be pounced. This was also done with some on-glaze stipple printing. Sometimes a difference can be detected between a print made from a plate charged with the pigment, and one that has had the pigment added only by pouncing. In the first case the intensity of each line or dot varies according to the amount of colour, controlled by the depth to which the plate was engraved or etched. When the pigment is pounced it adheres only to the surface of the printed medium, and the quantity remains constant no matter how thin or thick the medium may be. A flat even quality is very noticeable on much early nineteenth-century stipple printing because of this.

Transfer printing on ceramics being a direct and immediate extension of the

---

[11] *Art and History of the Pottery Business*, 1846, p. 46.
[12] *Liverpool Herculaneum Pottery*, London, 1970, pp. 124–6.

process evolved for the decoration of enamel articles, it is of interest to read an account of this in the diary of the Countess of Shelburne, wife of the second earl, and later Marchioness of Lansdowne. While on a visit to Birmingham in 1766, she wrote for 16 May:[13]

> 'At Mr Taylor's we met again and he made and ennamel'd a landscape on top of a box before us which he afterwards gave me as a curiosity from my having seen it done. The method of doing it is this: a stamping instrument managed only by one woman first impressed the picture on paper, which paper is then laid even upon a piece of white enamel and rubbed hard with a knife [sic], or instrument like it, until it is marked upon the box. There then is spread over it with a brush some metallic colour reduced to a fine powder which adheres to the moist part and, by putting it afterwards into an oven for a few minutes, the whole is completed by fixing the colour.'

From the start monochrome transfer printing took place in a number of colours. Most of these in the early years were pallid and unreliable, and a good black was most troublesome to obtain. As the formula above shows, Sadler used manganese, which he later changed to calcined verdigris (acetate of copper). Others used iron oxide, but it was probably the inclusion of chromium, at a later date, which did most to produce a fine jet black. Shades of red and puce were obtained from calcined copperas (ferrous sulphate, or green vitriol), lead chromate, chromium-tin compounds or mixtures of other metallic oxides. Green was a bothersome and unreliable pigment mostly procured from copper compounds. Chromium and its derivatives were not in use before the nineteenth century.

When prints were hand coloured after transfer it was quickly found that if they were in red, puce or brown, in preference to black, the printed lines were more easily obscured by the painting. Superficially the results could then pass for hand painting. Black had a tendency to 'grin' through all but the most opaque of enamels.

JAPANNING AND ENAMELLING

Transfer printing having first developed as a decoration of japanned and enamelled wares, it is necessary to understand the basic manufacturing process for these articles. The body of all British japanned ware was sheet iron. This after stamping and shaping was cleaned and coated with a paint which was

[13] Lord Petty-Fitzmaurice, *Life of William, Earl of Shelburne*, London, 1912, p. 399. (Brought to notice by R. J. Charleston, 'Petition for Patents, Part 1B', *E.C.C. Transactions 1966*, Vol. 6, Part 2, p. 80.)

stoved at between 125 and 150°C. After shaping the process required a minimum of plant and equipment, and could well be carried out in a private house—and fired in a bread oven, provided this was not allowed to get too hot. The common black japan paint was made from asphaltum mixed with gum anime, dissolved in linseed oil, and thinned with turpentine. Transparent and coloured japan was made from copal varnish with a little oil and turpentine. It could be coloured by a variety of pigments both mineral and organic. The use of organic dyes was made possible by the low stoving-temperatures.

Enamelling was a more complicated process although it had been carried out for thousands of years, in Egypt certainly before the reign of Rameses III (1204–1172 BC), and has been used in Europe probably without a break from Roman times to the present day.

The body of painted, and later printed, enamel was a thin metal sheet of gold, silver or copper. Usually it was the last named metal, and of a thickness of only a third of a millimetre, or less; the thinner the better. The copper plate was scrupulously cleaned in nitric acid and after washing and drying in oak sawdust it was covered back and front in what was termed flux or fondant. This was merely flint glass in fine-powdered form. Preparatory to painting or printing, after the first coat had been fired, a second was applied. This was similar to the original except that stannic acid or arsenious acid was added, which resulted in an opaque, white outer coating. Enamels of different hues were made by the addition of metallic oxides, in a similar manner to coloured glass.

The coated metal was placed on a refractory or iron platform called a *planché*, and put in a muffle kiln to fuse. The enamel pieces being so thin and of such high thermal conductivity required firing for only a few minutes. Further, because of their thinness, there were few, if any, annealing problems, and the articles could be withdrawn immediately firing was complete. A temperature of between 600° and 800°C was required, and the moment of withdrawal was judged by the article reaching brick red in colour, and then shining brightly at the instant that the enamel fused. Because of the absence of annealing problems, and of the short time required for firing, intermittent kilns were never used. Quite small ovens, much about the size of a present-day domestic-cooker oven, were heated first thing in the morning, and wares were continually inserted, fired and withdrawn throughout the working day.

There is no similarity at all between an enamelling oven, and a ceramic glost kiln or firing-on oven with contents of perhaps thousands of pieces requiring days to fire, anneal and cool. For enamelling, fuel-stocks and storage of products required a comparatively small area; therefore the land and buildings needed were in no way comparable to those necessary for the decoration of pottery or porcelain. The disparities of sizes of premises, and between the operation, working-temperatures and capacities of japanning stoves, enamelling ovens and ceramic kilns are of considerable importance when tracing the probable movements of John Brooks.

JOHN BROOKS IN BIRMINGHAM (1750 to 1753)

It now seems certain that transfer printing was invented by John Brooks in Birmingham in 1753. He was by profession an engraver, who was born in Dublin but is known to have been working in London in 1746 and perhaps earlier. He had an establishment in the Strand, and confirmation of this is in a quotation from the *Gentleman's Magazine* of December 1746, recorded by Bernard Watney.[14] It is unfortunate that the dates of Brooks's birth and death are unknown, but particulars are recorded of two of his more famous pupils. The *Dictionary of National Biography* states that Richard Houston (1721?–75), mezzotint engraver, was a pupil of John Brooks, as also was James Macardell (1729?–65), another mezzotintist. The dates of birth of these men are not definitely established, but assuming those shown are approximately correct, and that the men who subsequently proved themselves such gifted and competent artists were unlikely to have been pupils after the age of twenty-five, then it seems probable that Houston worked in London under Brooks sometime between 1738, when he was seventeen years of age, and 1746, and Macardell between 1746 and 1754. If this were accepted as a reasonable postulate, and that three years would be the shortest period for a pupil to serve his master, we would arrive at the probability that the minimum period that Brooks was in London was between 1743 and 1749.

That Brooks was in Birmingham in the autumn of 1751 is established by a patent application referred to below. On the basis above, at that date he could at the most have been there only for two years. Why did he go? He had built a reputation for himself, had his own establishment, and was thought sufficiently highly of to have very talented pupils. In the light of present knowledge it can only be conjectured that he went to experiment with transfer printing. Japanned ware was not made in London.

That Brooks was still in Birmingham in 1752 is proved by an advertisement in his name in *Aris's Birmingham Gazette* of 27 November 1752, offering to print waiters (japanned trays) on reasonable terms.[15] His address was given as New Church Yard, which was then on the western outskirts of the city, round what is now the pro-cathedral of St. Philips. The advertisement stated:

'Such Gentlemen as are desirous of having WAITERS printed, may apply to John Brooks, Engraver of New Church Yard, Birmingham, who is willing not only to treat with them on reasonable Terms, but also engages to execute the work in the most elegant Manner, with Expedition, and further, to disabuse those Gentlemen, who, as he is assur'd, have been told to the

[14] 'Petitions for Patents Concerning Porcelain etc.', *E.C.C. Transactions*, Vol. 6, Part 2, 1966, p. 61.
[15] Brought to notice by Eric Benton in 'John Brooks in Birmingham', *E.C.C. Transactions*, Vol. 7, Part 3, 1970, p. 162.

contrary, that he never intended to encourage a Monopoly in that Branch of the Trade.

N.B. He also recommends that his Work may not be spoiled, by committing it into the Hands of unskilled Daubers.'

This advertisement has given rise to the suggestion that others, at the time, were practising transfer printing in Birmingham, and that Brooks then had no intention of applying for a patent and creating a monopoly. The very opposite is the implication. That the advertisement is a trade one is self-evident, and what is conveyed is that the advertiser did not intend to confine his process to his own products, but was willing to print for others in the trade. His later applications for patents in 1754 and 1755 effectively dispose of any theory that he was willing to abandon his invention, or that others were practising the process. It has further been discovered that in the Poor Law rate-books for Birmingham for both 1752 and 1753 John Brooks is recorded as the occupier of 1 and 2 Colmore Row.[16] This was, and is, the north-west side of the pro-cathedral precincts, and is the address of the same premises as referred to in the advertisement.

In 1751 Brooks made an unsuccessful patent application which:[17]

'SHEWETH, That the Petitioner has by Great Study Application and Expence, found out a Method of printing, impressing, and reversing upon Enamel & China from engraved, etched, and Mezzotinto Plates, & from Cuttings on Wood and Mettle, Impressions of History, Portraits, Landskips, Foliages, Coats of Arms, Cyphers, Letters, Decorations, and other Devices.

'That the said Art and Method is entirely New & of his own Invention.'

This was 'allowed in the usual form' by the Secretary of State, the Duke of Newcastle, on 10 September 1751, which presumably means that it was referred to the Attorney or Solicitor General for report. What happened after that is not known.

There is no reason to suppose that in the eighteenth century the basic motives behind a patent application were any different from those prevailing today. When an inventor has a new idea his first thought is to put in an application based on a prototype, a model, or even a drawing or description, and to seek protection covering as wide a field as possible for every conceivable application of the process, and to spread the net to embrace the use of all possible materials by congeneric trades. Such petitions cannot be interpreted too literally. In the present instance it is most improbable that the invention had been put to any practical use at the time of the application. It is ironical that with all the care taken to seek protection covering as many substances as could be envisaged, printing should be first recorded as having taken place on a

[16] Eric Benton, ibid., p. 163.
[17] Public Record Office S.P.44/260.

different material from enamel and 'china', namely japanned ware, which was advertised fourteen months later. It cannot seriously be believed that Brooks had printed the nine types of impressions, by means of five printing methods, on both enamels and 'china'. What is clear is that he had thought out the method of transfer. This is apparent by the use of the word 'reversing'. In 1752 he advertised his ability to print japanned ware, and if he could then have printed on enamels, then what explanation is there for him not to have stated the fact?

Having once hit on the key of transference, the remaining problems for printing japanned ware could not have been difficult for an experienced engraver and printer. The colour paints in use for hand decoration of the ware, made of copal varnish, linseed oil, turpentine and pigment, would have needed very little modification to be made suitable for inking an intaglio plate and for transferring by means of tissue.

The composition of suitable pigments with which to print enamelled ware would have presented a much more intractable problem to him. It involved vitreous pigments as well as temperatures very difficult to achieve other than in a specially constructed kiln. As far as is known, Brooks had had no experience either in the materials or in working at the necessary temperatures, and it is doubtful if, when he left Birmingham in 1753—that is in the year following the transfer-printing advertisement—he had done any printing on enamels at all. That this was his aim is obvious from the patent application of 1751, as we have seen, and it seems a reasonable hypothesis that his removal back to London was undertaken in furtherance of that ambition.

It is more unlikely still that printing on 'china' was carried out by Brooks at Birmingham, and at present there is not a shred of evidence direct or indirect to substantiate it. There were no potteries in the near vicinity, and Brooks could not have obtained any local ceramic experience. Back in London he became a partner in the Battersea Enamel Works, and made two further patent applications.

BATTERSEA ENAMEL WORKS (1753(?) to 1756)

The Battersea Enamel Works played an important role in the development of transfer printing towards its application to ceramics. York House stood on Thames-side near Battersea Creek, on the right bank opposite where now stands the Fulham Power Station. It was a fifteenth-century building created by Lawrence Booth, Bishop of Durham, as a residence for himself and his successors when they had occasion to visit London. This exiguous palace was acquired sometime between 1750 and 1753 and turned into a factory by one Stephen Theodore Janssen (d. 1777), a London stationer. The precise date that he opened the works is not known, but in 1753 he took two partners, John

Brooks and Captain Henry Delamain. The latter was another Irishman, and seems to have been something of a swashbuckler. In 1752 he had purchased from the bankrupt Davis and Company the World's End Pottery in the North Strand, now called Eden Quay, near Mabbot Street, Dublin. It was run by his confidential clerk called William Stringfellow. On 1 November 1753 Delamain petitioned the Irish parliament for a grant, stating among other things that he 'had purchased the Art of Printing Earthen Ware with as much Beauty, Strong Impression and Despatch as it can be done on paper'.[18] After his petition had been considered by Sir Arthur Gore and a committee of the Commons, on 8 November 1753 the Irish Committee of Supply voted one thousand pounds to be given to Delamain; at today's values something just short of a hundred thousand pounds. The remarkable expedition with which the matter was dealt should be a salutary example to the present-day establishments both here and in Ireland. It seems virtually certain that Delamain obtained the idea from Brooks, to whom he may, or may not, have paid a sum of money; probably not.

From his letters and his will of 17 December 1753 it is known that Delamain was very friendly with the potters of Liverpool.[19] He claimed to have fired and glazed earthenware and porcelain by the use of coal, at one-third of the expense of wood, which had been used exclusively up to 1753. He offered to build the Liverpool potters special coal-firing kilns, although at the time he had not even built himself one. It would have been out of character for such a man not to have talked freely — perhaps too freely — of his new interest in transfer printing, and this is an important point to bear in mind when later the claims of John Sadler are considered.

John Brooks while at Battersea lodged two further patent applications. In 1754 he petitioned from York House, and stated that he:[20]

'SHEWETH THAT your Petitioner has found out and discovered the Art of printing on Enamels Glass China and other Ware History Portraits Landskips Foliages Coats of Arms Cyphers letters Decorations and other Devices. . . .

'That your petitioner is advised and verily believes that his Method of printing on enamel Glass China and other Wares will be of publick Utility. . . .

THAT the said Art and Method of printing upon Enamel Glass China and other Wares is entirely new and of his own Invention.'

The opening eight words of the second paragraph above are of significance, for it can be inferred from them that he had not then printed on all the materials

[18] *Journal of the House of Commons of Ireland*, AD 1753, 1 November, George II, Vol. V, p. 175.
[19] The most convenient reference for Delamain's correspondence is in Hugh Owen, *Two Centuries of Ceramic Art in Bristol*, 1873, pp. 393–7, and details of his will are in the monograph by Aubrey J. Toppin, 'The Will of Henry Delamain, the Dublin Potter', *E.C.C. Transactions*, Vol. 2, No. 8, London, 1942.
[20] Public Record Office, S.P.44/261.

named. If he had done so he could have stated the benefits unequivocally. The application was referred on 25 January by the Secretary of State, the Duke of Newcastle, to the Attorney or Solicitor General for consideration and report. Again there is regrettably no record of the result.

Once more, in 1755, and again from York House, Brooks petitioned stating that it.[21]

'SHEWETH That your Petitioner has by great Labour Study & Expence, found out a new Method of Printing on Enamel China Glass, Delft & other Wares, whereby your Petitioner has brought that Art, to a Degree of Perfection never yet known, exercised or practiced by any Person or Persons whatsoever to the Knowledge or Belief of Your Petitioner by which Your Petitioner can execute curious Performances, which are Pictures themselves, without the Help of or any Assistance from the Pencil, the Method used by Your Petitioner in Printing on Enamel China Delft, and other Wares far exceeding every Practice hitherto in use for printing thereon, by any other Person or Persons whatsoever, . . .

'That Your Petitioner is the First & sole inventor of the aforesaid Method of Printing on Enamel China Glass Delft, & other Wares, and that no other Person or Persons to the best of his Knowledge and Belief have ever practiced or been capable of performing the Same, in the manner used by Your Petitioner either before or since the Time of finding out & practicing the same by Your Petitioner.'

This was referred on an unspecified date in April 1755 to the Attorney or Solicitor General by the Earl of Holderness, who had succeeded the Duke of Newcastle as Secretary of State. Once more there is no record of the fate of the application, and it can only be assumed that it was rejected.

Why these three applications failed has been the subject of much conjecture. It is most unlikely that the 1751 petition was rejected because others were using the process. If Brooks, by accident or intent, had wrongly stated that his process was 'entirely New & of his own Invention', and it was in fact in use, it is beyond reason that he would have repeated the same assertion in 1754 and 1755. At the time of the petitions, if a patent was granted, the applicant was obliged to lodge within four months a full specification setting out details of the process, which then became part and parcel of the protection accorded. A probable explanation as far as the first application is concerned is that Brooks had been impetuous, and was unable within the four months to lodge a satisfactory specification. It is difficult to think of any other reason.

With the later applications the circumstances are somewhat different. That the Battersea Works was transfer printing on enamels in 1753, is supported by the statement of R. W. Binns that he owned an enamel box which he averred was of 'Battersea' manufacture, bearing the Masonic date 4753—that is

[21] Ibid.

AD 1753.[22] If articles so decorated had been on the market this would have jeopardized the success of the 1754 application, which sought protection for printing on enamels. The 1755 petition differs from that of the previous year by acknowledging that others were using some process, but in a manner which necessitated touching up by pencil, which he claimed his method did not. It is probable that by 1755 the enamel-makers of Bilston and elsewhere, with the help of renegade former Battersea employees, were trying to copy the Battersea products and their transfer printing was rather cruder. The inclusion of delftware in the petition leads to the speculation that Brooks had heard by then of the early efforts of Sadler and Green in Liverpool. It is worth remarking that Brooks again averred in 1755 that he was the inventor of the process, *and that no others, to the best of his belief, were using his method.*

It seems that he was ill advised for possibly, by omitting enamel from the 1754 and 1755 applications, he might well have succeeded in obtaining protection for the use of the process on glass, 'china', delftware and earthenware. There is little doubt that at the time of the 1754 and 1755 applications he had not successfully transfer printed on anything but japanned ware and enamel.

The evidence suggests that after the insertion of the advertisement in *Aris's Birmingham Gazette* on 27 November 1752, Brooks moved to London in early 1753. The Battersea partnership seems to have been composed of the financier, Janssen, the ceramics expert, Delamain and the artist and engraver, Brooks. Delamain would have been able to provide Brooks with the invaluable advice that he most needed, which was on the composition of pigments to withstand the high temperatures of the enamel kilns. It would seem that the problems were quickly overcome, and that before the end of 1753 transfer printing was taking place on enamel. This would account for Delamain's hurriedly returning to Dublin to petition the Irish parliament on 1 November 1753, and for the existence of the Binns snuff box dated 1753.

Sadly the firm was very short lived, and Janssen was gazetted bankrupt on 12 January 1756, and Brooks fifteen days later, on the 27th. It is recorded,[23]

> 'The irregular and dissipated habits of Brooks, and the consequent bad management and neglect of the business (the Battersea Enamel Works) caused the failure of what promised to be a successful enterprise, involving not only the ruin of Brooks himself, but disastrous consequences to Janssen and others who had joined in it.'

Although Brooks achieved fame as a mezzotintist, it is a puzzling fact that, as far as is known, no transfer printing has survived which can with absolute certainty be attributed to him. None bears his initials or signature.

[22] *A Century of Potting in the City of Worcester*, London, 1865, 2nd ed., 1877, p. 62.
[23] Walter W. Strickland, *Dictionary of Irish Artists*, Dublin, 1913.

One of the first written references to transfer printing was made in early 1755 by the Swiss painter and enameller Jean André Rouquet (1702–59), who spent most of his adult life in England.[24] Writing of Chelsea, and presumably referring to Battersea just across the river, he stated:

'Not far from hence they have lately erected another manufacture, where they paint some of their work in brooches by a kind of stamp. Having formerly imagined some such method of painting porcelain, I made several essays of it; and yet I do not pretend that what I am going to say concerning it is exactly the practice of its manufacture.

'The subject you want to stamp or imprint must first be engraved on a copper-plate; the cut of this engraving must be so open as to contain a sufficient quantity of the substance appropriated to the operation.

'The plate is covered with the substance which should be the calx or lime of some metals, mixed with a small quantity of proper glass.

'The impression is made on paper, the printed side of which is afterwards applied to the part of the porcelain intended to be painted, having first rubbed it with thick oil or turpentine; the paper is then taken off properley, and the work is put in the fire.'

Although inaccurate in detail this must be accepted as conclusive evidence that the process was in operation at Battersea by 1755 or earlier. It is important that this publication in both French and English revealed to all the key of transference.

Next to consider is an etcher and engraver, in the history of transfer printing the most important of them all, Robert Hancock (1730–1817). He was the son of John Hancock, and is thought to have been born in Burslem, Staffordshire, in 1730. On 28 January 1746, for a fee of thirty pounds, he was apprenticed to George Anderton, an obscure engraver of Temple Street, Birmingham. This was one of the short roads leading from New Street to the south corner of the pro-cathedral square. The premises in Colmore Row occupied by John Brooks from c. 1750 to 1753 were just around the corner, and little more than one hundred and forty metres (one hundred and fifty yards) distant. It would have been strange indeed if, living in a small community and working so close, the engraver in his late forties had not been acquainted with the young apprentice in the same profession. That Brooks left Birmingham in 1753 and went to Battersea is certain and beyond dispute. For many years it had been accepted without question that Hancock also worked at Battersea from 1753 until 1756. All the evidence conclusively points to this. However it has more recently been suggested that he never came to London at all. This is largely due to a mistaken belief that transfer printing on enamels originated and was perfected in the Midlands, which theory is scotched by Brooks's attempts right up to April 1755 to obtain a patent covering this—which would have been a waste of time if

[24] *L'Etat des Arts en Angleterre*, Paris 1755, English translation, London, 1755.

10 *The Tea Leaves Fortune Teller*: An early-state impression of an over-engraved etching by Robert Hancock, after Louis Peter Boitard. Copper plate 77 by 115 mm (3 by 4.5 in) (design 89 mm (3.5 in) wide)
   In parts strengthened by an unknown person, by pen and ink, particularly the etched imprints. Unfamiliarity with the name Hancock has caused an 's' to be added. Imprinted 'Boitard delin', 'Hancocks Sculp' and 'According to Act 1754'.
   See page 60 British Museum
11 *Les Jeux et Plaisirs de l'Enfance*: Disputed transfer print on TEAPOT with scroll handle and duck-head spout, of porcelain, made at DOCCIA, ITALY. 180 mm (7.1 in) high
   Underglaze blue decoration, thought by some to be printed in the centre, and hand-pencilled surround and landscape. *See page 25*
   Victoria and Albert Museum

the process was already being worked. There is no evidence to prove that Hancock was anywhere but in London for the four vital years, and the considerable circumstantial indications corroborate that he was.

It would have been the most natural thing in the world for Brooks on leaving Birmingham to take with him the very talented and ambitious young engraver from around the corner, who had just finished his apprenticeship. It has long been asserted that Hancock continued his studies under Simon François Ravenet (1721?-74) at Battersea, and a comparison of the styles of work of these two men very much confirms this. Ravenet, like Brooks, was an older and more experienced man than Hancock—he was in fact ten years Hancock's senior.[25] Hancock acquired a pronounced French style which stayed with him all his life, and which he passed on to his pupils, thereby influencing the whole early style of transfer printing. Another of Ravenet's pupils was the engraver John Hall (1738-97), although his indentures were in fact with 'Janssen & Co'.

A typical and very famous example of his early work, signed 'R.H.f.' is *The Tea Party*. There are many different later versions, some by Hancock and others by plagiarists. This original edition is on an enamel watch-back (Plate 13). It will be seen that although the style is very fluid, as a transfer print it is immature and lacks polish.

Another engraver of renown very probably working at Battersea was Louis Peter Boitard, who was born in Paris and studied under La Farge. As a young man he came to London, and in 1751 was living in Lambeth Marsh.[26] That he worked either whole or part time at the Battersea Enamel Works, about two kilometres (one and a quarter miles) distant, is highly probable. In the British Museum there is a small and now famous album containing six engravings. Of these, two, *Peeping Tom* and *The Pledge*, are unsigned: one, *The Round Game*, has at the foot 'R.H.Sc.', and in addition indistinctly 'R. Hancock Sculp'; one, *The Shepherd Lovers*, is signed 'Boitard Sculp', and the remaining two, *The Tea Leaves Fortune Teller* and *The Singing Lesson*, are marked 'Boitard delin', 'Hancocks Sculp' (or in the latter case 'Sc'), and with the words 'According to Act 1754' (Plate 10). These appear to be early-state impressions, from etched and over-engraved copper plates for printing on paper. What is rather puzzling is that all the imprints have been etched only, while those on *The Tea Leaves Fortune Teller* and *The Singing Lesson* have been strengthened after printing by careful script writing, during the course of which an 's' has been added in both cases to the name Hancock. Furthermore all the imprints are large, and seem grossly out of proportion to the very small prints. This album unequivocally confirms that Hancock and Boitard were well known to each other, and some time in 1754 or after worked together. All the above engravings except *The Pledge*, have been found on what are generally accepted as being Battersea

---

[25]This theory had the support of Aubrey J. Toppin, 'Notes on Janssen and the Artists at the Battersea Factory', *E.C.C. Transactions*, Vol. 1, No. 4, p. 65.

[26]Lens's Drawing Book (brought to notice by Aubrey Toppin, 'Battersea Ceramics and Kindred Associations', *E.C.C. Transactions*, Vol. 2, No. 9, 1946, p. 174).

12 '*KING OF PRUSSIA*': SAUCER of steatitic porcelain by WORCESTER PORCELAIN
    COMPANY. 139 mm (5.5 in) diameter
    Erroneously thought to be a coloured transfer print, but hand-pencilled in graphite
    colour and enamelled in grass green, Prussian blue, biscuit, primrose and puce,
    with border of primrose garrya-husks and rose-du-Barry ribbons. Crossed swords
    and 9 mark in underglaze blue. 1757. Cf. Plate 24. *See page 26*
13 *Tea Party No. 1*: on enamel WATCH BACK by BATTERSEA ENAMEL WORKS. 42 mm
    (1.6 in) diameter
    Etched and over-engraved by Robert Hancock, and printed in deep brown-black.
    Imprint 'R.H.f.'. 1753–6. *See page 60*
    Dyson Perrins Museum

14 *The Pet Lamb*: on enamel PATCH BOX from BIRMINGHAM or BILSTON. 51 mm (2 in)
wide.
Etched and engraved and printed in deep brown-black. Border and box of sky blue,
with lemon-yellow and white ovolo border. 1760–5. *See page 63*

enamel pieces. Fortunately Hancock often signed his copper plates with *Sculp.*
or *fecit*, or their abbreviations. He became a very proficient artist and mixed
with fellow artists, and he obviously appreciated the difference between an
engraver's and an etcher's imprint. It follows that the plates with his name and
sculp. were mainly engraved and those with *fecit* predominantly etched.

The Battersea Works had a very short life, for on the bankruptcy of Janssen
it closed, and later the contents were sold. Hancock very probably went to Bow
for a short period, and then perhaps in late 1756, and certainly by 1757, turned
up at Worcester. Boitard, it seems, went to Worcester before Hancock, but his
stay there was short.

It is not known exactly when transfer printing on enamels reached the
Midlands, but a working knowledge of the process perhaps was taken there in
1755 or 1756 by redundant Battersea employees. It certainly was flourishing
there ten years later, as is proved by the Marchioness of Lansdowne's diary,
and in all probability it continued in use until the close of the century. It must
be emphasized that the manufacture of enamel wares is known to have
flourished in Birmingham from 1749, and probably much earlier, and what is
being referred to here is only its decoration by transfer printing. An enamel

patch-box with a picture *The Pet Lamb* could have originated either at Birmingham or Bilston in Staffordshire, which is some twenty kilometres (twelve miles) north-west of Birmingham, and was another centre of production of enamel wares (Plate 14). It is of interest that this is in a dark brown–black, and not jet black, so that it probably dates from 1760 to 1765.

Chapter 3

TRANSFER PRINTING
ON GLAZED PORCELAIN

The progression from the transfer printing of enamelled surfaces to that of porcelain was a much easier one than the earlier leap from japanned ware to enamelled ware. The vitreous pigments used were much the same, and little increase of firing temperature was needed for on-glaze printing, but as earlier explained, because of the ceramic body, completely different equipment and firing techniques were required. In recent years it has been suggested that Bow porcelain was transfer printed at York House, and after it closed, was sent to Birmingham for decoration. This could not have occurred on any commercial scale without the erection of special intermittent muffle kilns at both Battersea and Birmingham, of which there is not the slightest factual or circumstantial evidence. These unsupported theories ignore all practical difficulties, and run contrary to the known facts, at the same time creating many unnecessary problems for which answers cannot be found.

It seems that to some degree these conjectures are inspired by the fact of Josiah Wedgwood having sent creamware to Liverpool for printing. What is so conveniently overlooked is that Liverpool was a ceramic and transfer-printing centre, and that from Bow to Birmingham and back is some three hundred and seventy kilometres (two hundred and thirty miles): nearly three times the distance from Burslem to Liverpool and back. This in good weather would have been a fortnight's return journey by un-sprung wagon, or pack horse, and in the winter could well have taken a month or more. It must be remembered that porcelain in those days was—and still is—immeasurably more fragile than creamware. The owners of eighteenth-century porcelain factories were sensible and most capable business men, and although they were denied modern techniques, were as cost conscious as any modern entrepreneur. What a money-wasting, time-wasting and material-wasting (breakages) operation such journeys would have involved. It is difficult to imagine any business men of any generation embarking on such an enterprise.

Birmingham, since Tudor times, had been famous as the home of small

A. '*the PRUSSIAN HERO*': on TEAPOT of bone china, by BOW CHINA WORKS.
187 mm (7.3 in) high
Attributed to Robert Hancock, based on an engraving by Jean G. Wille, after
Antoine Pesne, printed in deep Venetian red, and polychrome over-enamelled.
1756. Moulded and enamelled floral decoration. *See page 68*
Victoria and Albert Museum

B. *Temple Ruins*: on BREAD AND BUTTER DISH of steatitic porcelain, by WORCESTER
PORCELAIN COMPANY. 180 mm (7.1 in) diameter
From an etched and engraved plate, intended for monochrome decoration, by
Robert Hancock, printed in deep amethyst, and heavily over-enamelled in semi-
opaque terracotta, primrose, verdigris, dark drab, plum, tawny, grey salmon-pink
and grey-ultramarine. Heightened in gold. 1760–5. *See page 88*

metalwares, with a concentration of cutlers, lorimers, nailers and smiths, and by the turn of the eighteenth century it was the centre of manufacture of swords, guns, locks, hinges and snuff-boxes. It was natural for the production of enamelware to develop there, but at no time had there ever been any porcelain or pottery made in the vicinity, and therefore there was a total absence of ceramic kilns, and men with ceramic 'know-how'. Muffle kilns existed at the Bow works for enamelling, as well as experienced staff to operate them. How much simpler to get the engravers to work there. This has ever been the accepted theory of what happened, and in the author's opinion should continue as such, until the production of convincing evidence to the contrary.

BOW CHINA WORKS (c. 1747 to c. 1776)

The porcelain factory at Bow was founded by yet another Irishman, Thomas Frye (1710–62), a few years before the opening of the Battersea Enamel Works. He had two partners, Edward Heylyn (1695–1765), a local glass-merchant, and George Arnold (d. 1751), a man of some standing and one time president of St. Thomas's Hospital and Master of the Haberdashers' Company. Sometime prior to 1757 two new partners were admitted. These were John Crowther and John Weatherby (d. 1762). The former was also a London glass-merchant, and son of Ralph Crowther, a Cheshire farmer. In 1725 he had entered into partnership with Weatherby, who came from Staffordshire. It seems that Frye and Heylyn carried out their early porcelain experiments at premises on the north side of Bow Road, but to the west of Bow Bridge, on what was then the Middlesex side. Sometime about 1747 a factory was built on the other side of Bow Bridge, still north of the high road, but in Essex. This was some two hundred and fifty metres (two hundred and seventy yards) to the east of the River Lea, just past Marshgate Lane. The works was, it seems, the pioneer of three most important developments in the English ceramic industry. It was the first to use china clay, or kaolin, from America; it introduced bone ash into the composition of porcelain; and it may have been where transfer printing was first employed commercially on ceramics.

There exist many pieces of Bow porcelain decorated with on-glaze transfer prints, usually in a dull red-oxide colour — possibly obtained from ferric and zinc oxides. Many of the prints are in the distinctive style of Hancock, and four are known which carry his imprint. That Hancock worked at Bow was originally suggested by R. W. Binns and both W. B. Honey[1] and Cyril Cook[2] considered that all the available facts supported the theory. No proof to the contrary has been produced.

[1] *European Pottery and Porcelain*, 1933, p. 180.
[2] *Life and Work of Robert Hancock*, London, 1948, p. 38.

The Battersea works closed probably towards the end of 1755, but at the latest in mid-January 1756, and the earliest certain date of Hancock's presence in Worcester is sometime in 1757. This leaves a period of between eleven months and perhaps two years during which he could have worked at Bow. It is important to remember that until the commencement of underglaze transfer printing, and in fact for many years later, it was traditional for the intaglio printing process to be looked upon as part of the art of the engraver or etcher. This may well have had a big influence over the movements of Hancock, Boitard and others. There is nothing inconsistent in Hancock's engravings having appeared in *The Ladies' Amusement* for there is little doubt that these were executed and printed by him some years before he went to Worcester. In the list of potters and allied trades in *A Topographical Survey of the County of Stafford*, c. 1786, although several enamellers are listed, there are no engravers, and there is only one printer mentioned. On the map of the *Staffordshire Pottery Directory* published sixteen years later there are five printers shown, and no less than thirteen engravers—not described as printers. In the thirty-two years between 1753 and 1785 a vast quantity of ceramic printing was done at various potteries and by specialist on-glaze engraver-printers, but there are few records of printing done before 1785 from plates engraved by artists other than those who worked at the places of printing. Hancock worked at both Worcester and Caughley, where his engravings were transfer printed, and it is both inconsistent and incomprehensible that earlier he should have been so indifferent as to the use to which his unsigned and sometimes signed plates were put, as he would have had to have been if he sold his plates to either Battersea or Bow without working there.

There is a simple and very credible reason for his subsequent move to Worcester. Having lost his job at Battersea through the bankruptcy of Janssen, he would have been dismayed by the financial difficulties of Heylyn which terminated in his insolvency in 1757. He could justifiably have imagined that, like the closure of the York House factory in similar circumstances, the Bow works would be shut as a consequence.

Of the extant pieces of Bow porcelain decorated with prints from engravings by Hancock is a mug in the Cyril Cook collection, which has on one side printed in red a picture called *The Whip Top*. This is based on a design, *Le Jeu de Sabot* by Hubert François Gravelot (1699–1773), a great friend of David Garrick. A similar print exists on a Worcester mug, part of the Arthur Hurst bequest to the Victoria and Albert Museum (Plate 20). Cook, referring to this print, stated: 'Side by side comparison of these Bow and Worcester specimens has shown that the prints of *The Whip Top*, like those of *Battledore and Shuttlecock*, were taken from the same copper plate.'[3] The second named print is based on another of Gravelot's pictures, *Le Jeu Volant*, and copies are on the opposite sides of both the Bow and Worcester mugs. There is no credible

[3] Op. cit., 1948, Item 117.

15 *Tea Party No. 1* and *The Wheeling Chair*: on PLATE of bone china by Bow CHINA
    WORKS. 191 mm (7.5 in) diameter
    Engraved by Robert Hancock and printed in Venetian red. Border polychrome-
    enamelled. 1755–7. *See pages 68, 95*
    British Museum

16 *Manchu Lady Purchasing Haberdashery*: on 'TANKARD' of bone china by Bow
    CHINA WORKS. (A cicatrice proves it to be the body of a coffee pot.) 150 mm (5.9 in)
    high
    Outline printed in burnt umber, and over-enamelled in canary yellow, powder
    blue, puce, viridian, deep lavender and jet. 1756–8. *See page 68*

explanation as to how the printing plate went from Bow to Worcester other than that it was taken there by Hancock, and if this be admitted then he must have worked at both places. In case it should be doubted that the plate was engraved by Hancock there is on the Worcester mug a third print, *Blind Man's Buff*, based on another Gravelot picture, *Le Colin Maillard*, which is a decisive link. Llewellynn Jewitt found in 1862, at the Coalport factory, a copper printing-plate from which this picture was taken with also on it a version of *The Tea Party* signed 'R. Hancock fecit'.[4] After leaving Worcester in 1774 Hancock worked for a time for Thomas Turner of Caughley, whose business was later acquired by the Coalport organization. Hancock when he left Turner left the ceramic industry, and no doubt left any of his 'reversed' copper plates with his associate.

W. B. Honey thought that Ravenet accompanied Hancock to the Bow China Works for a short period.[5] This would explain why some prints on pieces from the factory appear to be much more in his style than that of Hancock. The suggestion is very probable, and there is nothing to disprove it.

Hancock's design *The Tea Party* is sometimes found as the left side and centre of a larger picture incorporating *The Wheeling Chair*, an example of which is shown printed in red on a Bow porcelain plate (Plate 15). The fashion set at Battersea of hand colouring some transfer prints before firing was followed at Bow. Illustrated is a teapot of 1756, showing a deep Venetian red print, '*the PRUSSIAN HERO*', over-painted in vitreous polychrome washes (Colour Plate A). It represents Frederick II (1712–86), 'The Great' of Prussia, who was cousin-german of George II and an ally of Great Britain at the beginning of 1756. It is probable that the teapot commemorates the signing in January 1756 of the convention between Great Britain and Prussia, rather than Frederick's victory at Lobositz in August of that year. This theory is corroborated by the fact that the king holds a scroll in his right hand, which presumably represents the treaty. The portrait, like others of both Liverpool and Worcester transfer printing, is derived indirectly from one of the paintings of Antoine Pesne (1638–1757), a portrait painter to the Prussian court. The Bow transfer print is a modified form of a published engraving by Jean Georges Wille (1715–1808), based on a three-quarters length picture of the king in a tricorn hat and heavily embroidered and frogged uniform. The other factories used transfer prints derived from a mezzotint by Richard Houston, originating from another of Pesne's portraits of the king in armour.

A large and most unusual print, showing a strong Pillement influence, is on a tankard which in reality is the mutilated remains of a baluster-shaped Bow coffee pot (Plate 16). This is printed in burnt umber, and enamelled in the same colour, with yellow, black, mauve, puce, blue and green. The brown of both the printing and the over-wash has coagulated into tiny spots, giving an effect

---

[4] *The Ceramic Art of Great Britain*, 1878, Vol. 1, p. 234 and Plate II.
[5] *The Connoisseur*, 1932, Vol. 89, p. 167.

17 *Manchu Lady with Handmaid and Child*: The reverse of 'TANKARD' shown in
Plate 16
Printed and over-enamelled in same colours with the addition of grass green. *See
page 70*
18 *L'Amour*: on bone china PLATE by BOW CHINA WORKS. 191 mm (7.5 in) diameter
Engraved by Robert Hancock, and printed in Venetian red, with polychrome
hand-enamelled border. After a design by C. N. Cochin *fils*. 1755–7. *See page 70*
Victoria and Albert Museum

as of chalk line-etching. The printing plate was first etched in line and then over-engraved. The subject, *Manchu Lady Purchasing Haberdashery*, is from a book of designs published in 1754.[6] On the reverse is *Manchu Lady with Handmaid and Child*, a more conventional Chinese scene of two women with a small boy (Plate 17). This is more representative of on-glaze transfer printing on Bow china.

A delicate print in typical Hancock style, which later became very popular at Worcester, is *L'Amour*, after a design by C. N. Cochin *fils* (1750–90) (Plate 18). This illustration on a Bow plate should be compared with the Worcester and Herculaneum versions (Plates 31 and 124). In the style of Ravenet, but thought by some to be the work of Hancock, is a rare transfer print of *Æneas and Anchises* fleeing from burning Troy (Plate 19). This picture depicts Æneas carrying his father pick-a-back, and is copied from a drawing by Hubert Gravelot.

A great Victorian collector of ceramics, Lady Charlotte Schreiber (1812–95) had in her possession the memoranda and books of the sales manager of the Bow China Works, one John Bowcocke. He, unfortunate man, died of lockjaw at six o'clock in the evening of 26 February 1765. The records have regrettably now vanished, but by great good fortune lengthy extracts were published before this happened.[7] Here was written confirmation that in 1756 transfer-printed Bow porcelain was on the market. Notes for that year contained the following entries:

> May 28 ... Mr Williams: 12 setts blue teas, at 2s. 10d.; a set compleat of the second printed teas
> June 18 Mr Fogg: 1 pint printed mug, 5s., 1 half-pint do., 3s. 6d. ...

It is significant that there exists no on-glaze transfer-printed Bow porcelain that can with certainty by attributed to a later date than 1757; this in spite of the fact that the factory struggled on for nearly twenty further years. This can be construed as denoting that after the presumed departure of Hancock the use of the on-glaze process ceased. A small amount of underglaze blue transfer-printed ware from the later period, 1761–3, has survived, and there exists a theory that this was under the surveillance of Richard Holdship, between his leaving Worcester and arriving at Derby.

THE WORCESTER PORCELAIN COMPANY (1751 to date)

More is owed to the Worcester Porcelain Company for the development of transfer printing, including the invention of printing underglaze, than to any factory. On 4 June 1751 a deed of partnership was engrossed to inaugurate a

---

[6] *A New Book of Chinese Designs*, published by Edwards and Darly, London, 1754, p. 32.
[7] *The Art Journal* of 1869.

19 *Aeneas and Anchises Fleeing from Troy*: on PLATE of bone china by Bow China
    Works. 203 mm (8 in) diameter
    Engraved in the style of Simon Ravenet, but believed to be by Robert Hancock,
    after a drawing by Hubert Gravelot, and printed in Venetian red. Hand-enamelled
    trefoil border. 1756–8. *See page 70*
    Sotheby, Parke Bernet and Company Limited
20 *The Whip Top*: on baluster-shape MUG of steatitic porcelain by Worcester
    Porcelain Company. 140 mm (5.5 in) high. (Also, *Blind Man's Buff* and
    Battledore and Shuttlecock.)
    Engraved by Robert Hancock, after Hubert François Gravelot, 1757–65. *See
    page 66*
    Victoria and Albert Museum

manufactory at Warmstry House, on the left bank of the river Severn, in the parish of St. Alban, in the City of Worcester. This was on a site where now stands the technical college. Richard Holdship, a Quaker and glove manufacturer in the city, on 16 May 1751 granted a lease of the property to a firm to be formed. The *raison d'être* of the undertaking was to finance the exploitation of the secret of porcelain manufacture stated already to have been discovered by a certain Dr. John Wall (1708–76) and William Davis (d. 1783), an apothecary, both of Worcester. They were each to be paid the sum of two hundred and fifty pounds for their discovery of the 'new Earthen Ware . . . under the denomination of Worcester Porcelain'. The material referred to, before the acquisition of Lund's licence in the following year, was probably very similar to the soft-paste porcelain then being made in large quantities at St. Cloud, and currently manufactured at Chelsea.

The deed mentioned two working potters to be employed on a wage and bonus basis: Robert Podmore and John Lyes. In spite of this special treatment Podmore left the firm, and according to William Chaffers went to work for Josiah Wedgwood.[8] He could not have been with him long, for on 14 July 1755 he signed an agreement with Richard Chaffers and Philip Christian of Shaw's Brow Pottery I at Liverpool, to show them the secrets of making steatitic porcelain, and to be their manager.[9]

Richard Holdship and his brother Josiah were both partners in the Worcester firm, and have in the past been much confused. Richard played a considerable role in the management, and could well have given up his business of glover, and become the whole-time manager under Wall. When he left the firm after his bankruptcy in 1760 his knowledge of the process of transfer printing suggests that he must have spent much time in the factory. Josiah in all probability also worked in the undertaking, for there is evidence which suggests that he had an executive position. The confusion between the two brothers is in some measure due to the notice in the *Gentleman's Magazine* as detailed below.

Nine months after its formation the firm had its capital fully employed. Because of this it was forced to buy through the agency of Richard Holdship, and much to his advantage, the licence of Benjamin Lund of Bristol to acquire steatite from Gew Graze, a very inaccessible cove five kilometres (three miles) north-west of the Lizard in Cornwall. Purchased at the same time were the stock, plant and knowledge of the processes of the Bristol firm of Benjamin Lund, then being liquidated. The steatite, known today as talc and at the time as soapy rock or soapstone, is a soft unctuous rock composed of approximately seventy-three per cent silica, with a lime and alumina content of only eleven per cent but a twelve per cent magnesia constituent. When pulverized it acted as a powerful flux, which with powdered calcined flint and china clay produced

[8] Op. cit., Vol. 2, p. 120.
[9] See p. 136.

21 *The Four Seasons* and *The Four Ages of Man*: on double-lipped and double-handled SAUCE BOATS of steatitic porcelain by WORCESTER PORCELAIN COMPANY. 184 mm (7.2 in) overall
Engravings for books by Louis P. Boitard, printed in dark drab in mirror image. *Old Age* with imprint 'L. P. Boitard delin.' in reverse. 1754–6.
See page 74
Sotheby, Parke Bernet and Company Ltd.

a strong soft-paste porcelain with a much higher resistance to thermal shock than other soft-paste porcelains. The licence proved a most valuable acquisition by the Worcester Company, and ensured a reliable source of supply of what at the time was a rare commodity.

Much has been written about the amalgamation of the Worcester and Bristol factories, but the evidence proves that no such union ever occurred. As part of the deal, and as is usual today in similar circumstances, Lund went to Worcester for a short period to explain and leave in operation the processes purchased. He is known to have been there in 1753, but after that his movements are obscure. A quite untenable theory is that the Worcester concern was created with the intention of taking over that at Bristol. It is preposterous to suppose that fifteen able and respected business men should enter into a partnership which disguised its real purpose, and then should involve their considerable capital to such an extent as to be unable, in seven months, to give effect to their real intent without the aid of the private resources of one of them—this very much to his benefit and to their detriment. It must be accepted that it was pure coincidence that Lund's licence became available; and a very fortunate one for Worcester. One thing about Lund's factory is quite clear, and that is that no porcelain made there was transfer-printed, unless it was so decorated at a later date at Worcester. The works were shut before the process was invented.

There exists a number of what are known as 'smoky primitive' pieces of transfer-printed Worcester porcelain. These carry prints either signed by, or very much in the style of, Louis Peter Boitard. The specimens are mostly sauce boats of silver shape, heavily potted and in the Bristol tradition. It is generally agreed that these were made before 1756. They are probably of Worcester production between 1752 and 1756, although a few may be old undecorated Bristol stock transfer-printed later at Worcester. The prints are invariably small, nearly always fitted into moulded cartouches, and are printed in a dark drab rather than black. Most have the appearance of having been printed from plates made for work on paper, and they look as if they were printed in a vitreous pigment similar to that used at Battersea. Amongst these prints are some of the pictures in the Boitard and Hancock album at the British Museum. One subject, *Old Age*, on one of a pair of two-handled sauce boats, has the imprint 'L.P.Boitard delin' in reverse, showing unequivocally that it was transferred from a plate originally intended for printing on paper (Plates 21 and 22). The second sauce boat has further examples of known Boitard designs, *The Four Seasons*. Yet another recorded example is on a waste bowl carrying the picture *Les Amusements Champêtres* which has the imprint again in reverse 'Boitard Sc' (Plate 23). This is proof positive that the copper printing-plate was engraved by Boitard. On the opposite side is *La Cascade*. Both engravings are after paintings by Antoine Watteau (1864–1721), and were intended when executed for printing on paper. The imprint is in mirror image when transferred to porcelain, and not as stated by another author in 1972, in reverse

22 Detail of *Old Age*: on right-hand SAUCE BOAT in Plate 21
    Clearly shows reversed imprint, proving that engraving was made for printing on
    paper (with only one reversal). *See page 74*
    Sotheby, Parke Bernet and Company Ltd.

23 *Les Amusements Champêtres*: on a WASTE BOWL of steatitic porcelain by WORCESTER
    PORCELAIN COMPANY. 153 mm (6 in) diameter. (On the reverse *La Cascade*.)
    From engravings for books by Louis P. Boitard, printed in dark drab, in mirror
    image. *Les Amusements Champêtres* with imprint 'Boitard Sc' in reverse. 1754–6.
    See page 74

when printed on paper. None of these very early Worcester transfer prints is in the style of Hancock, and none carries his imprint.

Every factor suggests that, irrespective of when these pieces were potted, they were transfer-printed between 1754 and 1756. It will be remembered that the album in the British Museum could not have been compiled before the earlier date, as the engravings carry a reference to the Act of that year. The only acceptable theory as to how these plates came to be used at Worcester is that Boitard went there for a short period, after the closure of the Battersea Works, and prior to Robert Hancock's arrival. Any suggestion that Hancock took Boitard's plates to Worcester is untenable. It is generally accepted that Hancock did not arrive at Worcester until late in 1756, or more probably in 1757. The primitive prints were done prior to that date. Furthermore it is impossible to envisage a valid reason why Hancock should experiment with, or use at all, plates engraved by Boitard in preference to his own. A new employee before he had thoroughly demonstrated his own skills and accomplishments would hardly be likely to work with the creations of a rival.

The only acceptable explanation is that Boitard, probably in 1756, visited Worcester, while Hancock was at Bow, and each man's work appears on the wares of his respective employer. It is interesting and significant that Boitard's engravings have never been found on Bow porcelain. Boitard for any possible reason may not have been happy away from London, and therefore returned. Hancock, on learning from him the size of the Worcester undertaking, could most naturally have seized the opportunity of returning close to the scene of his birth and upbringing, and, as remarked, this decision may have been helped by shadows cast before Edward Heylyn's bankruptcy in 1757.

A thorny problem is solved by acceptance of the above rationale, and this is why these primitive prints are so inferior to Hancock's work on Bow porcelain. The '*King of Prussia*' and other Hancock prints on Worcester porcelain from 1757 onwards are a natural progression from his work on Bow wares, and no amount of theorizing has been able to provide a satisfactory alternative explanation for the otherwise seeming regression shown by these very simple little prints. Unfortunately, acceptance of this postulate brings no nearer the answer to the vexed question as to whether the Bow China Works transfer printed on porcelain before the Worcester Porcelain Company, or vice versa.

Six years after the Worcester project had been started it is known that Robert Hancock had arrived, presumably with full knowledge and experience of the methods used at Bow. His presence is well documented, and he was to settle there to become a partner in 1772, and he remained nineteen years at the factory before he quarrelled with his colleagues and left in 1775. The first signed and dated print he produced was the famous '*King of Prussia*' portrait (Plate 24). The transfer print is after a mezzotint by Richard Houston (1721?–75), a pupil of John Brooks, based on one of Pesne's portraits, and it carries Hancock's monogram, the anchor rebus of Richard Holdship and the word Worcester, together with the date 1757 (Plate 25). The imprint is a

24 '*KING of PRUSSIA*' *No. 2*: on bell-shape MUG of steatitic porcelain by
WORCESTER PORCELAIN COMPANY. 119 mm (4.7 in) high. (On the reverse *Winged
Victory* with two trumpets, and in front *Military Trophies and Flags* showing
'Reisberg, Prague, Collin, Welham, Rossbach, Breslan [sic], Neumark, Lissa,
Breslan'.)
Engraved by Robert Hancock after a mezzotint by Richard Houston based on a
portrait by Antoine Pesne. Printed in deep grey-brown. Imprint 'RH Worcester'
and anchor. 1757. *See pages 26, 76*

classical example, derived from print publishing, of the initials of the engraver,
the name of the publisher and the date of publication, but with the rebus of the
vainglorious departmental director. There are several different versions of this
portrait by Hancock and others. If further confirmation is sought that Hancock

was at Worcester by 1757, this is provided by an engraving on paper entitled *A West Prospect of the Worcester Porcelain Manufactory with Mr Holdship's New Buildings*. This is signed 'R. Hancock delin. et sculp. 1757', and was doubtless an example of his desire to propitiate his new employer.

The confusion of identity that sometimes occurred between the two Holdship brothers has already been mentioned. Further complication was caused by the fact that Robert Hancock's and Richard Holdship's initials were the same. There is really no necessity for this if it is remembered that there is no evidence whatsoever to suggest that either of the Holdships ever engraved a line. Richard Holdship made Hancock engrave a small anchor as his rebus as printer, and when two of these are found side by side it is thought that they refer to both of the Holdship brothers.

Richard's having been a working partner and works manager, with overall responsibility for the transfer printing department, to some extent justifies his rebus appearing on prints. There is no record of his having any artistic ability, nor are there any examples extant of his work as a painter, draughtsman, engraver or etcher. If he had been capable of engraving the plates bearing his rebus, it is incredible that he would not also have used his talents in some other media, and that a trace or record of this would not have survived. He was certainly a vain and egotistic man, and if capable of engraving or etching would have signed his work with *sculpt.*, *fecit*, or some other imprint which could not have been mistaken either for that of his brother or of Hancock. His rebus on the '*King of Prussia*' engraving, manifestly in Hancock's style, proved to be an unsuccessful attempt to cash in on the circumstances. An edition of the *Gentleman's Magazine* in 1757 contained a woodcut of Frederick the Great with underneath a poem of twenty-seven couplets, referring to the Worcester mug carrying his portrait.[10] It included the lines:

> What praise, ingenious Holdship! is thy due,
> Who first on porcelain the fair portrait drew!
> Who first alone to full perfection brought,
> The curious art, by rival numbers sought!

One of the Holdships' founder partners in the porcelain company was Edward Cave (1691–1754), the son of a Rugby snob, who owned the *Gentleman's Magazine* from 1731 until his death. It seems that one of his successors with the pseudonym Cynthio, with which the poem was signed, wanted to give his late colleague's friend some praise and a little flattery, for which no doubt he was aware that he had an appetite. Unfortunately he made the additional confusion of Josiah with Richard. This eulogy was at the expense of Hancock, the employee really responsible. The following month the local paper championed Hancock's cause by a riposte in the form of a reprint of

---

[10] 20 December 1757, Vol. 27, p. 564.

25 Detail of imprint on MUG in Plate 24. *See page 76*

Cynthio's poem, at the request of an anonymous correspondent who signed his letter Philomath, but with the addition of a tailpiece:[11]

> Extempore on the compliment of imprinting the King of
> Prussia's bust being attributed to Josiah Holdship
>
> Hancock, my friend, don't grieve,
>   though Holdship has the praise,
> 'Tis yours to execute,
>   'tis his to wear the bays.

The Worcester Company quickly improved its black printing pigment, and achieved what was known at the time as jet enamel ware, although this in fact varied between deep brown–black and deep Payne's grey. A true jet black was never attained. The advance in depth of pigment was approximately as below:

(?)1754   (?)1755   (?)1756   1757   1758   1759   1760

Dark drab
Deep grey-brown
Deep Payne's grey   To end of
Deep brown-black   on-glaze
                                                     printing

[11] *Berrow's Worcestershire Journal*, January 1758.

26 *Tea Party No. 3* and *The Maid and Page*: on TEA BOWL and SAUCER of steatitic
porcelain by WORCESTER PORCELAIN COMPANY. Saucer 120 mm (4.7 in) diameter.
(On reverse of bowl a smaller version of *Tea Party No. 3*.)
The intermediate and rare variation, engraved by Robert Hancock, and printed in
deep grey-brown. 1757–9. *See pages 82, 95*

27 *Tea Party No. 2* and *The Maid and Page*: on TEA BOWL and SAUCER of steatitic
porcelain by WORCESTER PORCELAIN COMPANY. Saucer 118 mm (4.6 in) diameter.
(On reverse of bowl a smaller version of *Tea Party No. 2*.)
The last and much copied variation, engraved by Robert Hancock, and printed in
deep brown-black. 1760–5. *See pages 82, 95*

Inevitably *The Tea Party* figured on early Worcester pieces, originally in a very similar form to the prints found on enamels (Plate 26). In 1948 attention was drawn to some sheets of intaglio prints published by John Bowles and Son in 1756.[12] Two of these are from etched and over-engraved plates, very much in the manner of Hancock, and most probably are by him. They resemble in style those designed by Boitard and engraved by Hancock in the British Museum album. The imprints record that the sheets had been printed *for* John Bowles and Son, similarly to the *Ladies' Amusement* prints *for* Robert Sayer. The first sheet is numbered 37, and imprinted 'Published according to Act of Parliam! 24 Nov! 1756', and Bowles's address is stated as 'at the Black Horse, Cornhill.' It contains *The Tea Party* in almost exactly the same form as the transfer print on the enamel watch-back already considered, as well as *The Fortune Teller*, *The Singing Lesson* and three other vignettes.

Another sheet bears the same date, and was 'Printed for Jn? Bowles at 13 Cornhill.' This carries *The Wheeling Chair* and five other engravings in the same style. A third sheet and some loose cut-out engravings, supposedly from the same source, are in a quite different mode, and manifestly by another engraver. It is apparent that, like Sayer, Bowles may have employed a number of engravers to produce sheets for him. In the first instance he probably sold these loose, and then had them bound to make a book of designs.

Later a modified version of *The Tea Party* made its appearance on Worcester porcelain. This showed the lady and gentleman seated on opposite sides of the table, and without the page in attendance. Although a number of printing plates were engraved, which is proved by minor differences, it is probable that they were in use for only a short period, as the print is quite a rare one today. Unfortunately this version was numbered three by Cyril Cook, for it preceded his number two. The latter reverted to showing both persons on a settee, but this time on the right-hand side of the table (Plate 27). Again, the page is absent. This *Tea Party No. 2*, in all probability, was first in use about 1760, but it continued in production at Worcester for a number of years. Both the second and third varieties of *The Tea Party* are almost invariably associated with *The Maid and Page*, which was used to decorate the opposite sides of bowls and pots. *The Tea Party* is probably the most popular of all on-glaze transfer-printed designs, and was copied in many forms right up to the present century. It is of interest that as late as the nineteen-twenties, this *Tea Party No. 2* and *The Milkmaids* were faithfully copied by H. Fennell in line-etched and engraved transfer prints, on-glaze, on bone-china tea canisters by the New Chelsea Porcelain Company of Longton (c. 1912–51) (Plate 28). These canisters were made in pairs, superbly potted and printed. Nevertheless the pictures are inclined to be a little stilted, and lack the freedom and spontaneity of the originals. Of considerable interest is the picture, *The Chapman*, on the

[12] Aubrey J. Toppin, 'The Origins of some Ceramic Designs', *E.C.C. Transactions*, Vol. 2, Part 10, p. 271, and Plates XCVII a and b.

28 *Tea Party No. 2* and *The Milkmaids*: on a pair of TEA CANISTERS of bone china by
   NEW CHELSEA PORCELAIN COMPANY, LONGTON. 137 mm (5.4 in) overall height
   From engravings by H. Fennell, after Robert Hancock, printed in ivory black.
   Imprint 'H. Fennell', and back-mark anchor, and printed in red script 'New
   Chelsea Staffs.', with green pattern-number 1326. 1920–5. *See pages 82, 224*
29 *The Chapman*: on reverse of right-hand CANISTER in Plate 28
   Imprint 'H. Fennell'. The other engravings on these pieces are after Robert
   Hancock, but no original of this design has so far been recorded. *See pages 84, 224*

reverse of the second canister (Plate 29). The other engravings are after Robert Hancock, and one would assume that this had a similar derivation, but so far no original transfer print of this design has been recorded.[13] The threat that these high quality copies represent, should they fall into the hands of the unscrupulous, is considered in the last chapter.

Although all Hancock's copper plates were both etched and engraved, the use of the two techniques was complementary and differed from the freer style adopted by the Liverpool school of transfer printers. The engraving was very faithfully and painstakingly employed to deepen already etched lines, and very often it is difficult to detect that there was any prior etching. Occasionally, because the engraved line is a millimetre or so short of that etched, the end of the finer line can be detected. Magnified detail from the '*King of Prussia*' mug shows clearly the high proportion of engraving, and the care with which this has been superimposed over the etching (Plate 43). Examination of the cross-hatching behind the shoulder of the figure distinctly shows the deepened engraved lines crossing the lighter etched ones. When both techniques were employed on one copper plate invariably the etching preceded the engraving. A number of Hancock's original plates remain today in the archives of the Worcester Royal Porcelain Company, and these all show that they were both etched and engraved (Plate 8).

It did not take long for the Worcester factory to perfect on-glaze printing in maroon, puce, pale violet and brown. Prints covered many subjects, including some based on paintings by such masters as François Boucher, Jean Pillement and Antoine Watteau. *The Milkmaids* is an example of a transfer print based on a painting by the last-named artist, and Hancock's version printed in puce is illustrated on a saucer with *The Tease* on the coffee cup (Plate 30). One of the most attractive and popular subjects, to be found in a number of different forms, is *L'Amour* (Plate 31). This is shown on the lid of an early covered sucrier, but it is a somewhat unusual variety, for the more general Neptune fountain is omitted from the left background, and in the right background is a gardener rolling a lawn. The lid also carries two sprays of flowers, and a version of *Garden Statuary*, without the customary dog and roller. Both *L'Amour* and this print are similar in detail, but not identical, to the engravings on one of Hancock's surviving copper plates in the Dyson Perrins Museum. The print on the side of the bowl, shown in the illustration, is *The Fortune Teller No. 2*, and this again is an uncommon variant, which has been found on enamels. The bowl also carries outside *The Maid and Page*, and *Tea Party No. 2*, but with the omission of the terrace and statue in the right background. Amongst the many portraits are likenesses of George II, William Pitt, George III and Queen

---

[13] During the course of publication, it has come to notice that an original Hancock print of this subject was known over twenty-five years ago, on a baluster shape tea canister, but its whereabouts were then not disclosed and are unknown today: G. W. Capell, 'Some Transfer-Printed Pieces', *E.C.C. Transactions*, Vol. 3, Part 5, London, 1955, Plate 93a.

30 *The Tease* and *The Milkmaids*: on fluted COFFEE CUP and SAUCER of steatitic porcelain by WORCESTER PORCELAIN COMPANY. Saucer 134 mm (5.3 in) diameter *The Tease* is loosely derived from an engraving by Amiconi. Printed in puce, with imprint on saucer 'Hancock fecit'. Fretted square back-mark. 1758–62. *See page 84 Cheltenham Art Gallery and Museum*

31 *L'Amour* and *The Fortune Teller No. 2*: on covered SUGAR BOWL of steatitic porcelain by WORCESTER PORCELAIN COMPANY. 155 mm (6.1 in) high overall. (Also on bowl *Tea Party No. 2* and *The Maid and Page*, and on lid *Garden Statuary*.) Engravings by Robert Hancock, printed in deep Payne's grey. 1758–62. *See pages 70, 84*

32 *Queen Charlotte*: a marriage commemorative MUG of steatitic porcelain by
WORCESTER PORCELAIN COMPANY. 90 mm (3.5 in) high
From a magnificently etched and engraved plate by Robert Hancock, after an
engraving by James Macardell, published in 1762, printed in puce. 1762–5. *See
pages 88, 96*
Dyson Perrins Museum

33 *Pastoral Serenade*: on moulded cabbage-leaf JUG with mask spout, of steatitic
porcelain by WORCESTER PORCELAIN COMPANY. 179 mm (7 in) high
A very rare print engraved by Robert Hancock, and printed in deep Payne's grey.
1760–5. *See page 88*

Charlotte (Plate 32). The last two were probably on coronation and marriage commemorative pieces from 1760 to 1761 respectively. The very beautiful transfer print illustrated is probably the first issued of the queen, and deserves close study. The combinations of line and stipple, and etching and engraving are masterly. A later version, with a title, is a copy, and not a very good one. It is virtually certain that the original is the work of Hancock, and is after an engraving by James Macardell, published in 1762. Occasionally it is still possible to find very rare, or previously unrecorded, prints by Robert Hancock on Worcester Porcelain, and an example is *Pastoral Serenade* (Plate 33).[14] This is on a standard cabbage-leaf jug with mask spout, and shows a seated shepherd serenading, with a flute, a shepherdess reclining beneath some trees. Their dog is in the foreground, and the sheep in a distant meadow. It forms a trilogy with the better-known *Rural Lovers* and *Milking Scene No. 1* (Plates 34 and 35). These prints are in deep Payne's grey; again it is emphasized that at Worcester they never achieved a real jet black in their on-glaze printing — no matter what were the contemporary claims.

Following the mode of both Battersea and Bow, at Worcester they sometimes hand-coloured transfer prints by enamelling them before the hardening-on. Illustrated is a saucer dish with the print *Temple Ruins* printed in deep amethyst, over-enamelled in eight lack-lustre semi-opaque colours, and picked out in gold (Colour Plate B). The engraving is a complete picture with all shading and hatching, and when it was prepared it is obvious that there was no intention that it should form the basis of a coloured picture. The result is heavy, muddy and lifeless, and the gold seems to have been an unsuccessful attempt to try and give some sparkle and vitality. It forms a miserable comparison to the delightful enamelled prints of the Bow China Works, where special plates were engraved mostly in outline, with the clear intention that the prints should be coloured. It might be thought that this dish has been 'clobbered' by an outside decorator, except for the fact that most enamelled Worcester prints of this period suffer from the same improvisation. (See also Postscript, page 233.)

An exception that is very much a paradox, is the *Red Bull* pattern, which is generally accepted as being found on Worcester porcelain, as well as on porcelain by Chaffers and Christian of Liverpool. Illustrated is a waste bowl attributed seemingly with good cause to Worcester, and it will be seen that the print, which is of graphite colour, is an outline one, designed for over-enamelling — very much in the tradition of similar Chinese designs on Bow porcelain (Colour Plate C). Most noticeable is the hatching on the bull to the left, which it is not intended should be coloured, contrasted with the outline only of the other which is red enamelled. On the other side of the bowl is a design *The Horizontal Tree* (Plate 36). What is even more perplexing is that

---

[14] The only previous record of this pattern was forty-five years ago on a mug, the property of C. W. Dyson Perrins: Bernard Rackham, 'Some Unusual Worcester Porcelain', *E.C.C. Transactions*, Vol. 1, Part 5, London, 1937, Plate XIIa.

34 *Rural Lovers*: on front of JUG in Plate 33
Engraved by Robert Hancock after an engraving by François Vivares, after a
painting by Thomas Gainsborough. 1760–5. *See pages 88, 144, 150*
35 *Milking Scene No. 1*: on left side of JUG in Plates 33 and 34
Engraved by Robert Hancock after an engraving by Luke Sullivan. 1760–5. *See
page 88*

these patterns seem to have been isolated ones at Worcester, but prints from plates quite obviously etched and engraved by the same hand are found on Chaffers and Christian porcelain (see page 138 and Colour Plate E). If there is no error in the attributions, it would seem that an engraver-enameller must have moved, like Podmore, from Worcester to Liverpool.

Hancock was evidently the man in charge of the engraving department at Worcester, and at first he worked directly under Richard Holdship. The latter in the four years before he left in 1760 acquired from Hancock a knowledge of all there was to know about the transfer-printing process. There was a strong team of engravers and apprentices, some of whom achieved eminence at a later date in the ceramic industry. Hancock's foreman was George Lewis, in remembrance of whom there was formerly a tablet in the nave of St. Alban's Church, Worcester.[15] This is the small church remaining next to the technical college. The tablet read:

> GEORGE LEWIS who departed this life on the 29th day of September 1790, aged 57. He was the conductor of the printing business of the Porcelain Manufactory in the City upwards of thirty years, in which capacity his indefatigable attention and integrity were worthy of imitation.

Probably Lewis took sole charge after the departure of both Holdship and Hancock. Valentine Green (1739–1813), a famous artist, mezzotintist and author, who recorded the above epitaph, had been a pupil of Hancock from 1760 to 1764. Others working under him were James Ross (1745–1821) and John Lewick, both apprenticed in 1765, and William Underwood, who later went with Richard Holdship to Derby and, according to Simeon Shaw, afterwards worked for John Turner senior (fl. 1762–86) of Lane End.[16] The apprentice who achieved greatest fame in the ceramic world was undoubtedly Thomas Turner (1749–1809). He was indentured in 1765, at the age of sixteen, and although in 1772, soon after his term expired, he left the Worcester factory, he remained in the city and set up as a middleman handling the products of his ex-employers. By the summer of 1775 he had moved to the Caughley factory, as is proved by a change of address in the books of James Giles (1718–80), a London dealer. After he left Worcester he confined his transfer printing to underglaze blue.

On-glaze transfer printing may have continued at Worcester until 1770 and later — some ten or more years after the introduction of underglaze printing. All on-glaze printing from the factory is found on hollow ware, small dishes, saucers and stands. It seems that, unlike its contemporaries manufacturing soft-paste porcelain, it experienced great difficulty in the production of large plates and dishes of the steatitic bisque.

The departure of Richard Holdship must have thrown a great strain on Dr. Wall, but fortunately by then the factory was fully established, and Hancock

---

[15] Valentine Green, *History of Worcestershire*, 1796, Vol. 2, Appendix p. cix.
[16] Op. cit., p. 214.

36 *The Horizontal Tree*: on opposite side of WASTE BOWL in Colour Plate C
    Outline engraving printed in graphite colour, and over-enamelled in the same six
    colours as the main picture. 1758–61. *See pages 88, 138*

was well able to control all the transfer printing. On his bankruptcy in 1760
Holdship ceased to be a partner, and his next proven place of work was at
Derby in 1764. It is thought that he left Worcester in 1761, and, as has been
mentioned (page 70), there is a most attractive and probably theory that he
then worked at Bow for a short period, and taught them to transfer print under
glaze.

MICHAEL HANBURY, DUBLIN (fl. 1758 to 1762)

The first free-lance transfer printer, after Sadler and Green (see page 101), of
whom there is record, was Michael Hanbury, who worked in George's Lane,
Dublin—a small turning off King Street North. He exhibited to the Dublin
Society in 1758 several pieces of transfer-printed pottery for which he was
awarded a prize of twenty guineas.[17] This ranks him as one of the earliest of all
engravers and transfer printers. It seems that he must have obtained details of
the process either from his fellow citizen Henry Delamain, or from John
Brooks who is reputed to have returned to Dublin after his bankruptcy in 1756.

In the Irish National Museum there are two delftware plates decorated with
transfer-printed heraldic achievements emblazoned with colour enamels

[17] M. S. D. Westropp, *Irish Pottery and Porcelain*, 1935, p. 14.

(Plates 37 and 38). On the base of one is written in longhand 'Made by John Stritch Limerick 1761', and on the other 'Made by John Stritch Limerick 4 June 1761'. The achievement on the first is of Francis Pierpoint Burton, and on the second of Edmond Sexton Pery, Viscount Pery (1719–1806), speaker of the Irish Parliament 1771–85, member for Wicklow 1751–60 and for Limerick 1760–85. Another copy of the Pery plate is back-marked '6 July 1761 made by John Stritch'. The escutcheons, insipid mantlings, and scrolls under, have been printed from the same copper plate, while the arms, wreaths (helmets missing), crests and in one case the motto, and in the other the name, have been hand pencilled in outline to match the printing, before the whole in each case was enamelled. The printing is very similar to that of Bow and in the same burnt-umber colour, but the enamelling is much inferior. Sprigs printed on both condiments-rims are identical. It would seem a reasonable assumption that both are examples of the work of Michael Hanbury.

DERBY: POT WORKS (1751 to 1780) and PORCELAIN FACTORY (1756 to 1848)

The Derby Pot Works were situated at the south-west corner of Siddals Road, between Cock Pit Hill, which is the north end of Eagle Street, and Rivett Street. There was then no Traffic Street which now runs diagonally across the site. The factory was opened in November 1751, and by a deed dated 25 December 1753 it was owned by a partnership composed of John Heath, William Butts and two other men. Shortly after the formation, Christopher Heath (1718–1815), brother of John, joined the firm. In 1780 the two Heaths were declared bankrupt, a malady which seems to have been extraordinarily infectious amongst potters in the eighteenth century. This resulted in the closure of the Cock Pit Hill Works and five subsequent auctions when the stock was sold at knock-down prices.

The second Derby factory was near the end of St. Mary's Bridge, and about one hundred and fifty metres (one hundred and sixty-four yards) down the north side of Nottingham Road, between Wood Street and Alice Street. This was nearly two kilometres (a mile and a quarter) distant from the Cock Pit Hill Works, and on the opposite bank of the River Derwent. This factory manufactured porcelain, and it is now believed that it was opened in 1752, or perhaps earlier, because of a newspaper report in January 1753 of the drowning of an employee of 'the China Works near Mary Bridge'.[18] The founder partners were John Heath and Andrew Planché (1728–1809).

In 1756 William Duesbury (1725–86) joined the Nottingham Road partnership. He was born at Longton Hall in Staffordshire on 7 September 1725, the son of a father of the same name, a hide and leather dresser of

---

[18] *Derby Mercury*, January 1753.

37 *Heraldic Achievement* of Francis Pierpoint Burton, showing motto '*Dominus Providebit*': on delftware PLATE by JOHN STRITCH, LIMERICK. 220 mm (8.6 in) diameter
Probably engraved by Michael Hanbury of Dublin, and printed in burnt umber, emblazoned with polychrome over-enamelling. Base marked in script 'Made by John Stritch Limerick 1761'. *See page 92*
Ard-Mhúsaem Na hÉireann an Roin Oideachais (The Director, National Museum of Ireland)

Cannock. He married Sarah James of Shrewsbury, and before coming to Derby was an enameller in London. It is believed that he spent a short time at the Longton Hall Works immediately prior to going to Derby, and that when that factory closed in 1760 he purchased some of the undecorated stock, which he took to Derby. Llewellynn Jewitt possessed a draft partnership agreement dated 1 January 1756 between John Heath, Planché and Duesbury.[19] In 1770 Duesbury, with financial assistance from John Heath, took over the Chelsea

[19] *The Ceramic Art of Great Britain*, 1878, Vol. 2, p. 64.

38 *Heraldic Achievement* of Edmond Sexton Pery Esq.: on delftware PLATE by JOHN
STRITCH, LIMERICK. 220 mm (8.6 in) diameter
Printed from the same copper plate as that used on the plate shown in Plate 37.
Condiments-rim washed in biscuit colour. Base marked in script 'Made by John
Stritch Limerick 4 June 1761'. *See page 92*
*Ard-Mhúsaem Na hÉireann an Roin Oideachais (The Director, National Museum of
Ireland)*

Porcelain Works, and six years later purchased from John Crowther the
moulds and plant of the Bow China Works. After the bankruptcy of the Heaths
he ran both the Derby and Chelsea factories for fourteen years, before closing
the latter in 1784, and transferring much of the plant and some of the most
skilled craftsmen to Nottingham Road, Derby.

Although until 1780 the two Derby firms had a common partner in John
Heath it is clear that they were very largely independent of each other, and
there is nothing to show that Duesbury ever had a financial interest in the pot
works. The precise business relationship of the two factories is obscure,
although evidence indicates that they worked in close harmony.

In 1764, four years after his bankruptcy at Worcester, Richard Holdship turned up at the Derby Porcelain Works, accompanied by a capable engraver, William Underwood, also from Worcester. By another agreement once in the possession of Jewitt, Heath and Duesbury undertook to employ Holdship, and to pay him for his knowledge of transfer printing one hundred pounds down, and thirty pounds per annum.[20] Holdship on his side was to show them how to make first-class porcelain and to 'print with enamel and blew', and to keep the processes secret. Soapstone was introduced into the bisque immediately, but bone ash not until 1770. This deed shows that no successful printing either over or under the glaze had taken place at Derby before 1764.

Clearly Holdship was to organize the engraving and transfer-printing departments, but there are several pointers to suggest that his management did not reach the standards demanded by Duesbury. He is recorded as constantly complaining that he had no pieces for his presses. It is only possible to surmise about the arrangements made for transfer printing at the two Derby factories. It is probable that William Underwood worked as engraver at the porcelain works, and that another engraver, Thomas Radford, was engaged to work at the Pot Works—both under the control of Holdship, who supervised the transfer printing at the two places. This is confirmed by his vanity in demanding that his anchor rebus, as manager, should on occasion be engraved on copper plates used at both establishments.

Radford's origins are a complete mystery, but he was a competent engraver. It is generally assumed that he stayed at Cock Pit Hill until the factory closed in 1780, but this is unlikely, and evidence suggests that he was in Staffordshire at the latest by 1778, where besides being a free-lance on-glaze transfer printer he later built up a substantial business as an engraver of plates for underglaze printing. The movements of William Underwood are more obscure. When he left Derby is unknown, but it is thought that this was in 1769, when Holdship departed. The next definite news of him is that sometime before 1786 he was doing work for John Turner senior of Lane End.

There exists a rather crude creamware teapot, dating from about 1765, printed on-glaze with on one side *The Tea Party* and on the other *The Wheeling Chair* (Plate 39). It is interesting to compare these prints with Hancock's earlier editions on Bow and Worcester porcelain (Plates 15, 26 and 27). It will be noticed that the Derby versions are in mirror image, which suggests that they may have been copied by an engraver unfamiliar with the transfer-printing process. This piece is in fact signed by Thomas Radford, so that the pictures could be some of his earliest efforts at engraving for transfer printing. Another similarly shaped creamware teapot has on one side a print of *The Imperial Russian Arms*, and on the other a portrait of *Catherine II* (1729–96), 'The Great', who reversed most of her late husband's policies and in 1764 became the ally of Frederick the Great, which was presumably the reason for her portrait appearing on a British teapot (Plate 40). The shape of the design suggests that originally it was intended as a decoration for mugs and jugs.

[20] Ibid, p. 87.

A creamware plate has a pattern *La Pêcheuse Chinoise* (Plate 41). This piece has the characteristic Derby pale lime glaze, which in places is lineally crazed, as is often found on Cock Pit Hill products. This was caused by the use of a glaze excessively fluxed in relation to the bisque, and internal stresses transverse to the crazing being greater than those in the direction of it. The print shows a marked Worcester influence, but nevertheless the style and technique of the engraving are very much those of Thomas Radford.

An early example of transfer printing on Derby porcelain is illustrated by a mug bearing portraits of George III and Queen Charlotte (Plate 42). Similar mugs are marked with Holdship's anchor and the word 'DERBY', either beneath the handle, or in the centre front. It is of interest that the cherub bears a ribbon inscribed 'Crownd Septr 22d 1761', but it is impossible for the mug to have been a coronation souvenir, for the agreement with Holdship proves that he was not at Derby before 1764. If there is any doubt as to the reason for Duesbury's dissatisfaction with transfer printing at Derby, a comparison should be made between the almost caricature portrait on this mug and the beautiful and dignified likeness by Hancock on the Worcester mug (Plate 32). If it were not for the anchor imprint, the style of the Derby engraving is such that it could easily be thought that the pieces had been printed in Liverpool, by Sadler and Green, from plates engraved by Thomas Billinge. It is sad, but all Derby transfer printing on porcelain is markedly inferior in quality to that of Worcester, as well as lacking crispness and spontaneity.

After Holdship left Derby in 1769, the possibility is that on-glaze printing ceased at both works, and that underglaze printing only as a base for hand enamelling was continued at the porcelain factory. While the use of the underglaze process rapidly proliferated, the continuance of on-glaze printing, as practised at Bow, Worcester and Derby, probably devolved solely on Thomas Radford, and his possible pupil, Thomas Fletcher (see page 160).

THOMAS RADFORD, SHELTON AND STOKE-ON-TRENT
(fl. 1778 to 1802)

Probably sometime in 1778 Thomas Radford arrived at Shelton. He is known to have done much on-glaze printing about then for William Greatbatch at Fenton, two kilometres distant (see page 172). It has been suggested that Greatbatch was himself an engraver and printer, but this was not so, and is due to an incorrect interpretation of his publisher's imprint. Simeon Shaw when writing of Greatbatch stated that he 'had a most rapid sale of teapots, on which was printed, in black by Thomas Radford, the history of the Prodigal Son'.[21] Whether Radford was on Greatbatch's staff or a free-lance transfer printer is not certain, but the probability is that he had his own business. It has been

---

[21] Op. cit., p. 190.

C. *Red Bull Pattern*: on WASTE BOWL of steatitic porcelain, by WORCESTER PORCELAIN COMPANY. 106 mm (4.2 in) diameter
Outline printed in graphite colour, and over-enamelled in vermilion, bright cobalt, grey-emerald, lavender, primrose and shrimp. 1758–61. *See pages 88, 138*

D. *The Chinese Tea Drinker*: on TILE of delftware, LIVERPOOL. 128 mm (5 in) square
From a woodcut, after an engraving by Johann E. Nilson, printed in deep violet-
brown by Sadler and Green. 1756–8. *See page 106*

39 *Tea Party No. 1*: on globular TEAPOT of creamware, by DERBY POT WORKS.
103 mm (4 in) high. (On reverse *The Wheeling Chair*.)
Engraved by Thomas Radford, and printed in deep brown-black. Both pictures in
mirror image. Imprints 'Pot Works in DERBY' and 'Radford Sculpsit DERBY'.
1764–6. *See page 95. British Museum*

40 *Catherine II*: on TEAPOT of creamware, by DERBY POT WORKS. 105 mm (4.1 in)
high. (On reverse *The Russian Imperial Arms*.)
Engraved by Thomas Radford and printed in deep brown-black. Imprints 'T.
Radford Sc DERBY', '1765'. *See page 95*
Derby City Museum and Art Gallery

41 *La Pêcheuse Chinoise*: on Royal-pattern PLATE of pale reseda-colour creamware by
    DERBY POT WORKS. 209 mm (8.2 in) diameter
    With six different dead-game vignettes, printed in jet black. Enamelled black
    border. 1766–9. Cf. Plate 116. *See pages 96, 188*
42 *Queen Charlotte*: on MUG of porcelain by DERBY PORCELAIN FACTORY. 127 mm
    (5 in) high
    Engraved probably by William Underwood, under Richard Holdship's super-
    vision. (King George III's portrait on other side.) Anchor rebus and 'Derby'
    imprint beneath handle. This is almost a caricature compared with Worcester
    portrait of the Queen, Plate 32. 1764–6. *See page 96*
    Royal Crown Derby Porcelain Company Limited

suggested that these engravings are in a different style from that of Radford, and are not by him (Plates 97 and 98). A negative like this is very difficult to substantiate, for the style of every artist changes over his lifetime, and an additional complication is that the prints on Greatbatch creamware are almost entirely made for the purpose of being over-enamelled, whereas Radford's work at Derby was for monochrome printing. Although Shaw has often been proved to have been in error, he perforce had some reason to couple these specific engravings on Greatbatch's teapots with Thomas Radford.

While at Derby, Radford must have acquired a knowledge of the underglaze process from Richard Holdship, for he quickly changed his business at both Stoke-on-Trent and Shelton to supplying engraved copper plates for this purpose. He instructed his potential customers in the craft of underglaze printing, beginning with John Baddeley II. Shaw wrote:[22]

> 'Mr John Baddeley, of Shelton, some time employed Mr. Thomas Radford to print Tea Services by an improved method of transferring the impression to the bisquet ware; which was attempted to be kept secret, but was soon developed; and the glaze prevented the beautiful appearance which attached to the Black printed.'

As John Baddeley had died in 1771, it is certain that Shaw was referring to John II (b. 1760), one of his four sons. John II at the age of twenty-four, together with his brother Edward, who had just reached his majority, opened in 1784 a pottery next door to that of their late father, which was then being run by the eldest brother, Ralph. It is possible that Thomas Radford began to work for them immediately afterwards.

Radford must have built up a considerable engraving business because in the *Staffordshire Pottery Directory* map of 1802 he is shown as operating from establishments both at Shelton and at Stoke-on-Trent. It is significant that he was then described as an engraver, and not as an engraver and printer, so the likelihood is that he had completely relinquished transfer printing.

[22] Ibid., p. 213.

Chapter 4

THE NORTHERN SCHOOL OF TRANSFER PRINTING

Inventions mostly represent the application of known principles to new uses, or the combination of two or more existing procedures to achieve novel results. Nevertheless, original thought is needed: the rarest of all human capabilities. It is difficult, and perhaps impossible, to find any instance where an invention has taken place more than once completely independently: if that is not an Irishism. Ideas, simple in retrospect, often failed to materialize thousands of years after conditions were seemingly right for their discovery. It is now incredible that the ancient Greeks, with their advanced scholarship, mathematics and architectural abilities, never found out how to put the arch to practical use. The Incas in the sixteenth century AD were city dwellers of mature civilization, but had no knowledge of the use of the wheel, five and a half millennia after its discovery. This clearly demonstrates the effect of a lack of communication on the dissemination of an invention. Stories abound of the lifetime toils of an inventor having been in vain, because at the moment of triumph glory was snatched by another. It is impossible to authenticate any cases where it was impracticable for there to have been any communication or linking factors.

These rather trite observations have been made because ceramic printing depended upon a combination of a number of well-known principles, and the keystone was the idea of transferring the print instead of attempting to print directly upon the article. Like many discoveries, it seems so simple and obvious with hindsight that there is a temptation to think that it could easily have been thought of by more than one person. This is most improbable, and the odds against such a duplication of an original idea are astronomical. Although it will in some quarters be held to be contentious the theory is advanced in this book that once having been discovered, the idea and details of the process of transfer printing were disseminated only by those with experience of the craft. After examples appeared on the market, ceramic history records many stories of attempts to use the process without the help of those completely familiar with it. All were unsuccessful in spite of public knowledge of the principle of transference.

SADLER AND GREEN, LIVERPOOL (1749 to 1799)

John Sadler (1720–89) was born in Liverpool on 9 January 1720, the son of Adam Sadler (1682–1765). He was duly apprenticed as printer to his father in New Market, Liverpool, and in 1748 he started his own business in Harrington Street, from a house owned by his father, who let him have it for the sum of five shillings per annum—even in those days a nominal rental. This street runs parallel to, and just north of, Lord Street, and was in a central and advantageous position. He remained a bachelor until the age of fifty-seven, and resided at his place of work, employing a housekeeper named Hanah, who looked after him from 1763 until at least 1774, and probably up to the time of his marriage. This was not until 1777, after his retirement from business, when he married a young girl of twenty-three, Elizabeth Parker (1754–1842), the daughter of a watchmaker of Seal Street. They had a daughter, Elizabeth Mary, born in 1782, who never married, but survived until 1857, and provided an important link three years before her death by supplying information to Joseph Mayer.

In 1749 John Sadler took as partner Guy Green, who had also been apprenticed to Sadler senior. Together they ran a thriving printing business until 1761, when they sold the plant and machinery. This was ten years after they had started their ceramic printing, and only four years prior to Sadler's retirement in 1770.

According to their own account Sadler and Green invented transfer printing, and perfected it in the summer of 1756. What in fact were the circumstances?

(1) Transfer-printed japanned ware had been on the market for more than three and a half years.

(2) There is evidence that transfer-printed Battersea enamel wares had been sold in quantity for at least two and a half years.

(3) Jean Rouquet had published in 1755 in both Paris and London an equivocal account of the process, which nevertheless gave away the basic principles.

(4) Brooks had made no less than three unsuccessful patent applications in 1751, 1753 and 1754.

(5) Transfer-printed Bow porcelain was on the market in May 1756, and probably some months earlier.

(6) Henry Delamain, who knew the process, had passed through Liverpool from time to time between 1753 and 1756. He was intimate with the Liverpool potters in December 1753, and it is unlikely that such an extrovert would not have mentioned his knowledge of the new transfer-

printing process. His character may be easily judged from his letters referred to earlier (page 55).

Is it credible that in August 1756 neither Sadler nor Green, nor the Liverpool potters who supported them, were aware that transfer printing was already discovered, and in use? They must have known, but rightly thought that as yet nobody had applied the process to delftware.

Subject to these reservations, however, they did develop a process different in a number of respects from that already in use. This was principally due to the fact that their approach to the problem was from a quite different starting-point. At Bow and Worcester the invention had been perfected by professional engravers with the help of men experienced in the manufacture and decoration of porcelain. At Liverpool the method evolved was by printers aided, at the start at any rate, by makers of delftware and earthenware. It is as well to emphasize here that neither Sadler nor Green was an artist, engraver or etcher, any more than were the Holdships.

Because of their printing experience their approach to the problem differed from that of Hancock and his friends in a number of fundamental ways:

(1) At the commencement they used surface-printing woodcuts with which they were familiar.

(2) They soon changed to the employment of etched plates strengthened by engraving, but this was less carefully carried out than at Worcester, where the engraved line always deepened the etched line. At Liverpool the engraving for many years was only for a heavier effect, and this was achieved without regard to the underlying etched lines.

(3) They realized the disadvantages of charging intaglio plates with pigments including vitreous ingredients, and introduced their system of pouncing.

(4) Being printers and not potters they never seriously embarked on a programme of underglaze printing.

Having taken all the necessary steps preliminary to a patent application, they swore a joint affidavit on 2 August 1756. It was short, not without interest, and read:

I, John Sadler of Liverpoole, in the County of Lancaster, printer, and Guy Green of Liverpoole aforesaid, printer, severally maketh oath, that on Tuesday, the 27th day of July instant, they, these deponents, without the aid or assistance of any other person or persons, did, within the space of six hours, to wit, betwixt the hours of nine in the morning and three in the afternoon of the same day, print upwards of twelve hundred earthenware tiles of different patterns, at Liverpoole aforesaid, and which, as these deponents have heard and believe, were more in number and better and neater, than one hundred skilful pot painters could have painted in the like space of time in the common and usual way of painting with a pencil; and these deponents say that they have been upwards of seven years in finding out the method of printing tiles and in making trials and experiments for that purpose, which they have now, through great pains and expense, brought to perfection.

John Sadler
Guy Green

This affadivit was supported by an equally interesting certificate signed by the two potters who fired the printed tiles, after Sadler and Green had finished their exhausting day's labour. Thomas Shaw and Samuel Gilbody, the Liverpool potters in question, stated:

We, Alderman Thomas Shaw and Samuel Gilbody, both of Liverpoole in the County of Lancaster, clay potters, whose names are hereunto subscribed, do hereby humbly certifye that we are well assured that John Sadler and Guy Green did, at Liverpoole aforesaid, on Tuesday, the 27th day of July, last past, within the space of six hours, print upwards of 1,200 earthenware tiles of different colours and patterns, which is, upon a moderate computation, more than 100 good workmen could have done of the same patterns in the same space of time by the usual way of painting with the pencil. That we have since burnt the above tiles, and that they are considerably neater than any that we have seen pencilled, and may be sold at little more than half the price. We are also assured that the said John Sadler and Guy Green have been several years in bringing the art of printing on earthenware to perfection, and we never heard that it was done by any other person or persons but themselves. We are also assured that as the Dutch (who import large quantities of tiles into England, Ireland. &c.), may by this improvement be considerably undersold, it cannot fail to be of great advantage to the nation, and to the towne of Liverpoole in particular, where the earthenware manufacture is more extensively carried on than in any other town in the Kingdom, and for which reasons we hope, and do not doubt, the above persons will be indulged in their request for a patent to secure to them the profits that may arise from the above useful and advantageous improvements.

The intention to obtain a patent, and therefore the reason for the preparation of the foregoing documents, is confirmed in the following brief letter addressed to Charles Poole, the then member of parliament for Liverpool, at the time resident in London:

Liverpoole, Aug 13, 1756

Sir,

John Sadler, the bearer, and Guy Green, both of this town, have invented a method of printing potters' earthenware tyles for chimneys, with surprising expedition. We have seen several of their printed tyles and are of opinion that they are superior to any done by the pencil, and that this invention will be highly advantageous to the Kingdom in general, and to the town of Liverpoole in particular.

In consequence of which, and for the encouragement of so useful and ingenious an improvement, we desire the favour of your interest in procuring for them his Majesty's letters patent.

Ellis Cunliffe
Spencer Steers
Charles Goore

There are many points of interest in these documents, but firstly the fact that several different patterns were printed suggests that their experiments were mature, and the petition not rushed through on success with the first block. In this it differed markedly from the hasty patent applications made by John Brooks. The neatness of the results is confirmation of this.

It does seem from these documents that in all probability less than justice has been done in ceramic history to Thomas Shaw and Samuel Gilbody. Neither Sadler nor Green would have known the first thing about vitreous pigments, and presumably they were greatly aided in their essential chemical experiments by the two potters who eventually did the firing for them. Finally, one wonders at the singular emphasis in the affidavit that experiments had been taking place for upwards of seven years, only half-heartedly supported in the potters' certificate. The interval claimed conveniently brings the supposed commencement back to 1749. The question must be asked, was it by coincidence that this was comfortably before Brooks had attempted to print by the transfer process?

The letter to Charles Poole leaves little doubt that Sadler went to London with the intention of personally lodging the application, but the events that followed are unrecorded. The explanation generally advanced is that Sadler and Green consulted with friends—anonymous—who advised them that it was imprudent to take the matter further, because of the expense and delay that would be involved, and the fact that they would have had to disclose details of their process. Alternatively, if they were careful and prudently guarded their secret a long time must elapse before their process became known to their competitors. This explanation is singularly unconvincing, and as far as can be ascertained it was originally proffered by Joseph Mayer in a paper read in 1871 to the Historical Society of Lancashire and Cheshire, and given additional respectability three years later by William Chaffers.[1] This is one of Mayer's suspect deductions that have time and again been repeated. We know he visited Elizabeth Mary Sadler in 1854 at her late grandfather's farm at Aintree, which she had inherited. It was she who gave to him the copies of the affidavit and supporting documents, now in the Merseyside County Museums.[2] She could

[1] Op. cit., Vol. 2, p. 125.
[2] Joseph Mayer, *The Art of Pottery and the History of Its Progress in Liverpool*, 1873, pp. 56–7.

well have suggested to him the explanation of why no patent was granted to her father, but it must be remembered that Mayer met her a century after the events, and sixty-five years after the death of her father. Elizabeth was then only a little girl of seven years of age, and Sadler had retired from business nineteen years previously. Her mother had only married her father seven years after his retirement, and could have had no firsthand knowledge to pass on to her daughter. Elizabeth Sadler was an old lady of seventy-two talking of events of which she had no memory, and her unsupported statement can carry no real authority, any more than the information which she presumably gave to Mayer, that her father was an engraver.

There are two alternative explanations, both very much more probable. The application could have been made and rejected, which theory receives some support from the fact that Elizabeth Sadler gave to Mayer copies and not original documents. What more probably occurred was that the application was abandoned for quite different and more cogent reasons. In 1756 both Sadler and Green were experienced, ambitious and shrewd, with great business capabilities. These were hardly the kind of men to go to all the trouble of staging a demonstration, swearing an affidavit, and obtaining all the requisite corroboration, before consideration of the time and expense involved, neither of which was very great. It is inconceivable that they were unaware that at the time, on the grant of a patent, it was obligatory within four months to lodge a specification detailing the actual process patented. Even if they had been so ignorant, it is out of character that they would have been dissuaded by such weak arguments put to them at such a late stage. It is beyond all question that if the application was in fact lodged then it was rejected. The Secretary of State's office had already received three petitions, in 1751, 1754 and 1755 for protection of the process, and even without a patent having been granted these applications would have effectively blocked Sadler and Green's.

If Sadler did not lodge his petition, the most rational explanation of why he did not do so is that when he reached London he learned that he had been forestalled, and was advised that to proceed further was a complete waste of time and money. It is a sad speculation that if he and Green had not been so conscientious and, like Brooks, had applied for protection before bringing their process to such a degree of perfection, then they might well have achieved their goal.

It has been assumed by many that Green did not become Sadler's partner until sometime between 1761 and 1763, and this is based entirely on the omission of Green's imprint, and Sadler's name appearing alone at the foot of early engravings. It is obvious, however, that he was in some form of partnership in 1756 or earlier, as is proved by his swearing the affidavit, and from the inclusion of his name in the supporting documents. Any patent if granted would have been made out to them jointly. Guy Green has been sadly neglected by ceramic historians, and we know little of his private life or personal particulars, but it is a fairly safe assumption that he was Sadler's junior by at least ten years. He may well have been the chief experimenter, and his the inspiration behind the whole transfer-printing enterprise. It is difficult to think of any other reason for Sadler's having distinguished Green in the manner he did.

Because of their familiarity with woodcuts it is generally assumed that transfer printing by this method preceded that from intaglio plates, but it is more likely that they started with copper plates, but due to excessive wear they changed to wood-blocks, only returning to intaglio printing after they had evolved their method of pouncing the abrasive vitreous material. Had they persevered with their patent application it would be known for certain if in 1756 the idea had occurred to them to print from woodcuts or engraved plates, for the specification would have disclosed this. It is ironical that the use of woodcuts may have been responsible for the idea of pouncing some of the printing elements, but for quite different reasons from those dictating its use with copper plates. Being surface-printing devices wood-blocks may have been difficult to charge evenly with sufficient of the thick vitreous pigment, particularly where there were large solid areas. This could well have given rise to the idea of printing only with a viscid medium, and after transfer, of pouncing with the vitreous ingredients.

There are numerous examples of tiles printed by Sadler and Green from woodcuts, and many are in the United States of America with which country the firm did a considerable business. Fortunately some specimens remain in this country. An example shown has a picture, *The Chinese Tea Drinker*, which is based on plate 12 of *Caffe, The und Tobac Zierathen* by Johann E. Nilson. The transfer print is in deep violet-brown, which colour was popular with Sadler and Green in the early years of their transfer-printing enterprise, and was probably the most successful of their experimental colours (Colour Plate D).

Tiles are known printed from woodcuts in black, red and surprisingly in blue. Only very rarely are found ceramic examples of on-glaze transfer printing in blue. The reason for this is that the impure zaffre then used, containing a high proportion of nickel, required a considerably higher firing temperature than other on-glaze colours. When the printing was under the glaze, this was of no consequence, as the glost kiln was of the necessary heat. The specimen illustrated depicts *The Resting Huntsman*, which is based on another of Nilson's engravings from the same source, *The Smoking Huntsman*. In the original the lady is trying to encourage the reclining gentleman, who is smoking a large pipe of ogee shape, to resume the shoot, but on Sadler and Green's tiles the pipe is entirely missing, resulting in a rather fatuous-looking huntsman (Plate 48). Both figures are in shooting habit, with guns and dogs, in a rococo setting. The colour is king's blue.

There is only one other instance recorded of woodcuts having been used for on-glaze transfer printing, and unfortunately no surviving examples are known. Llewellynn Jewitt gave an account of a conversation he had with an aged, one-time manager of Sewell and Donkin of St. Anthony's Pottery, Newcastle-upon-Tyne. It included the following:[3]

'I came to the works in 1819, the description of the ware then produced . . . [included] all kinds of Biscuit Painted, Printed very dark engraved patterns, also stamping with *Glue*, and printing on the glaze from Wood Engravings also with *Glue*, I believe the first that was done this way.'

Jewitt added:

'I have been enabled to ascertain that engravings of Bewick were then brought into use; specimens are, however, very rare.'

Time has shown that this remark is very much an understatement; examples are both unknown and, apart from this reference, unrecorded. There is however evidence that Thomas Bewick (1753–1828), between 1775 and 1778 supplied six engraved copper plates to the North Hylton Pottery, Sunderland (see page 204).

Joseph Sewell certainly transfer printed from intaglio plates long before 1819, and it is difficult to understand why woodcuts with their shorter life and loss of detail should have been employed at so late a date. If, as Jewitt's words suggest, Bewick's small wood engravings were used to transfer print on-glaze in the manner of bat-printed stipple engravings, then there is possibly an exciting discovery awaiting some fortunate person who first identifies one. The best that can be done by way of illustration is a fine reproduction of Thomas Bewick's '*The Ring Dove*' on a small trinket-tray made by the Crown Staffordshire Porcelain Company in the middle of the present century (Plate 47). This has been made from an original print by means of a photographically produced line-block, and is an interesting study of a print originating from a woodcut, with no cross-hatching, and in fact without any one line crossing another. A further known use of woodcuts for transfer printing was made by the Belleek Pottery of County Fermanagh, Northern Ireland in the second half of the nineteenth century, but examples are underglaze.

Examination under magnification of Sadler and Green intaglio transfer prints clearly reveals the etching with stronger touching-up by the graver (Plates 44 and 45). This was for general effect, and was carried out without any attempt to deepen already etched lines, and the etching made no allowance for the subsequent engraving. Comparison should be made with the magnified detail of a Worcester print (Plate 43). This rather crude engraving over the etching of Liverpool transfer prints has led some to believe that individual prints have been strengthened by pencil, but this is not so.

If there be any doubts as to the method employed by Sadler and Green these

[3] Op. cit., Vol. 2, p. 6.

43 Detail of Robert Hancock transfer print on Worcester MUG in Plate 24
At A can be seen the ends of the engraved lines faithfully following the etched, in one direction of the cross-hatching, but ending before the dark edge of the collar. At B some of the etched armour-shading has been strengthened by engraving, but not quite to the full extent of the etched lines. *See pages 84, 107*

44 Detail of print on Chaffers and Christian SAUCER in Plate 63
The over-engraving pays little attention to the etched lines. At C will be seen how
random flicks of the burin have been used to enhance the bocage. At D the fold in
the dress has been engraved without any regard to the underlying etching. *See
pages 107, 180*

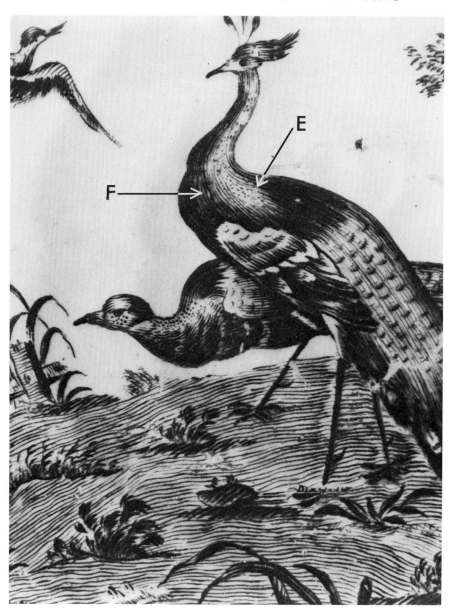

45   Detail of print on Wedgwood PLATE in Plate 71
At E and F the engraving makes no attempt to follow the etched lines, often crossing
them diagonally. *See pages 107, 144, 180*

46 Detail of print on Leeds PLATE on Plate 106
Similar disregard of the etching is shown as in the Wedgwood print on Plate 45,
being most noticeable at points G and H. The general style has more in common
with that of the Chaffers and Christian print on Plate 44. *See page 180*

should be quelled by a letter of 8 July 1763, from John Sadler to Josiah Wedgwood, which is proof positive of the process employed:

> 'The Tea Drinkers large teapots you'll see are very pale but the Engraver sent it down not $\frac{1}{2}$ finished, he left it just as it was etched without ever touching it with the graver and the Harlequin is not much better.'

That neither Sadler nor Green were engravers is confirmed by the fact that each man described himself in the affidavit as a printer, not as an engraver, or as an engraver and printer. This would have been the most ridiculous modesty if it were not the whole truth. Furthermore, no rate, or other contemporary records describe either man as an engraver. They were styled as printers, printed-ware manufacturers, china printers or china manufacturers; the last a forgivable, and at the time popular, conceit under the circumstances. Lastly, if either had been a competent engraver of wood or copper it is incredible that owning a printing business they published no works of their own.

They employed a number of artists of merit. One of these was Jeremiah Evans, a London engraver, who lived in Bear Street, a narrow lane between the Charing Cross Road and Leicester Square. It seems that in 1757 he decided to move to Liverpool, where he tried to set up an engraving business in Williamson's Fields, Liverpool. This was just to the east of where now stands the Post Office Tower, and about four hundred metres (four hundred and forty yards) from Sadler and Green's premises. On 3 June 1757 he inserted an advertisement as engraver in the *Liverpool Chronicle*. It is possible, although unlikely, that Evans survived very long as a master man, and the indications are that he became an employee of Sadler and Green on either a whole- or a part-time basis. E. Stanley Price illustrated a porcelain mug attributed to William Ball of Ranelagh Street, Liverpool, but now considered to be of Longton Hall origin, which carried a transfer-printed portrait, *King of Prussia, Elector of Brandenbourg*.[4] Beneath was the imprint 'Sadler Liverpl. Enl. Evans Sc.', and like Hancock's prints it was copied from a mezzotint by Richard Houston. The design embodied battle honours, and the mug could have been made at any time between 1757 and the end of the Seven Years' War in 1763. Another William Ball mug carries a portrait of *Major-General Wolfe*, and this is almost certainly the work of Evans (Plate 60). James Wolfe (1727–59) was only created a major-general in 1758, and died on 13 September 1759 on the plains of Abraham. The print is dated August 1763, and it is interesting that it carries the imprint 'J. Sadler Liverpool'. Yet another specimen of Evans's work with a portrait of the King of Prussia was thought to have been destroyed by enemy action in the 1939–45 war, but has recently been re-discovered at the museum. This was signed and imprinted 'Gilbody Maker, Evans Sculp.' Samuel Gilbody of Shaw's Brow Pottery II was adjudged bankrupt in the summer of 1761, so that the piece must have been made before then. If anyone had

---

[4] *John Sadler, A Liverpool Pottery Printer*, 1948, Plate 13.

47 'The Ring Dove': on PIN TRAY of bone china by THE CROWN STAFFORDSHIRE
    PORCELAIN COMPANY. 98 mm (3.8 in) diagonal
    From a photographically reproduced line-block taken from an original woodcut by
    Thomas Bewick. It will be noticed that no single line crosses another. Marked 'The
    Ring Dove by Thomas Bewick' and Crown Staffordshire badge. 1920–5. See pages
    29, 107
48 The Resting Huntsman: on TILE of delftware, LIVERPOOL. 128 mm (5 in) square
    From a woodcut, after an engraving by Johann E. Nilson, printed by Sadler and
    Green in king's blue. 1757–60. See page 106
    Victoria and Albert Museum

purchased the printing plate they would certainly have removed the imprint. It is virtually certain that the piece was printed by Sadler and Green. Since its reappearance this mug is considered to be of Worcester manufacture. If this attribution is correct, the most reasonable explanation is that it was a piece of Worcester porcelain purchased by Gilbody in the glazed white, and sent by him for transfer printing from his own engraved plate. In any other circumstances it would have been so simple, when trimming the tissues, to have snipped off the imprint. The custom of allowing engravers to sign their work seems sometimes to have been allowed by transfer printers in the early days of their trading. When they became properly established, for the most part they prohibited the practice. Much the same applied to potters permitting free-lance printers to have their imprint. Josiah Wedgwood never suffered Sadler and Green to put their names on his wares.

In 1767 a young boy of thirteen named Richard Abbey became an apprentice engraver with the firm. He proved a very apt pupil, for six years later he set up his own business as an engraver and printer to the ceramic trade. Another of Sadler and Green's employees was John Robinson, who probably about 1767 also left to set up as engraver and printer at Burslem.

Thomas Rothwell was an engraver with a distinctive style, who in early life lived in Liverpool. His later fortunes are more fully considered under Henry Palmer of Hanley, and subsequently the Melbourne and Swansea Potteries. He was a young man of sixteen in 1756, and there is little doubt that he was employed by Sadler and Green, and the possibility is that he was indentured to them. He seems to have used the technique of Robert Hancock, for his engraving was principally used to carefully deepen the already etched lines. He engraved deeply and as a result his transfer prints are very heavy. It is possible that later he dispensed with etching and entirely engraved his plates. Even when unsigned his distinctive style is often recognizable because of its overall heaviness. Examples of his work in his characteristically heavy manner are to be found on Chaffers and Christian's porcelain, and Melbourne and Swansea pottery (Plates 65 to 67 and 114 to 119). The initials 'T. R.' on Derby creamware have in the not too recent past been attributed to Rothwell, but of course they are nothing to do with him, and apply to Thomas Radford.

Sometime between 1785 and 1789 a second rival transfer printer set up in Liverpool. His name was Joseph Johnson, and it seems that he could only have gained his experience either with Sadler and Green or with Richard Abbey, but at the moment there is no evidence to indicate which, except that in later life he was very friendly with Abbey. He traded well into the nineteenth century.

Thomas Billinge (fl' 1766–1800) was a Liverpool engraver, also with an individual style, who was employed by Sadler and Green. Illustrated is an example of his work on a steatitic porcelain baluster-shaped mug made by Chaffers and Christian (Plate 64). It carries a portrait of '*The Right Hon. William Pitt Esq.*' very probably made between 1758 and 1761, at which date he resigned the office of prime minister. Another porcelain mug attributed to

Samuel Gilbody II's manufacture makes an interesting comparison. Also carrying a portrait of William Pitt, it is printed from a completely different copper plate, but seems assuredly to be the work of Billinge (Plate 59). This one has the imprint 'J. Sadler Liverp!'.

There remains one other who may possibly have worked experimentally for a short period, between 1771 and 1773, with Guy Green, and this is Peter Pever Burdett, the aquatintist, who conducted trials in Liverpool in ceramic transfer printing. A Liverpool character who it is fairly certain never worked for Sadler and Green, or took any part in ceramic transfer printing was the engraver Thomas Lawrenson (d. 1769). He donned the mantle of Jean Rouquet, and in 1757 published a pamphlet called *Secrets of Art and Nature*. He was a near neighbour of Jeremiah Evans and operated, probably from rooms, at an address in Williamson's Fields, but he lived some two kilometres (a mile and a quarter) from the city centre, in Lombard Street by Sheil Park. Unfortunately no copy of this brochure, which sold for half-a-crown, has been discovered, but Lawrenson advertised it twice in some detail in the local paper, and from this it is apparent that it comprised notes relevant to a variety of trades.[5] The fourth item read:

> 'The new and curious art of printing or rather re-printing from Copper-plate, Prints upon Porcelain, Enamel and Earthen Wares, as lately practised at Chelsea, Birmingham, &c. With a true preparation of suitable Colours; and necessary Rules of Baking.'

Whatever information Lawrenson possessed he probably gleaned in Birmingham, and from Rouquet's book. If a man is practising a new and secret process he does not tell the world its details, nor does he allow an employee to do so. It is therefore unlikely that Lawrenson ever transfer printed.

It is apparent from the number of artists they employed that Sadler and Green had a very considerable business. There is documentary evidence that strongly suggests the following were customers:

Ball, William (1747–67) of Ranelagh Street Pottery
Barnes, Zachariah (c. 1780–1800) of Haymarket Delph Works
Chaffers and Christian (1755–69) of Shaw's Brow Pottery I
Christian and Son, Philip (1769–76) of Shaw's Brow Pottery I
Gilbody II, Samuel (1754–61) of Shaw's Brow Pottery II
Pennington, James (1767–86) of Park Lane Pothouse, and later Copperas Hill
   Pottery
Shaw, Thomas (1743–74) of Dale Street Pottery I
Wedgwood, Josiah (1759–   ) of Burslem and later Etruria

There were others, and wares from many factories were purchased on their

---

[5] *Liverpool Advertiser*, 11 and 18 February 1757.

own account by Sadler and Green for decoration. Furthermore, some customers are believed to have bought pieces from distant factories which they sent to Sadler and Green to transfer print.

Tiles that were transfer printed in Liverpool have been very carefully catalogued, and omitting slight variations and border tiles there are in all three hundred and twelve recorded designs.[6] It is safe to assume that of these the prints from wood-blocks totalling twenty-two designs are all the work of Sadler and Green, and except for replacements probably date from before 1760. There are a further one hundred and twelve patterns which have what is known as the double-eight border, and these include forty-five pictures of Aesop's fables, which date from 1765 onwards. Illustrated is a picture, *The Salutation*, which is based on the design in the *Ladies' Amusement*, engraved by William Elliot after E. Walker (Plate 49). This particular example is printed in a deep grey-green. There are a dozen designs believed to have been the work of Richard Abbey, comprising four in the actor series with Adam-style husk borders (Plate 50), one of which he thoughtfully signed, six in the urn series and two overall or wallpaper designs. The remaining one hundred and seventy-six are, so far as is known, attributable to Sadler and Green. These include thirty-six in the main actor series which comprises contemporary actors in stage costume, striking attitudes. They are surrounded by a continuous ribbon-border with outer trellis-pattern, with on the left torches and on the right musical instruments and masks. Illustrated is '*Mr Lewis in the Character of Douglas*', and the figure is taken from an engraving by John Goldar (1729–95), after the painter Daniel Dodd (fl. 1760–90), published in Lowndes' *New English Theatre*, 1777 (Plate 51). Dodd was a fashionable portrait-painter in oils and crayon. The tile is printed in jet black, as were most of the series. As both actor series were mainly based on engravings in the *New English Theatre*, the *British Theatre* and Bell's *Shakespeare*, they must have been produced after they first appeared in print on paper in 1777, therefore if they are Harrington Street products they were issued by Guy Green, after the retirement of Sadler.

As at Battersea, Bow and Worcester in the early days, great difficulty was experienced by Sadler and Green in obtaining a jet-black print, and until about 1764 their transfers were a dark drab. In that year an ivory black was achieved, but not until about 1770 was a real jet black accomplished. Green was a very critical colour which needed most exact firing-temperatures. For this reason variable tints are often found on single tiles. This is particularly noticeable in the print *Harvest Carousal*, where the right-hand border is in bronze-green, while the remainder of the picture is in a very much paler tint (Plate 52). Similarly, in the case of a tile bearing *The Itinerant Dentist* the very deep Brunswick green in the lower-right corner fades to a bronze-green in the upper-left corner (Plate 53). It has been suggested that the firm used iron boxes

[6] Anthony Ray, 'Liverpool Printed Tiles', *E.C.C. Transactions* 1973, Vol. 9, Part 1, p. 36 et seq.

49 *The Salutation*: on TILE of delftware, LIVERPOOL. 128 mm (5 in) square
An engraving, in a double-eight border, taken from another by William Elliot, after
E. Walker, in *The Ladies' Amusement* (see Plate 7). Printed by Sadler and Green in
deep grey-green. 1760–5. *See pages 41, 116*
50 '*Mr Foote in the Character of the Doctor, in the Devil upon Two Sticks*': on TILE of
delftware, LIVERPOOL. 127 mm (5 in) square
Engraved by Richard Abbey, after an anonymous engraving published by Robert
Sayer, in a garrya-husk festoon border. Printed in ivory black. Imprint 'Abbey
Liverpool'. 1780–5. *See page 116*
Merseyside County Museums

as saggars, or muffles, in which to fire tiles, and the pale edges were presumably nearest to the sides of the boxes. To a lesser degree the same characteristic can be seen in the print *The Salutation*. From John Sadler's notebook we know that in 1766 he made the green pigment from calcined verdigris (a product of acetic acid on copper) mixed with eight times its weight of a flux or borax. This was for enamelling, and he varied it later by substituting calcined copper for the verdigris. Presumably he used this pigment, powdered and mixed with oil and mastic, for his printing. This is a temperamental compound which requires oxidizing conditions in firing, and it is doubtful if Sadler realized this, for his green printing is not of his best.

Brown was another of Sadler's not altogether successful colours, and this usually fired in random patches of light and dark areas. An example is illustrated: a tile with the picture *The Blind Carrying the Halt*, which has a double-eight border (Plate 54). This picture is copied from an engraving in *Select Fables*, published in 1761 by Robert Dodsley (1703–64), a colourful character who started life as footman to the Hon. Mrs. Lowther, but later became poet, playwright, bookseller and publisher for Dr. Johnson, Alexander Pope, Oliver Goldsmith and others. The colour varies between grey-brown and burnt umber. It is not without interest that the Bow China Works experienced similar difficulties when printing in brown. Like their contemporaries, Sadler and Green hand-enamelled some of their prints, and an early example is provided by *A Pastoral Celebration*, which is over-enamelled in three colours, and shows a shepherdess and her beau drinking from trumpet-shaped glasses (Plate 55). This is an adaptation of *Les Amours Pastorales*, a painting by François Boucher (1703–70).

More particularly on tableware, Sadler and Green, like others in the trade, copied their competitors' designs, and inevitably their versions exist of *The Tea Party* and '*King of Prussia*' portraits. Their renderings of the latter are easily identified for, as on their plaques, they are wrongly titled '*Frederick III, King of Prussia*', whereas they should of course be Frederick II.[7]

There is much confirmation that a very friendly relationship was maintained with the potters in the city so that they allowed Sadler to conduct many of his experiments on their premises. In November 1781 he noted that a green enamel ran entirely away through Pennington's crucible; that is, bleached out. This was at Copperas Hill Pottery, then being run by James Pennington. In September 1784 he made a note about a flux, and that he had burnt it under the 'Haymarket Delft kiln'. This was at the time in the hands of Zachariah Barnes and James Cotter.

There exist some porcelain tankards apparently of Worcester origin, first noted by R. L. Hobson over seventy years ago, which are decorated with transfer-printed landscapes, imprinted 'I Sadler, Liverpool'.[8] If the

---

[7] There was not a Frederick III, King of Prussia, until 1888. Frederick II was succeeded in 1786 by his nephew, Frederick William II.
[8] *Worcester Porcelain*, 1910, p. 78.

51 '*Mr Lewis in the Character of Douglas*': on a TILE of delftware, LIVERPOOL. 127 mm (5 in) square
Engraving taken from another by John Goldar, after Daniel Dodd, printed by Guy Green, in jet black. 1777–82. *See page 116*
52 *Harvest Carousal*: on TILE of delftware, LIVERPOOL. 130 mm (5.1 in) square
Engraving printed by Sadler and Green in bronze-green. Apart from the right-hand border the print is over-fired, resulting in a grey-green colour. 1765–70. *See page 116.*

attribution is correct, and they are not of Chaffers and Christian's make, then they must have been purchased glazed in white from the Worcester Company, either direct or through a wholesaler.

For many years the firm had a virtual monopoly, but their prices were always reasonable. In 1783 Guy Green's charge to Josiah Wedgwood for printing a tea and dinner service of two hundred and fifty pieces worked out at a little less than eight (old) pence per piece. This included etching and engraving the printing plates, of which there were probably a number of different sizes and shapes as well as those for borders, transferring the prints to the pieces, many of which would have carried between two and seven transfers, and firing them. Wedgwood hired a waggon from Morris, a carrier to Lawton, a hamlet eleven kilometres (about seven miles) north of Hanley on the Warrington road, to take a fortnightly load of Queen's ware to Sadler and Green for printing, and to return with the previous fortnight's load. It speaks for the quality of their printing that it satisfied such a perfectionist as Josiah Wedgwood right up to the time of his death.

It is very obvious that throughout his life John Sadler enjoyed experimenting, in preference to ordinary business routine, and this is what led to his early retirement from work in 1770, at the early age of fifty. He had for some years been leaving affairs more and more to Green, and it is obvious that when he did retire he retained a financial interest in the firm, otherwise the experiments he conducted and noted in the 1780s would have been pointless. After Sadler's death in 1789, Guy Green continued to run the business for a further ten years, although as far as the customers were concerned he had been doing so since 1770. With his own retirement on the eve of the nineteenth century the firm ceased to trade.

RICHARD ABBEY, LIVERPOOL (fl. 1773 to c. 1785 and c. 1810 to 1819)

The dates given by Joseph Mayer in respect of Richard Abbey (1754–1819) are now known to have been completely wrong. The correct facts are that Richard was the son of William Abbey (1711–86), an excise officer, and his wife Alice (née Bolton) of Walton, then a village four kilometres (two and a half miles) to the north of Liverpool. He was born in 1754, and at the age of thirteen apprenticed to John Sadler. On the termination of his indentures in 1773, this extremely capable and precocious young engraver and transfer printer set up his own business at 11 Cleveland Square, Liverpool. This is now bisected by the continuation of Whitechapel, called Paradise Street. On 31 July of the following year he married Rachel Gardiner.

53 *The Itinerant Dentist*: on TILE of delftware, LIVERPOOL. 125 mm (4.9 in) square
Engraving in an arabesque border printed by Sadler and Green in deep Brunswick
green, fading on the left-hand side to bronze-green, through over-firing. 1765–70.
See page 116

54 *The Blind Carrying the Halt*: on TILE of delftware, LIVERPOOL. 127 mm (5 in)
square
Engraving after another in Robert Dodsley's *Select Fables*, 1761, printed by Sadler
and Green in burnt umber, fading to grey-brown in the firing. 1761–5. *See
page 118*

When he launched his business he caused to be inserted in the local newspaper the following advertisement.[9]

RICHARD ABBEY
Late Apprentice to Messrs. Sadler and Green
Begs Leave to inform his FRIENDS and the PUBLIC
That he has Open'd his SHOP, at No. 11, in Cleveland Square,
Where he Manufactures and Sells all
Sorts of QUEEN'S WARE,
Printed in the neatest Manner, and in a Variety of
Colours N.B. Orders for Exportation
Also Crests, Coats of Arms, Tiles, or any other
particular Device will be completed at the shortest Notice
By their most obedient humble Servant
RICHARD ABBEY

There exist many pieces of creamware decorated with prints carrying Abbey's imprint, and more that have prints that by their style leave little doubt that they are his work, but in no case is it recorded that any early pieces are back-marked. For about ten years details of Abbey's life are vague. Mayer averred that he taught engraving and transfer printing at a pottery in Glasgow, and also in the Rue de Crussol in Paris. He certainly had the advantage of John Sadler, Guy Green and Joseph Johnson, inasmuch as he personally was both an engraver and a printer. At some period he appears to have worked for Joseph Johnson, as is proved by prints carrying the imprint of both their names.[10] This arrangement probably started near the turn of the century. Prints very much in his style are found on Leeds ware, and it seems that he probably did work for that pottery.

An example of his work, which could well be on a Leeds Pottery jug, is the print *Youthful Lovers* (Plate 56), with beneath:

Dear to the Mother's flutt'ring heart
The tender Brood must be
But not so dear a thousand'th part
As Delia is to me.

On the reverse is the print *Hudibras*. The imprint is 'R. Abbey Sculp'. Abbey's quite distinctive style is very apparent in these prints, and they form a good basis for judging other unsigned works.

Many of Mayer's facts have been proved wrong, and he was responsible for the statement, repeated by William Chaffers, 'A pottery was established on the south shore of the Mersey, near Liverpool, about 1790, by Richard Abbey, in conjunction with a Scotchman named Graham, where they carried on business

---

[9] *The Liverpool Advertiser*, 10 December 1773.
[10] A creamware teapot in the Colonial Williamsburg Museum, Virginia, has the print *The Upright Man*, with the imprint 'Rd Abbey Sculpt. Jph. Johnson Liverpool'.

55 *A Pastoral Celebration*: on TILE of delftware, LIVERPOOL. 128 mm (5 in) square
    A woodcut after a painting by François Boucher, over-enamelled in blue, green
    and yellow by Sadler and Green. 1757–60. *See page 118*
    Victoria and Albert Museum

56 *Youthful Lovers*: on JUG of creamware possibly by LEEDS POTTERY. 216 mm (8.5 in)
    high. (*Hudibras* on other side.)
    Engraved and printed in jet black by Richard Abbey. Imprint 'R. Abbey Sculp'.
    1795–1800. *See pages 122, 184*
    Stoke-on-Trent City Museum

with good success for a time'; and later, 'He retired from the concern in 1796, when the works were taken by Worthington & Co., who called the site the *Herculaneum Pottery*; he died at Aintree in 1801, at the age of 81.'[11] In fact the site was on the north-east shore, or the right bank of the estuary, and it is now known that Richard Abbey was buried in Walton churchyard on 21 January 1819, at the age of sixty-five. There was considerable confusion by Mayer over dates, places and possibly over identity. It is known that as late as 1794 the works on the site were still in the hands of Charles Roe, a copper smelter, for in that year he advertised the lease for sale.[12] Twenty-nine months later Samuel Worthington, the proprietor of the future Herculaneum factory, also advertised:[13]

> On Saturday last the NEW POTTERY (formerly the Copper Works) near this town, was opened, and a plentiful entertainment given by Mr. WORTHINGTON, the PROPRIETOR, to upwards of SIXTY PERSONS employed at his Manufactory.

It is very improbable that in a little over two years there was sufficient time for Abbey and Graham to have acquired the site, erected a pottery and closed it, and for Worthington to have purchased and staffed it. In that event there would have been no justification for his advertising 'the NEW POTTERY (formerly the Copper Works)... was opened'. Abbey was never a potter, but he may have merchanted or transfer printed from a building on the site.

He undoubtedly did a considerable trade with the Herculaneum concern, either on his own account or through Joseph Johnson, and there exist many examples of the pottery's wares transfer printed from his plates. For some unknown reason it is generally assumed that Abbey worked on the staff of the Herculaneum firm, but again there is nothing to substantiate this. The evidence is that the factory never did any on-glaze printing, and for many years was without its own engravers of copper plates for underglaze printing.

JOSEPH JOHNSON, LIVERPOOL (fl.1789 to 1810)

At the end of the eighteenth century there lived a number of Joseph Johnsons, either with connections with Liverpool, or with printing, or both. One of these was an independent on-glaze transfer printer of earthenware. Several pieces exist which carry prints with the imprint 'Joseph Johnson', or 'J. Johnson' with, or without, 'Liverpool' added. Some of these transfers are of military figures, and one which calls for special mention is a spirited portrait of '*Colonel Tarleton*', with captured guns and colours, after the fall of Charleston in 1788

[11] Op. cit., Vol. 2, p. 129.
[12] *Gore's General Advertiser*, 3 July 1794.
[13] Ibid., 15 December 1796.

57 '*The Death of Gen. Wolfe*': on a JUG of creamware, 257 mm (10.1 in) high
Engraved by Richard Walker and printed by Joseph Johnson in jet black. Imprints
'R. Walker Sculp' and 'I. Johnson Liverpool'. 1790–1800. *See page 126*
Merseyside County Museums

(Plate 129). It is based on a painting by Sir Joshua Reynolds P.R.A. (1732–92). Sir Banastre Tarleton (1754–1833) was made a colonel in 1790, and a general in 1812. The imprints are 'Wedgwood & Co.' and 'J. Johnson Liverpool'. The printing was certainly done for the Knottingly Pottery (1796–1801) situated near Pontefract in Yorkshire and owned by William Tomlinson and Ralph Wedgwood. It was later known as the Ferrybridge Pottery. The jug bearing this print therefore dates from between 1796 and 1801.

A teapot in the Colonial Williamsburg Museum, Virginia, with the print *The Upright Man*, has the imprint 'R. Abbey sculpt. Jph. Johnson Liverpool', clearly showing that at some time Abbey engraved for Johnson, which is borne out by many more of the latter's prints being in Abbey's style—although without imprint. This was unlikely to have occurred while Abbey had his own competitive business, which suggests that this particular relationship commenced in the closing years of the century. *The Upright Man* was derived from an engraving published by Carrington and Bowles of 69 St. Paul's Churchyard, London on 16 August 1785. Bowles had previously had a partner called Carver, and they were responsible for publishing the famous *Toby Philpot* mezzotint which was copied by Abbey and transfer printed by Johnson on a mug attributed to the Herculaneum Pottery (Plate 128).

Another engraver employed by Johnson in the early years, and one whom he allowed to sign his own plates was Richard Walker (fl.1789–1808). He resided in 1790 at 23 Edmund Street, in 1794 at Bevington Bush, in 1803 in Castle Street, in 1805 in Harrington Street, in 1808 in Temple Street, and after retiring he was living in 1839 in Rose Place.[14] This restless gentleman was certainly not a transfer printer, for obviously he could not have built kilns at all these addresses. That he engraved for Joseph Johnson is proved by a jug showing a print of '*The Death of Gen. Wolfe*', which has the imprints 'R. Walker Sculp' and 'I. Johnson Liverpool' (Plate 57). Although this depicts the death of General James Wolfe (1727–59) on the plains of Abraham, Quebec, on 13 September 1759, it is an historical, not a contemporary, commemorative piece. It is based on an engraving made in 1776, derived from a painting by Benjamin West P.R.A. (1738–1820), which was exhibited in 1771. Versions of *The Farmyard* print, '*The Farmers Arms*' and '*Box the Compass*' with Johnson's imprint exist on Herculaneum pottery. These confirm that the Herculaneum Pottery did not transfer print on-glaze, for had it purchased some of Johnson's copper plates second-hand, as has been suggested, there is no reasonable explanation for its not having taken the elementary precaution of removing the imprint of a comparatively obscure competitor by snipping it off the transfer tissue.

There is little doubt that Johnson in the early nineteenth century ran a thriving transfer-printing business, and with Richard Abbey's help he did a

[14] Alan Smith, *Liverpool Herculaneum Pottery 1796–1840*, 1970, p. 35.

considerable turnover with the Herculaneum Pottery, and perhaps with the Leeds Pottery, and some of those in Staffordshire. Little is really known of either Johnson's or Abbey's circumstances in the early years of the nineteenth century, but the possibility exists that either together, or with Abbey as an independent engraver and Johnson transfer printing, they may well have had a business as great as that of Sadler and Green in their halcyon days. They were lucky to have survived as long as they did, for by the early nineteenth century scores of potters had their own printing departments, mainly for underglaze work, and the days of the specialist printer were nearly over. The age of the free-lance engraver, who did no printing, had arrived.

Chapter 5

CUSTOMERS OF THE LIVERPOOL TRANSFER PRINTERS

It is not generally realized that in the middle of the eighteenth century Liverpool housed, after Staffordshire, the second largest concentration of ceramic manufacturers in Britain. There were nearly two dozen separate potteries within a two-kilometres (mile and a half) radius of the city centre, and although most made delftware and earthenware, eight are reputed to have manufactured procelain. The evidence strongly suggests that no Liverpool factories transfer printed on-glaze, but relied upon the services of the local transfer printers. It is useful to remember the approximate dates between which these firms operated:

	1756		1799
Sadler and Green	├─────────────────────────────┤

	1773 c. 1785	1810 ? 1819
Richard Abbey	├──────┤	├──────┤

	c. 1789	1810
Joseph Johnson (probably employing Richard Abbey)	├────────────┤

From this it is apparent that Sadler and Green enjoyed a local monopoly for the first seventeen years. A list has already been given of the firm's customers for whom there is documentary evidence in one form or another. Seven of the eight were Liverpool firms. There existed in addition three other factories in the city which also could well have used their services. These were:

The Liverpool China Manufactory (1756–61),

The Flint Potworks (c. 1770–95) and

The Islington China Manufactory (1743–1800)

It is easiest to consider these ten factories in the date order in which they shut.

58 *'Fred. yᵉ : IIIᵈ : KING OF PRUSSIA'*: on a TANKARD of porcelain by SAMUEL
GILBODY. 118 mm (4.6 in) high
Engraved by Jeremiah Evans, and printed in deep brown-black, probably by
Sadler and Green. Imprint 'Gilbody maker, Evans Sc.' 1757–60. *See page 130*
Merseyside County Museums

SHAW'S BROW POTTERY II (1754 to 1761)

This was situated a few metres east of Richard Chaffer's Shaw's Brow Pottery I in what today is called William Brown Street, and where now stands the City Library. It was one of the smaller Liverpool potteries and was run by Samuel Gilbody (b. 1714). This was the Gilbody who swore the affidavit in support of Sadler and Green's abortive patent application. Gilbody is thought to have commenced his business in 1754, and operated until his bankruptcy in 1761. He made delftware, but also merchanted porcelain hollow ware. An example of the latter is a tankard with a head and shoulders portrait of '*Fred. ye III^d* (sic): *King of Prussia*', wearing a tricorn hat, which has the imprint 'Gilbody maker, Evans Sc.' (Plate 58). Some authorities are of opinion that this mug is of Worcester potting. There is little doubt that the printing plate was engraved by Jeremiah Evans for Sadler and Green, who transfer printed porcelain merchanted by Gilbody. Another tankard which is attributed to Gilbody has already been referred to, and this shows a head and shoulders portrait of William Pitt. It is believed to have been engraved by Billinge, and carries the imprint 'J. Sadler Liverp^l.' (Plate 59).

LIVERPOOL CHINA MANUFACTORY (1756 to 1761)

This was an ambitious enterprise situated on the south side of Brownlow Hill, and backing on to Chapel Lane. It was run by William Reid and Company. The factory opened in 1756, under the management of Lawrence Harrison, and in modern parlance it never seemed to get off the ground. After operating for less than five years it crashed, resulting in the bankruptcies in 1761 of four of its partners. What happened to Harrison is not known, but John Sadler entered in his notebook in February 1767 the formula of his yellow enamel. Obviously the men were intimate. If there are any surviving transfer-printed products of the factory they are unrecognized. The most interesting fact about the firm is that one of the partners, Henry Baker, is described as an enameller, and was almost certainly one and the same man as the Harry Baker referred to by Simeon Shaw, and for whom he made exaggerated claims.[1] It is probable that he unsuccessfully tried to transfer print at Brownlow Hill, with the assistance of Hugh Milligan, an engraver. When working at Hanley about 1777, he could neither engrave nor transfer print; he is further considered at the start of the following chapter.

William Roscoe (1753–1831), the lawyer, historian, banker and member of parliament for Liverpool 1806/7, wrote of his childhood at the Bowling Green Tavern on Brownlow Hill and mentioned that there was on the staff of the adjacent pottery an engraver and painter, Hugh Milligan.[2]

[1] Op. cit., pp. 192, 212 and 213.
[2] Henry Roscoe, *Life of William Roscoe*, 1833, Vol. 1, p. 10. (Brought to notice by Alan Smith, op. cit., p. 32.)

59 *'WILLIAM PITT Esq.'*: on TANKARD of porcelain, by SAMUEL GILBODY. 140 mm
(5.5 in) high
Printed in deep brown-black by Sadler and Green. Imprint 'J. Sadler Liverp!'
1756–60. *See pages 115, 130*
Royal Pavilion, Art Gallery and Museum, Brighton

RANELAGH STREET POTTERY (c.1747 to 1769)

Sometime prior to 1747 there was a pottery situated near where now stands the Central Station. This was run by William Ball until 1767, and afterwards for a year or so by Richard Ball. There exists a number of transfer-printed pieces which some attribute to the factory. One of Major-General Wolfe by Jeremiah Evans has been mentioned (Plate 60). Others are commemorative of royalty, and of the Seven Years War. Illustrated is a cylindrical mug with a head and shoulders portrait, '*Charlotte, Queen of Great Britain*', which has the imprint 'I. Sadler, Liverpool'. It is a royal marriage commemorative mug of 1761, and is printed in red (Plate 61). Another very interesting piece is a teapot printed in black, and with a metal spout. It has a most distinctive handle, and the lid an acorn knop. The print, which is marked 'Sadler Liverpl', is *The Courted Shepherdess* (Plate 62). It must in fairness be mentioned that some authorities now consider this teapot to be of Longton Hall bankrupt stock (see page 218). A similar print exists on a Chaffers and Christian teapot, and others on tiles. William Ball was sufficiently friendly with Sadler to tell him his formula for glaze, which Sadler duly recorded.

DALE STREET POTTERY I (c. 1720 to 1784)

There were three potteries in Dale Street, but the one associated with Sadler and Green was on a site that is now a sea of concrete where Fontenoy Street joins Dale Street under the fly-over, and opposite the Technical College. It was opened by Samuel Shaw (d. 1725), the father of Thomas Shaw who signed Sadler and Green's supporting document for the patent application. Thomas Shaw sold the pottery in 1774 to Thomas Chorley, who ran it until 1784. Thomas Shaw for a period also ran the Islington China Manufactory (see page 138). The Islington factory, as its name implies, produced principally porcelain, but the Dale Street Pottery I concentrated upon delftware and must have produced vast quantities of tiles which were then transfer printed. At the moment there is regrettably no method of identifying these.

PARK LANE POTHOUSE (1755 to 1773)
COPPERAS HILL POTTERY (1773 to 1786)

The Park Lane Pothouse was situated on the site of the present goods station at the corner of Blundell Street, and about two kilometres (a mile and a quarter) south of the city centre. It was opened about 1755 by John Eccles and Company, who were succeeded by Richard Thwaites and Robert Willcock. In 1767 it was acquired by James Pennington. There were three brothers

60 *Major-General Wolfe*: on MUG of porcelain, probably by WILLIAM BALL. 92 mm (3.6 in) high
Engraved probably by Jeremiah Evans, and printed by Sadler and Green in black. Imprints 'J. Sadler Liverpool', and 'August 1763'. 1763–5. *See pages 112, 132*
Victoria and Albert Museum

61 '*CHARLOTTE, QUEEN OF GREAT BRITAIN*': on cylindrical MUG of porcelain, probably by WILLIAM BALL. 147 mm (5.8 in) high
Printed in red by Sadler and Green. Imprint 'I. Sadler, Liverpool'. 1761–5. *See page 132*
British Museum

Pennington, all potters, and there has often been confusion over them, so the following is what has now been established of their history and movements. John Pennington, a maltster, married in 1727 and had three sons, James (b. c. 1728), John (d. 1786) and Seth (b. 1744).

James, the eldest, took over the Park Lane Pothouse which he ran until 1773, when he removed to Copperas Hill Pottery. In 1775 he was joined by his brother John for four years, but for some reason John then separated and took over the Islington China Manufactory which he ran until his death in 1786. James continued to run the Copperas Hill works until John's death, when he moved and helped John's widow, Jane, and her son John II to look after the Islington works.

Seth, the youngest, became a partner in the Shaw's Brow Pottery I, previously owned by Richard Chaffers and Philip Christian, and probably the best known of all Liverpool porcelain factories. He was there for twenty-three years, from 1776 until 1799, after which for about five years he ran a china-merchanting business.

From the very beginning James appears to have been a customer of Sadler and Green, and for some reason he told them the composition of his bisque. Sadler noted this in his diary twice, the first time being on 18 March 1767. It is interesting that this body was composed of approximately one-third by weight of bone ash. The Copperas Hill factory to which James moved in 1773 was about the same distance from the city centre, and beside where now stands Lime Street Station, at the junction with Skelhorne Street. These factories of James Pennington are further examples where it has not been possible to identify any of the products.

THE FLINT POTWORKS (c. 1770 to 1795)

This was situated right on the boundary at the southern end of the city, in Parliament Street near the corner of Jamaica Street, and about seven hundred metres (seven hundred and sixty-five yards) east of the waterfront. Precisely when and by whom it was opened is not known, but it is thought to have been in about 1770, and by John Okill. As a result of his death in 1773 it was sold as a going concern to Rigg and Peacock, and later to John Sykes and Company. From the sales advertisement by James Okill, the executor of John, it is clear that the factory made cream-colour or 'Queen's Ware'.[3] No evidence survives of any trade connections with Sadler and Green, nor are there extant any identified examples of the pottery's products.

[3] *Liverpool Advertiser*, 29 October 1773.

62 *The Courted Shepherdess*: on barrel shape TEAPOT with metal spout, either by
WILLIAM BALL or LONGTON HALL. 134 mm (5.3 in) high
Printed in black by Sadler and Green. Imprint 'Sadler Liverpl'. 1760–5. *See pages
132, 218*
British Museum

63 *The Rock Garden*: on a TEA BOWL and SAUCER of steatitic porcelain by CHAFFERS AND
CHRISTIAN, LIVERPOOL. Saucer 134 mm (5.3 in) diameter
Engraved after an early Worcester hand-pencilled design and printed in ivory
black, probably by Sadler and Green. Characteristic Liverpool hand-pencilled
fancy border. 1764–70. *See page 136*

SHAW'S BROW POTTERY I (c. 1740 to 1799)

This pottery stood at the corner of the present Byron Street and William Brown Street, where now stands the Technical College, under the shadow of the overhead roads. It is thought to have been started by John Livesley in the second quarter of the eighteenth century. In 1747 it was acquired by Richard Chaffers (c. 1722–65). He was the son of a Liverpool shipwright, and had been apprenticed about 1736 to Samuel Shaw at the Dale Street Pottery, which was then about fifty metres (fifty-five yards) to the east of where was to stand the pottery he subsequently owned. Sometime prior to 1755 Chaffers took a partner, Philip Christian (d. 1785).

It has been recounted earlier how Robert Podmore, one of the original employees of the Worcester Porcelain Company, left there, and after having worked for a short time for Josiah Wedgwood, joined Chaffers and Christian as their manager on 14 July 1755. He left Worcester too early to know anything of transfer printing, but he did know all about the use of soapstone, and undertook to show them the secrets of making steatitic porcelain. Immediately after signing his agreement, which was for seven years, Podmore assisted Chaffers in discovering soapstone at Mullion in Cornwall. This was five kilometres (three miles) north of Gew Graze, where Benjamin Lund had found deposits then being used by the Worcester company.

After the deaths of both Chaffers and Podmore in 1765 the business was carried on by Philip Christian with Chaffers' two sons, Huniball and Edward. In December 1769 Christian bought out the Chaffers' interests for twelve hundred pounds, and then traded as Philip Christian and Company. After seven more years he sold the remainder of the lease of the mineral rights at Mullion to the Worcester company for five hundred pounds, and the pottery to Seth Pennington and John Part. Pennington and Part traded until 1799, when the business was put up for auction, and it is improbable that the premises were ever again used as a pottery. For the following five years Pennington traded as a china merchant from various addresses in Shaw's Brow. The manufacture of steatitic porcelain at Shaw's Brow Pottery I was therefore confined to the twenty years from 1756 to 1776.

Illustrated are a tea bowl and saucer by Chaffers and Christian, each of which carries a transfer print in ivory black of a picture which for some obscure reason has been named *The Rock Garden* (Plate 63). Similar designs are also found on enamel snuff boxes and on Derby and Worcester porcelains. On the reverse of the bowl is a small vignette of a sportsman with two gun-dogs. The prints are from etched plates, with considerable strengthening by the graver. A further example of the same period is the mug, already described, with the print engraved by T. Billinge of '*The Right Hon. William Pitt Esq.*' (Plate 64). A bowl made at the factory in the 1760s is printed in deep puce. This has a triad of interesting prints, with inside in matching colour a hand-pencilled sprig of

64 '*THE RIGHT HON. WILLIAM PITT ESQ.*': on baluster-shape MUG of
porcelain by CHAFFERS AND CHRISTIAN, LIVERPOOL. 153 mm (6 in) high
Engraved by Thomas Billinge and printed by Sadler and Green. After a mezzotint
by Richard Houston, from a painting by William Hoare. Imprint 'T. Billinge Sc'.
1758–61. *See pages 114, 136*
Victoria and Albert Museum

65 *Gallop on the Highway*: on a BOWL of steatitic porcelain by CHAFFERS AND
CHRISTIAN, LIVERPOOL. 162 mm (6.4 in) diameter
Engraved by Thomas Rothwell; the horsemen after detail in an engraving by
Sébastien Le Clerc. Printed in deep puce. With typical Chaffers and Christian
hand–enamelled inside border. 1774–6. *See pages 114, 138*

convolvulus and fancy enamelled border (Plates 65, 66 and 67). The subjects, *Gallop on the Highway, The Serenading Shepherd* and *Wood-pigeons Feeding Fledgling*, printed from heavily engraved plates are with little doubt the work of Thomas Rothwell. The figures in the first picture are based on detail from an engraving by Sébastien Le Clerc (1673–1714), and a later adaptation on a tea bowl has been attributed to the Islington China Manufactory.[4] The second print is known in mirror image, signed by Rothwell, on creamware, while the last-named vignette is based on a detail of a composition by the engraver and painter Francis Barlow (1626?–1702), published by Pierce Tempest (1653–1717) in *Various Birds and Beasts Drawn from Life*. Tempest is best known as the publisher of *The Cries of London*. The fact that Robert Hancock re-engraved this picture, and that this was published in 1798 in *Book of Birds*, by Laurie and Whittle, is of no significance.

Reference has already been made in the section on the Worcester Porcelain Company to a similarity in outline prints for enamelling, on pieces from that factory, and those made by Chaffers and Christian (see page 88, and Colour Plate C and Plate 36). An example of the latter is the design *Gifts for a Manchu Lady*, found on tea bowls and saucers (Colour Plate E). The Liverpool bowls, unlike the hemispherical bowls of Worcester, are more truncated, and stand on wider footrims. The glaze is distinctly of orange-peel surface-texture—a characteristic of Chaffers and Christian porcelain—and the bases of the bowls, in the Liverpool tradition, are even dirtier, through burst bubbles, than those of Worcester. Characteristic of Liverpool decoration is the combination of a transfer-printed main design with a hand-pencilled border. It will be seen from the captions to the respective illustrations that the enamels, other than vermilion and primrose, differ in hue. The Liverpool examples of this engraver's work are of somewhat later date than those of Worcester.

ISLINGTON CHINA MANUFACTORY (1743 to 1800)

This pottery was situated on the then eastern outskirts of the city, about two kilometres (a mile and a quarter) from the centre. It was on the north side of Folly Lane, now called Islington, near the corner of St. Anne Street. Started by Thomas Shaw in 1743, it was by 1779 in the possession of John Pennington. It has been related how on John Pennington's death in 1786 the pottery was kept going by his widow, Jane, with the help of her son John II and her brother-in-law, James. It seems that she was not considered credit-worthy, for in 1787 a new lease was granted to a Richard Gerard. He was not a potter, and he immediately granted a sublease back to Jane Pennington, but the arrangement was short lived. On 22 February 1790 a lease of the premises was granted to

[4]Recorded by Bernard Watney, 'Some Origins of Some Ceramic Designs,' *E.C.C. Transactions*, Vol. 9, Part 3, 1975, Plate 173.

66 *The Serenading Shepherd*: on BOWL in Plate 65
   Engraved by Thomas Rothwell and printed in deep puce. 1774–6. *See pages 114,
   138*
67 *Wood-Pigeons Feeding Fledgling*: on bowl in Plates 65 and 66
   Engraved by Thomas Rothwell, after an engraving by Francis Barlow published
   before 1717. 1774–6. *See pages 114, 138*

Thomas Wolfe, potter of Stoke-on-Trent. Presumably the Penningtons had ceased trading, and there are indications that for the next six years Wolfe merely used the site as a warehouse for his Staffordshire products. In 1796, however, the factory experienced a brief renascence. Wolfe took into partnership Miles Mason, who until then had been a china-merchant in Fenchurch Street, London, and John Lucock, a ceramic modeller and engraver from Stoke-on-Trent. The factory proved to be a white elephant, for within a space of three years it had ceased to operate, and the firm was gazetted bankrupt on 16 June 1800. Wolfe returned to his business in Stoke-on-Trent; Mason set up his own factory at Victoria Pottery, Lane Delph; and Lucock, after working for a few months as modeller for William and John Turner of Lane End, Longton, set up as an engraver of plates for underglaze printing, at Stoke-on-Trent, where he is shown as such in the map of the *Staffordshire Pottery Directory* of 1802.

Sadler and Green printing has not been identified on the wares of John Pennington, but very probably specimens exist. Wolfe, Mason and Lucock introduced underglaze printing in blue at the Islington Works.

THE HAYMARKET POTTERY (1751 to 1800)

This alas, is another pottery which stood on a site now completely obliterated. Today the city entrance to the Queensway Tunnel is right over, or more correctly under, where stood the Haymarket Pottery. Zachariah Barnes (1742–1820) was born at Warrington, and in due course developed into a Liverpool corn and flour merchant of considerable substance. Sometime about 1768 he became the proprietor, with a James Cotter, of the Haymarket Pottery, which had been opened in 1751 by John Livesley. Barnes had married in 1767 an Esther Livesley, so that it is probable that John Livesley was his father-in-law, and that his wife had inherited the property. In that case Cotter was probably manager of the factory raised to the status of partner by Barnes, who at that time knew nothing of ceramics. The date at which Barnes became owner of the works is supposition, but John Sadler made a memorandum in his notebook in September 1784 that he had experimented with some flux which was 'burnt under the Haymarket Delph Kiln'.

Principally the factory produced delftware druggists' pots and tiles, the latter in vast quantities. For unknown reasons it is generally supposed that the firm was responsible for the tiles on which appear one of the actor series. By 1790 Cotter had retired and it is thought that the pottery was shut by the turn of the nineteenth century. Barnes lived until 1820, and his youngest daughter, Margaret (b. 1785) in 1812 married Aaron Wedgwood, member of a cadet branch of the Wedgwood family.

JOSIAH WEDGWOOD (AND SONS), BURSLEM AND ETRURIA (1759 to date)

Probably more has been written about Josiah Wedgwood (1730–95) than any other single potter, and he certainly occupies most space in the *Dictionary of National Biography*. This is but justice, as in all probability there is no one man in ceramic history who has been responsible for more innovations and improvements. In 1759 he opened his first pottery at Ivy House Works in Burslem. The year 1762 saw his removal to the Brick House Works in the same town, which he rented at twenty-one pounds per annum. It had formerly been run by John Adams. Josiah operated from these works until 1770. In 1768 he took into partnership Thomas Bentley (1730–80) of Scropton, Derbyshire, who was a partner of Bentley and Boardman, Josiah's agents in Liverpool. In 1769 Wedgwood opened his famous pottery at Etruria, and in 1770 Bentley went to the London office in charge of sales. Etruria was situated a kilometre and a half (about a mile) west of Hanley, a few hundred metres north of the subsequent junction of the Trent and Mersey canal with the Cauldon canal. Josiah was very much a perfectionist and it is reported that of an evening he would stump round the works on his peg leg, and smash any piece that did not reach his standards, and chalk on the work bench by the broken fragments, 'This will not do for Josiah Wedgwood.'

One of Wedgwood's most famous ceramic bodies was Queen's Ware. This was of cream colour, caused by minute quantities of ferric oxide, ever the potter's greatest enemy until then. By great good fortune for Sadler and Green this ware proved a perfect base for transfer printing. According to John Sadler's notebook the account was opened on 23 September 1761; this probably through the advocacy of Thomas Bentley. In the two years and two months ending 10 November 1763 the business between them totalled £789. By 1770 it had grown to the extent that for eight and a half months to 6 September it amounted to £1,538. The figures may not be comparable because it is believed that in 1763 the arrangement was for Wedgwood to invoice his wares to Sadler and Green, and for the latter in their turn to charge him for the complete printed wares. By this method Sadler and Green were responsible for breakages, insurance and return freight. Later the method was altered, and no charge was made for the goods to be printed, and they were either returned or sent forward at Wedgwood's direction. Allowing for this, the increase in the average monthly turnover during the seven years must have been more than twelvefold.

A Wedgwood historian has written of the transfer printing: 'There [Liverpool] the transfers were laid on, and the ware returned to Staffordshire for firing, although in the case of consignments intended for export, firing may have been completed in Liverpool'. This would have been quite impracticable. Then, as now, the normal method of packing ceramic wares was in hay and straw in light wooden casks, and unfired there would have been very little printing left by the time Etruria was reached. Particularly would this have been so because of the deplorable condition of the roads, and the unsprung wagons, in the mid-eighteenth century.

In dating transfer-printed Wedgwood pieces it is important to consider both the colour of the creamware and of Sadler and Green's black printing. Originally Queen's Ware was a pale manilla-colour, and progressively over twenty years this became lighter and lighter until by 1780 or thereabouts a very pale stone-colour, which was near white, was achieved. It is convenient to summarize the above changes alongside the dates of Sadler and Green's progress towards jet-black printing:

Approximate dates	Colour of Wedgwood's creamware	Colour of Sadler and Green's black printing
1761	Cane	Dark drab
1763	Pale manilla	
1764		Ivory black
1765	Pale cream	
1768	Ivory	Jet black
1785	Off-white	

At the commencement in 1761 Sadler and Green used printing plates made for printing tiles to decorate Wedgwood's creamware. A number of fine examples exist, including a plate showing a square picture of Aesop's fable *The Wolf and the Lamb* which is a mirror-image derivation from an engraving by Sébastian Le Clerc (Plate 68). This is surrounded by an ordinary double-eight tile border, but with an outer Adam-style husk-and-ribbon frame in green enamel, and with printed floral sprigs on the condiments-rim. In the early days Wedgwood accepted Sadler's selection of subjects, and he did not escape the prevalent *Tea Party No. 1* (in mirror image), but with a difference. Some of the prints on Queen's Ware are believed to portray Josiah and Sarah Wedgwood themselves. Whether this is wishful thinking of today, or a pretty compliment of yester-year by John Sadler is debatable. One such example on a tea canister of about 1766, although in miniature, has figures which certainly bear a strong resemblance to them (Plate 69). On the reverse, as is almost invariable, is a rendering of *The Shepherd* (Plate 70).

Later, Josiah sent his own selected engravings to be copied in Liverpool. He personally ransacked the London printsellers' shops in his search for material suitable as a basis for designs for transfer printing. A variety of subjects were chosen which included genre scenes, portraits, classical groups, floral and shell studies, and bird designs. The latter, which have become known as *Liverpool Birds*, are found in various forms, and seem to have been adaptations and combinations of Charles Fenn's vignettes. Mostly they were used in the early 1760s, and one of the first is a variety, *Peafowl*, illustrated on a rose-moulded,

68 *The Wolf and the Lamb*: on PLATE of creamware by JOSIAH WEDGWOOD. 255 mm
(10 in) diameter
From an engraving for a tile, with double-eight border, and surrounding printed
floral vignettes, in jet black. Hand-enamelled garrya-husk festoons and ribbon.
Printed by Sadler and Green, based on an engraving by Sébastien Le Clerc, but in
mirror image. 1768–75. *See page 142*
The Victoria and Albert Museum

69 *Tea Party No. 1*: on flattened-oval TEA CANISTER with fluted corners and serpentine
top, of pale creamware, by JOSIAH WEDGWOOD. 104 mm (4.1 in) high
In mirror image, printed by Sadler and Green in ivory black. This is one of the
versions believed to be a portrayal of Josiah and Sarah Wedgwood. 1765–8. *See
page 142*

feather-edged plate (Plate 71). It is interesting to compare this with a very similar design on a Leeds Pottery creamware plate (Plate 106). If Sadler and Green also printed the latter version, it seems that it must have been before Josiah required his patterns to be confined to his own wares. All his later designs were modified in varying degree before appearing on competitors' products.

A little later, designs of birds which seem to be a hotchpotch of features of numerous species were used on Wedgwood pieces, and an example is *Exotic Birds*, on a triple-ridged plate with segmented rim (Plate 72). Not dissimilar is yet another design, this time on a feather-edged fruit dish, which for differentiation is best called *Fabulous Birds* (Plate 73). There are many other similar bird designs to be found on Wedgwood's creamware, and some patterns were occasionally used in mirror image. A comfiture dish has round its body two landscapes with *Liverpool Birds*, with floral motifs in-between, while the lid has four more different transfers of *Liverpool Birds* in branches; inside the bowl is a fifth. The whole piece is as thin as fine porcelain, and although 140 mm (5.5 in) high, weighs but 400 grams (14.1 oz) (Plate 74). This represents the acme of creamware manufacture, since apart from its opacity it is in every way comparable with the best bone china.

A magnification of one of Sadler and Green's bird prints clearly shows how the engraving made no attempt to follow the earlier etched lines (Plate 45).

Josiah Wedgwood may well have been the first industrialist to found a Masonic lodge for his employees, for there is in the Merseyside County Museum a creamware deep-plate decorated with a print of *The Most Worshipful Grand Master*, printed in pale sienna colour. It has at the top 'Etruscan Lodge 327', and beneath the hostlery wherein was the temple, 'Bridge Inn Etruria'. The engraving is either by James Ross, or copied from one of his used at Worcester in the period 1760 to 1770. A small Wedgwood mug printed in the same pale sienna colour, and made between 1780 and 1785, is illustrated (Plate 75). The print is similar to that on the Etruscan Lodge plate, except for some slight modifications to accommodate the different proportions, and is from an engraved plate by the same hand. The Grand Master and two other Masons are inspecting an open-air temple containing a large Masonic achievement surrounded by insignia of the order. Masonic mugs and jugs abound, but mostly they date from the turn of the nineteenth century, whereas these pieces are earlier, and the subject is much more delicately and artistically treated than on most of those that followed.

A very attractive example of Sadler and Green's printing on Queen's Ware is provided by a tea canister with the picture *Rural Lovers* based on an engraving by François Vivares (1709–80), published by him in 1760 and based on a painting by Thomas Gainsborough (Plate 76). This print is, as is usual on Wedgwood wares, beautifully proportioned to fit the piece it decorates, and on the reverse is a rural landscape, *Cows Fording Stream* (Plate 77). Both of these pictures are on the heavy side, as they have been taken from plates engraved

70 *The Shepherd*: on reverse of TEA CANISTER in Plate 69
    Printed in ivory black by Sadler and Green. *See page 142*

71 *Liverpool Birds (Peafowl)*: on rose-moulded PLATE, of pale manilla-colour
    creamware, with feathered edge (24 feathers), by JOSIAH WEDGWOOD. 236 mm
    (9.3 in) diameter
    Printed in dark drab by Sadler and Green. 1762–5. *See pages 41, 144, 180*

72 *Liverpool Birds (Exotic)*: on Queen's-pattern PLATE of pale creamware, by JOSIAH
WEDGWOOD. 242 mm (9.5 in) diameter
Printed in dark drab by Sadler and Green. 1765–8. *See pages 41, 144*

73 *Liverpool Birds (Fabulous)*: on cushion-shape FRUIT DISH, of pale manilla-colour
creamware, with feathered edge (28 feathers), by JOSIAH WEDGWOOD. 297 mm
(11.7 in) diagonal
Printed in dark drab by Sadler and Green. 1762–5. *See pages 41, 144*

74 *Liverpool Birds (Various)*: on COMFITURE DISH of pale manilla-colour creamware, with lid with floral knop, by JOSIAH WEDGWOOD. 140 mm (5.5 in) diameter
Printed in dark drab by Sadler and Green. 1760–5. *See pages 41, 144, 180*

75 *The Worshipful Grand Master*: on a MUG of off-white creamware, by JOSIAH WEDGWOOD. 95 mm (3.7 in) high
Copy of an engraving by James Ross, found on Worcester porcelain. Printed in pale sienna. 1780–5. *See page 144*

76 *Rural Lovers*: on flattened-oval TEA CANISTER, with fluted corners and serpentine top, of ivory-colour creamware by JOSIAH WEDGWOOD. 106 mm (4.1 in) high
Engraved without prior etching, after an engraving by François Vivares, and printed in jet black by Sadler and Green. Impressed 'WEDGWOOD'. 1775–85.
See page 144

77 *Cows Fording Stream*: on reverse of TEA CANISTER in Plate 76
Engraved without prior etching, and printed in jet black by Sadler and Green.
1775–85. *See page 144*

78 *Corinthian Ruins*: on Royal-pattern PLATE of off-white creamware by JOSIAH
WEDGWOOD. 245 mm (9.6 in) diameter
Printed in jet black by Sadler and Green. 1780–5. *See pages 150, 172*

79 *East Indiaman on the Starboard Tack*: inside of a PUNCH BOWL (one of a pair, Plates
80 and 81) of ivory-colour creamware, by JOSIAH WEDGWOOD. 213 mm (8.4 in)
diameter
Printed in jet black by Sadler and Green. Impressed 'WEDGWOOD' and broken
circle'( )'. 1780–5. *See pages 150, 226*

without prior etching. For this reason they lose delicacy, but gain in contrast with the creamware. The treatment of the former picture is very different from that of the same design on Worcester porcelain, where the print has to fight with the cabbage-leaf moulding over which it has been placed (Plate 34). Wedgwood wrote to Bentley:

'I have had a good deal of talk with Mr. Sadler, & find him very willing to do anything to improve his patterns. He has just completed a sett of Landskips for the inside of dishes &c., with childish scrawling sprigs of flowers for the rims, all of which he thinks very clever, but they will not do for us. He is trying the purple, and thinks he shall manage it, and is willing to have a sett of the red chalk stile, or Mezotinto flowers, but thinks they can do them at Liverpool best. I am afraid of trusting too much to their taste, but they have promised to offtrace & copy any prints I shall send them without attempting to *mend* or alter them. I have promised to send him the red chalk plates and a few prints of flowers immediately, & beg you will send him the plates &c. and pick out some prints of different size flowers to send along with them by the coach to Liverpool.'

It is not without its humour, this criticism from men of such impeccable taste as Wedgwood and Bentley of another with a proclivity to gaily sprinkle flowers in every vacant space. A probable example of the result of Josiah's efforts to improve floral border-patterns is on a plate with the picture *Corinthian Ruins* (Plate 78). The body of this piece is off-white and has a chalky look, contrasting well with the jet-black printing.

Interesting examples of the value of transfer printing in making, or confirming, attributions are to be found in four Wedgwood punch bowls. The most recently made, a pair, circa 1780, are impressed on their bases 'WEDGWOOD', and have inside *East Indiaman on the Starboard Tack* (Plate 79). This is a spirited engraving much superior to that inside the third bowl referred to below. Outside are two rare prints of genre subjects, *Buying Fish* and *Directing a Wayfarer* (Plate 80). They have been transferred from comparatively new printing-plates, which were somewhat heavily engraved. The remaining two prints outside each bowl are *Venus Rising from the Waves* and *Neptune in his Chariot* (Plate 81), which have both been taken from somewhat worn, and in places re-engraved, plates, earlier used to decorate the third bowl.

This latter bowl dates from about 1775, and has inside *East Indiaman on the Port Tack* (Plate 82). This is a rather flaccid picture, compared with the ship in the later bowls, giving the impression that in spite of a fair wind the vessel makes no progress at all. Outside are the Venus and Neptune prints referred to above, and made before it was found necessary to strengthen the engravings because of wear. Between these two fairly common prints are two more rare impressions, the first being *The Colonist's Departure* (Plate 83). The complementary picture *The Colonists Reunited* is opposite (Plate 84). These

80 *Buying Fish* and *Directing a Wayfarer*: on a pair of creamware PUNCH BOWLS
(interior of one shown in Plate 79)
Printed in jet black by Sadler and Green. 1780–5. *See page 150*

81 *Venus Rising from the Waves* and *Neptune in his Chariot*: on pair of PUNCH BOWLS
shown in Plates 79 and 80
Printed in jet black by Sadler and Green from the same plates after repair as used
on the outside of the punch bowl shown in Plates 82, 83 and 84. 1780–5. *See page
150*

82 *East Indiaman on the Port Tack*: inside of a PUNCH BOWL of ivory-colour creamware
   by JOSIAH WEDGWOOD. 248 mm (9.7 in) diameter
   Printed in jet black by Sadler and Green. (The floral sprays transferred from the
   same printing-plate as that used for the decoration of the bowl in Plate 85.)
   1775–80. *See page 150*

83 *The Colonist's Departure*: outside of the PUNCH BOWL shown in Plate 82
   Printed in jet black by Sadler and Green. 1775–80. *See page 150*

84 *The Colonists Reunited*: outside of the PUNCH BOWL shown in Plates 82 and 83
   Printed in jet black by Sadler and Green. 1775–80. *See page 150*
85 *Taking the Enemy's Wind*: inside of a large PUNCH BOWL of ivory-colour creamware
   by JOSIAH WEDGWOOD. 299 mm (11.7 in) diameter
   Printed in jet black by Sadler and Green. (The floral sprays transferred from the
   same printing-plate as that used for the decoration of the bowl in Plate 82.)
   1775–80. *See page 156*

86 '*JEMMY's FAREWELL*': on outside of the PUNCH BOWL shown in Plate 85
An incident from the *Song of Auld Robin Grey*, printed in jet black by Sadler and
Green. 1775–80. *See page 156*
87 '*JEMMY's RETURN*': on outside of the PUNCH BOWL shown in Plates 85 and 86
Another incident from the *Song of Auld Robin Grey*, printed in jet black by Sadler
and Green. 1775–80. *See page 156*

88 *Crowded Waters*: on outside of PUNCH BOWL shown in Plates 85, 86 and 87
Printed in jet black by Sadler and Green. 1775–80. *See page 156*

89 *'GOD SPEED THE PLOW'*: on outside of PUNCH BOWL shown in Plates 85, 86, 87
and 88
Printed in jet black by Sadler and Green. 1775–80. *See page 156*

at first glance might be thought to be just other versions of Jemmy's, or the sailor's, farewell and return, but the wagon train in the background of the second print effectively prevents such confusion.

The fourth is a very large punch bowl, which inside has one of the finest examples of on-glaze transfer printing, *Taking the Enemy's Wind*, which depicts a spirited naval duel between two ships of the line (Plate 85). It will be noticed that there are six floral vignettes round the inside edge of the bowl, and these have been transferred from the same printing plate as that used for the inside border of the previous bowl. Floral vignettes will be found round plates and bowls of many other manufacturers, but they differ considerably in detail. As has been remarked, it is inconceivable that Sadler and Green should have risked commercial suicide by using Josiah Wedgwood's printing plates for other customers, so that these printing links confirm the attribution of the two unmarked bowls. Two of the prints outside this bowl are found singly, or as a pair, on other Wedgwood pieces, so they deserve illustration. Of the opposing pair, one is '*Jemmy's Farewell*', with underneath '*Song of Auld Robin Grey*' (Plate 86). On the other side is '*Jemmy's Return*', with the same caption (Plate 87). They are based on a ballad, which on some pieces is underneath the pictures. It was published anonymously, but was in fact written by Lady Anne Barnard (1750–1825), the daughter of James Lindsay, fifth Earl of Balcarres. Between these prints there is on one side a rare engraving, *Crowded Waters*, which depicts six sailing vessels of different classes, in a seascape (Plate 88). The antipodal print is a version of '*God Speed the Plow*', which puts all other transfer prints of this theme to shame (Plate 89).

Predominantly, Queen's Ware is found printed in black or near-black, and less frequently in shades of brown, red, green and even yellow. Coloured hand-enamelling of prints on Wedgwood wares is more of a rarity. In 1776 Josiah wrote to Bentley: 'Yes. I make no doubt Painting and Printing may exist together. I hope we shall do both in quantities both in Table and Teaware.' This is ambiguous, and is hardly likely to be referring to printing and painting on the same pieces, for hand colouring of prints was probably a treatment which offended the susceptibilities of a man of the character of Josiah Wedgwood.

The evidence suggests that the firm itself never transfer printed on-glaze, but after Josiah's death in 1795 some creamware was printed in jet black underglaze. It was then that such famous patterns as *Wild Rose* and *Zebra* were introduced, to be plagiarized in underglaze blue by nearly every potter in the kingdom.

Chapter 6

THE DISSEMINATION —
FREE-LANCE TRANSFER PRINTERS

In the twenty years immediately following the invention of transfer printing the increase in the number of those skilled in the process was comparatively modest, but the next twenty years saw a great proliferation of those engaged in the art. Not unnaturally the rate of expansion of knowledge of the process increased in a geometrical progression, until by the end of the century there were really very few secrets left concerned either with transfer printing on glaze, or with that under glaze. Throughout the second half of the eighteenth century this expansion became channelled in two directions; one course was followed by specialist transfer printers like Sadler and Green, and the other by the potters who set up their own printing departments and directly employed engravers and printers on their staffs.

The first group flourished from 1756 until the beginning of the second decade of the nineteenth century. The great majority of the men engaged in the business during that period were the trained progeny of the first of them, Sadler and Green. Factories like Bow, Worcester and Derby guarded their secrets as best they could, and their employees became accustomed to the idea that transfer printing necessarily formed a small part of a greater undertaking, too large and costly to be set up independently. If they migrated it was usually to become employees at a competitive factory.

It has been explained that for transfer printing it was essential for the firing of the prints to be done at the place of printing, and for this reason whenever an engraver was described also as a printer — or in the language of the eighteenth century a 'black-printer' — he worked on glaze. Later, when underglaze printing became commonplace, a class of engraver came into existence composed of men divorced from the printing, who sold their etched or engraved plates to the potters for them to do their own printing and subsequent glazing. In contemporary documents these men were simply described as engravers. Eleven black-printers are known by name, and five of them were shown on the 1802 map in the *Staffordshire Pottery Directory*. Their output must have reached considerable proportions. Care must be exercised when reading nineteenth-century authors on ceramics, for it was a prevalent habit to write that Tom Scratchplate 'worked for' John Bakeclay, or that Bakeclay 'employed' Scratchplate, and these ambiguous phrases must be accepted with the reservation that Scratchplate could equally well have been an employee, or a free-lance with his own place of business. When the man is in fact known to have had a business of his own, or at the same time did work for more than one potter, it is safest to assume, unless there is evidence to the contrary, that he worked in a free-lance capacity.

First Harry Baker of Hanley calls for mention. There are no grounds for the belief that he ever successfully engraved or transfer printed on pottery or porcelain, and his name is known only through three sources. Firstly, Simeon Shaw wrote:[1]

> 'But, the first black Printer in the district, is said to have been Harry Baker, of Hanley, prior to Sadler and Green practising it; and from some plates borrowed from and belonging to a Book Printer.'

It is unfortunate that at the date mentioned by Shaw (1777), the process had been in use in London, Worcester and Liverpool for over twenty years. Shaw went on to explain at length that the paper was used in a dry state on a sometimes obviously cold plate, because if it was not transferred 'the instant it came from between the rollers' it failed. Later he stated that the method of damping paper adopted by copper-plate printers was tried 'and various essays were made by different persons, with different degrees of success'. It is extraordinary how Shaw's mention of this man Baker has been quoted time and again to the effect that Harry Baker was an engraver and transfer printer, and it is hoped that this misleading report can be shown up for what it is. If Baker himself had been an engraver it is difficult to see why he should have needed to borrow plates from a book-printer; also, if he had had only the most elementary knowledge of intaglio printing he would have been aware that since its invention three centuries earlier the printing plate was always kept warm, and the paper dampened in order that it should pick the ink from the etched and engraved lines.

The second probable source of our knowledge of this same Baker has already been mentioned when dealing with the ill-fated Liverpool China Manufactory that closed in 1761. One of the partners of this firm was a Harry Baker, described as an enameller. It is generally supposed that he was the Henry Baker of Simeon Shaw. What is certain is that this Baker tried to transfer print on glass, and this is proved by a patent granted to him on 20 October 1781.[2] This is described as 'A new method of ornamenting glass by a composition of colours or materials imprinted or made upon the glass, by means of copper or other

[1] Op. cit., pp. 192, 212 and 213.
[2] Patent No. 1296/1781 on Specification lodged 13 October 1781.

plates and wooden blocks or cutts.' There are details of the preparation of inks and pounces, and particulars of transference to glass by glue-bat and tissue. This is really a lifting of, by then, well-known, formulas and methods of transfer printing on pottery and porcelain, and their application to the decoration of glass. There is nothing original in the patent, other than the material to be decorated. As with John Brooks's applications, one of the secret keys to the whole process is omitted, namely the preparation of the slippery, unreceptive surface of the glass to give it a tooth to accept and retain the transfer. This failure suggests that his process could not have been very successful, and today it is impossible to form a judgement, as the only two recorded examples of his work were unfortunately destroyed by enemy action, 1939–45.

The third reference to Baker was made by John Sadler in correspondence with Josiah Wedgwood, when he dismissed Henry Baker's efforts as nothing to be feared, and observed that his transfer-printed pieces were so poor that 'the Londoners wd. buy none of them at any price'. Once more it is obvious that he was unable to carry out the process satisfactorily, and the evidence supports the theory that he could not obtain proper adhesion of the transferred print or medium to the glazed surface. What other possible reason could there have been for Londoners not buying them at any price? Colour or design could easily have been changed, but to remedy incorrect technique was a different matter, and as far as present information goes he never did succeed in his ambitions.

JOHN ROBINSON, BURSLEM (fl. 1768 to 1786)

Sometime about 1786 William Tunnicliff published *A Topographical Survey of the County of Stafford*, in which he listed seventy-six potters and china manufacturers, two enamellers, one merchant and factor, and one 'enameller and printer of cream-colour and china-glazed ware'. The last described was John Robinson of Hill Top, Burslem. Simeon Shaw in writing of the creamware of Enoch Booth of Tunstall recorded:[3] 'An excellent specimen is a Sauce Boat, made in 1768, of a fiddle head pattern, from a mould of Mr. A. Wood's, and enamelled by Mr. John Robinson, then recently come from Liverpool.' If Shaw's date is reliable, it would seem that Robinson was, after Thomas Rothwell, the second man with a knowledge of transfer printing to settle in Staffordshire.

Later Shaw stated:[4]

'About this time the late Mr John Robinson, of the Hill Top, Burslem, who understood enamelling and printing, left the service of Messrs. S. & G. and settled at Burslem, to print for Mr. Wedgwood; but he afterwards

[3] Op. cit., p. 177.
[4] Op. cit., p. 193.

commenced business as a Printer in Black or Red, on the glaze, and also as Enameller, for any of the manufacturers; the preserved specimens of his productions, are deficient in elegance.'

It could be inferred from Shaw's words that Robinson joined Wedgwood's staff for a short period, but there is no evidence that the latter had a printing shop at the Brick House Works—everything points to the contrary—and it is safer to assume that Robinson worked for him as an enameller.

Robinson maintained contact with Richard Abbey, a fellow employee while he was at Sadler and Green's Liverpool works, and after both had left he did sketches which Abbey engraved. An example of their joint work is a print called 'Hibernia' which has the imprint 'I Robinson Burslem pinxt R. Abbey Sculp'. Illustrated is a jug decorated with such a print (Plate 90). The apparent explanation for this is that Robinson was an artist, enameller and printer, but that, like John Sadler and Guy Green, he could not etch or engrave. The jug shows the female crowned figure of Hibernia seated beside an Irish harp, on a dockside with bales of merchandise consigned to France, Spain and America. On the ground are two broadsheets; one with 'Reduction of the Pension List', and the other 'Taxation of non-Residentials'. The picture is bordered by a garland of garrya-husks, with at the bottom 'Ye Sons of Hibernia rejoice in the Freedom of your extensive COMMERCE'. It would seem to have been an over-optimistic commemoration of the Act of Union of 1801.

THOMAS FLETCHER, SHELTON (fl. 1786 to 1810)

John Baddeley I ran a pottery in High Street, Shelton, and on 31 July 1761 admitted into partnership for a period of fourteen years a man called Thomas Fletcher. After John I's death in 1771, his eldest son Ralph honoured the partnership agreement, but at the end of July 1775 he bought out Fletcher. What the latter did for the next eleven years is uncertain, but in 1786 he was in business as a decorator and transfer printer with Sampson Bagnall II, whose father was a potter of Hanley. It is not known where Fletcher learned the transfer-printing process, but it seems that it could well have been from Thomas Radford, who had established his transfer-printing business in Shelton a year or two after Fletcher's partnership with Baddeley had been dissolved. By 1796 Bagnall had left Fletcher, who took as partners Thomas Thompson and John Hewitt. In 1800 the firm was dissolved and while Hewitt started a pottery at Lane End, Fletcher continued as transfer printer on his own. He was shown on the map of 1802 in the *Staffordshire Pottery Directory* at his residence, Boden Brook, Shelton, and described as a black-printer and enameller. He is believed to have continued in business until about 1810.

The usual problem is posed as to whether Fletcher's imprint is that of an engraver or printer, but the weight of evidence is against his ever having been

E. *Gifts for a Manchu Lady*: on TEA BOWLS and SAUCER of steatitic porcelain, by
CHAFFERS AND CHRISTIAN. Saucer 134 mm (5.3 in) diameter, and bowls 86 mm
(3.4 in) diameter
Outline printed in graphite colour, and over-enamelled in vermilion, king's blue,
apple green, primrose and lilac. The hand-pencilled husk-and-berry borders are in
apple green and bright puce. 1764–70. *See pages 90, 138*

F. *Liverpool Birds (Exotic)*: on a hexagonal PLATE of pearlware, probably by the
LEEDS POTTERY. 264 mm (10.4 in) diameter
From an etched outline printed in raw umber, and delicately over-enamelled in leaf
green, primrose, mandarin blue, chestnut and deep violet. Hand-pencilled border
of alternate swags and husk-festoons in the same enamels. 1785–95. *See page 184*

90 'HIBERNIA': on a JUG of creamware, potter unattributed. 217 mm (8.5 in) high
     Engraved by Richard Abbey, after a design by John Robinson, and printed by him
     in jet black. Commemorative of the Act of Union, 1801. Imprints 'I. Robinson
     pinxt' and 'R. Abbey Sculp'. 1801–2. See page 160
     Merseyside County Museums
91 Farewell of Louis XVI: on a cylindrical MUG of creamware. Potter unattributed
     Printed in black by Thomas Fletcher, with imprint 'Fletcher & Co Shelton'.
     1793–8. See page 162
     Victoria and Albert Museum

reponsible for any artistic work. The prints with his name as an imprint are much too professional to have been the work of a man who had taken up art in late middle age, and one of these imprints is 'Fletcher and Co, Shelton' (Plate 91). The engraving of a copper plate is a personal achievement, and no artist, even if he owned a transfer-printing business, would sign a plate with his firm's name in preference to his own, any more than an author-publisher would omit reference to his authorship. The illustration is of a mug with an on-glaze black print of Louis XVI taking leave of his wife, sister and children at eight o'clock in the evening of Sunday, 20 January 1793, before he went to the guillotine on the following morning. This is decidedly the work of no amateur, and could possibly be that of Thomas Radford. William Turner illustrated a jug with hunting prints with the imprint 'T. Fletcher Shelton'.[5]

THOMAS BADDELEY, HANLEY (fl. 1797 to 1822)

On the map of the 1802 *Staffordshire Pottery Directory* Thomas Baddeley is shown as an engraver and black-printer at Chapel Fields, Hanley. The Baddeleys were a large family of Staffordshire potters, and Thomas (b. 1762) was probably the third son of John I, referred to under Thomas Fletcher immediately above. Where Thomas Baddeley received his artistic training and his knowledge of transfer printing is not known, but what is certain is that unlike many of his contemporary transfer printers he himself was an engraver. This is corroborated by some of his prints carrying the imprint 'Printed and engraved by Thos. Baddeley Chapel Field Hanley'. He was a very competent engraver, and printed in both black and sepia. Illustrated is a portrait by him of Admiral Adam Viscount Duncan (1731–1804), who was created an admiral in 1795, and Viscount Duncan of Camperdown in 1797, after winning that battle against the Dutch admiral, De Winter (Plate 92). The engraving possibly dates from that year or 1798. Under the portrait is the verse:

> Long as the Sea shall fence our envi'd Land,
> Long as our Navy shall that Sea command:
> So long shall Admiral Lord Duncan's Name,
> Be grav'd by Memory on the Rock of Fame:
> The Page of History shall his Deeds repeat,
> With Britain's Triumph and the Dutch defeat.

On the reverse, under the title '*Britain's Glory*', are pictured a youth and child beside a spinning machine, with beneath 'Success to the Friendly Association of Cotton Spinners', and another verse. A creamware plaque, or tile, with a circular transfer print entitled '*Plenty*,' one of a pair with '*Peace*,' shows firm, confident stipple engraving (Plate 93). It is signed 'T. Baddeley Hanley'.

[5] Op. cit., pp. 84/5 and Plate A30.

92 *'ADMIRAL LORD VISCOUNT DUNCAN'*: on JUG of creamware. Potter
   unattributed. 224 mm (8.8 in) high. (On reverse, *'Britain's Glory'*.)
   From line-and-stipple etched and engraved plates printed in ivory black. Imprint
   'Printed & Engraved by Thos. Baddeley, Chapel-Field, Hanley'. 1797–8. *See page*
   162
   City of Coventry Museums
93 *'PLENTY'*: on PLAQUE of creamware. Potter unattributed. 178 mm (7 in) high
   Stipple-etched and engraved and printed in tobacco colour. Imprint 'T. Baddeley
   Hanley'. 1805–15. *See page 162*
   Stoke-on-Trent Museum

GEORGE BRAMMER, SHELTON (fl. 1802)
JOHN JOHNSON, SHELTON (fl. 1802)
FRANCIS MORRIS, SHELTON (fl. 1802)

Three transfer printers, George Brammer, John Johnson and Francis Morris were all shown on the map in the *Staffordshire Pottery Directory* of 1802 as black-printers residing at Shelton, which is now part of southern Hanley. There are no other records of their activities, and nothing is known about them except that Morris lived at Vale Pleasant, and there is a record in a 1967 auction catalogue of a jug with a medallion of Sir John Jarvis, K.B., with the imprint 'Mollart Sculp. Morris print', which confirms that Morris was not an engraver.[6]

The known sources of eighteenth-century engraving and on-glaze transfer-printing can be summarized in their respective categories:

Free-lance engravers and transfer printers:

Abbey, Richard	Liverpool
Baddeley, Thomas	Hanley
Hanbury, Michael	Dublin
Radford, Thomas	Stoke-on-Trent

Free-lance transfer printers reliant on employed engravers:

Brammer, George	Shelton (probably)
Fletcher, Thomas	Shelton
Green, Guy	Liverpool
Johnson, John	Shelton (probably)
Johnson, Joseph	Liverpool
Morris, Francis	Shelton (probably)
Robinson, John	Burslem
Sadler, John	Liverpool

Factories with engraving and printing departments:
Bow China Works
Derby Porcelain Works
Derby Pot Works
Worcester Porcelain Works

Staff transfer printers, unable to engrave:

Holdship, Richard	Worcester and Derby (also possibly underglaze at Bow)
Lewis, George	Worcester

[6] The author is indebted to Norman Stretton for this information.

Staff engravers:

Abbey, Richard	Sadler and Green, Joseph Johnson (also possibly free-lance)
Billinge, Thomas	Sadler and Green
Boitard, Louis Peter	Worcester (possibly)
Burdett, Peter Pever	Sadler and Green (possibly)
Evans, Jerimiah	Sadler and Green
Green, Valentine	Worcester
Hancock, Robert	Bow and Worcester
Lewick, John	Worcester
Radford, Thomas	Derby Pot Works, later free-lance
Ravenet, Simon	Bow (possibly)
Robinson, John	Sadler and Green, later free-lance
Ross, James	Worcester
Rothwell, Thomas	Sadler and Green, Henry Palmer, Melbourne Pottery and Swansea Pottery
Turner, Thomas	Worcester (underglaze at Caughley)
Underwood, William	Worcester, Derby Porcelain Works and John Turner of Lane End
Walker, Richard	Joseph Johnson

It is interesting that for the first thirty-five years at least there was no union of the separate lineages springing from Battersea and Liverpool, as is shown by the following development chart (see pages 166–7):

PROLIFERATION OF ON-GLAZE TRANSFER PRINTING

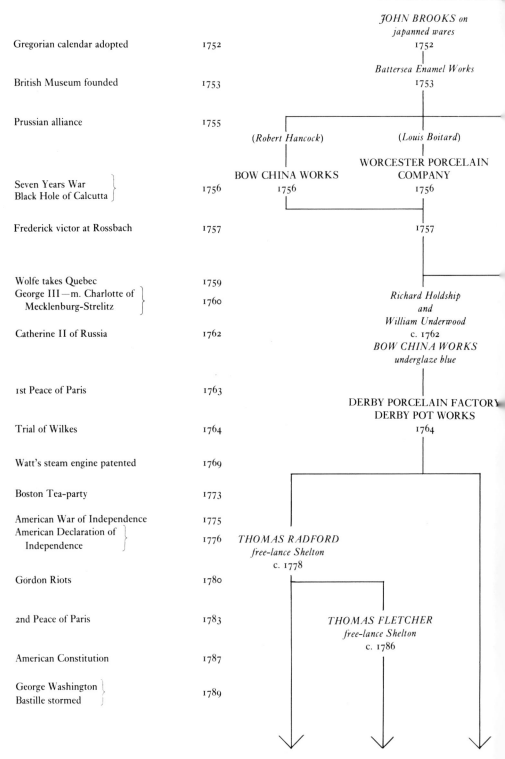

UP TO 1790, BY MIGRATION OF EMPLOYEES

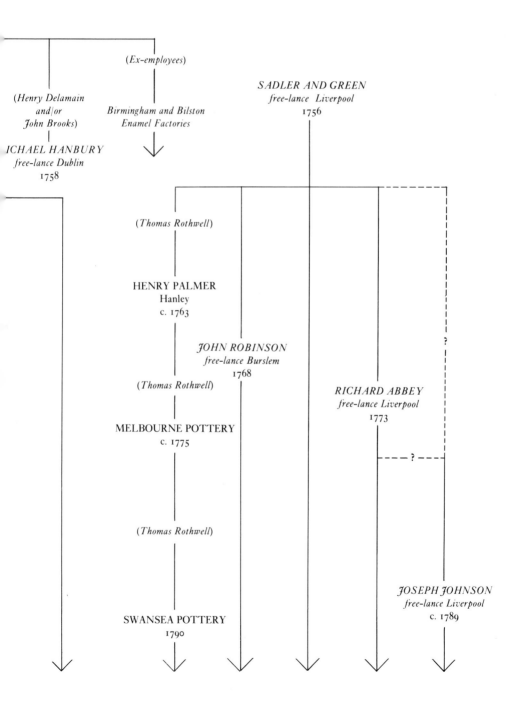

Chapter 7

THE DISSEMINATION —
POTTERIES AND FACTORIES

There is no doubt that Josiah Wedgwood, with his impressive reputation, by subcontracting his transfer printing to specialists, set a pattern for other creamware and earthenware manufacturers, and it is possible that his example was copied very much more than is generally appreciated. It is worthwhile pausing to consider that although the Liverpool potters and porcelain manufacturers were manifestly the customers of Sadler and Green, and did not themselves transfer print on-glaze, there is little documentary evidence to prove it. Were it not for the continued existence of Josiah Wedgwood and Sons, with its well-protected archives, it is unlikely that today there would be any written confirmation of the relationship that existed between that firm and Sadler and Green. This is a factor which must be borne in mind when the on-glaze printing of wares of Herculaneum, Leeds and other factories is considered.

HENRY PALMER, HANLEY (fl. 1760 to 1776)

Thomas Rothwell (1740–1807) was the son of a cabinet-maker of the same name of Common Garden, Liverpool. He was born on 19 May 1740, and when he was twenty years of age he married a girl named Esther Johnson, and they set up home in Frog Lane, Liverpool. It seems that sometime after 1762 they moved to Staffordshire. Simeon Shaw stated:[1]

> 'About this time Thomas Rothwell, possessed of great skill as an enameller, engraver and printer, was employed by Mr. Palmer, at Hanley, and specimens yet remaining evince considerable ability; but like all the other attempts, they do not equal the productions of S. & G. for Mr. Wedgwood.'

[1] Op. cit., p. 192.

94 *The Haymakers' Return*: on olive-shape TEAPOT of creamware, probably by HENRY
     PALMER. 148 mm (5.8 in) high. (On other side *Shepherd and Sheep*.)
     Printed in black, with imprint 'T. Rothwell Delin et Sculp'. 1763–8. *See page 170*
     Merseyside County Museums
95 *The Sleeping Beau*: on TEA CANISTER of creamware, by HENRY PALMER. 133 mm
     (5.2 in) high
     Probably engraved by Thomas Rothwell, and printed in black. Imprint 'Palmer
     Enamel Hanly'. 1762–72. *See page 170*
     E. Norman Stretton Esq.

In this instance it is safe to assume that Rothwell joined Palmer's staff, for there are no contemporary records which suggest that Rothwell ever acted as a free lance while in Staffordshire.

Henry Palmer (d. 1778) is thought to have been the son of John Palmer, and to have started the Church Works, Hanley in 1760. He was Wedgwood's plagiarist, and the partner and brother-in-law of James Neale. He got into financial difficulties in 1776, which resulted in Neale taking over the entire business. The rate-books and directories of Birmingham have been searched and it is apparent that Rothwell was in that city by May 1773.[2] There were, however, many books published from 1769 onwards containing engravings by Rothwell, so that it is a reasonable assumption that he had left the ceramic industry by that year. The known facts suggest that he was in Staffordshire between 1763 and 1768. As, until 1773, Sadler and Green were the only transfer printers in Liverpool, it appears that Rothwell must have been trained by them.

There is a remarkably fine creamware teapot in the Liverpool City Museum which has on one side a print *Shepherd and Sheep*, and on the other *The Haymakers' Return* which is signed 'T. Rothwell Delin. et Sculp.' (Plate 94). It is possible that this is an example of Henry Palmer's ware. Of the few pieces which can positively be attributed to this potter one certain and delightful example is a creamware tea canister with a bucolic transfer print of a young maiden awaking a sleeping beau beside a blighted tree-stump (Plate 95). The very extraordinary imprint is 'Palmer Enamel Hanly', and it can only be assumed either that it is a very early example of Rothwell's work in Staffordshire and that Palmer gave instructions that he should be described in the manner that he then used for his existing business, or the copper plate was engraved with the intention that prints from it should be colour enamelled. After his stay in Birmingham the next record of Rothwell is sometime between 1775 and 1785 at the Melbourne Pottery. By 1790 he had become an employee of the Swansea Pottery. The indications are that Rothwell, unlike other ex-employees of Sadler and Green, at no time set up as a free-lance engraver and printer to the ceramic industry.

NEALE AND COMPANY, HANLEY (1776 to c. 1802)

Reference has been made above to James Neale taking over his brother-in-law Henry Palmer's business in 1776. Neale had originally been in charge of the London office and showrooms in Shoe Lane, but moved to Church Works, Hanley, when Palmer got into financial difficulties. For a few years round 1780, a man called Bailey was a partner, but had left by 1786 when Neale took into partnership Robert Wilson, who ultimately became the sole proprietor. By

[2]Norman Stretton, 'Thomas Rothwell, Engraver and Copper Plate Printer', *E.C.C. Transactions*, Vol. 6, part 3, 1967, p. 251.

96 *Pheasants with Chick*: on Royal-pattern PLATE of pale reseda-colour creamware, by
    NEALE AND COMPANY. 221 mm (8.7 in) diameter
    With four simple sprigs round rim, all printed in jet black. 1775–85. *See page 172*
97 '*The Prodigal Son in Excess*': on a TEAPOT of creamware, made or merchanted by
    WILLIAM GREATBATCH. 140 mm (5.5 in) high. (On reverse '*The Prodigal Son in
    Misery*'.)
    Outline print engraved by Thomas Radford and printed in burnt umber, with
    polychrome over-enamelling. 1775–80. *See pages 99, 172*
    Stoke-on-Trent Museum

1802 the pottery was owned by Wilson's brother and sole beneficiary, David.

There exists a number of pieces of transfer-printed creamware from this factory, and some are marked. The potting is of top quality, the body of fine even texture, and the glaze usually of reseda colour and uncrazed. The engravings used for the transfer printing of these wares is not in the style of Thomas Radford, who had probably left at least eight years before Neale took over; nevertheless they are very professional, and it is very probable that some of the printing is the work of Sadler and Green. Plates from the factory are often of Royal pattern with gutter edges, but the scallops between the indentations are rather more serpentine than is usual. An example is illustrated featuring *Pheasants with Chick*, printed in a jet black (Plate 96). Another example, with the picture *Frigate on the Starboard Tack*, has sprigs round the border.[3] Sprigs of the same design are found in Sadler and Green printing, but in anticlockwise order, as on the Wedgwood plate bearing the print *Corinthian Ruins* (Plate 78).

WILLIAM GREATBATCH, FENTON AND LANE DELPH (fl. 1760 to 1788)

William Greatbatch (1735–1813) of Fenton was the son of a farmer and coal merchant of Berryhills. William was indentured between 1750 and 1756 to Thomas Whieldon, and during the latter part of his apprenticeship met Whieldon's junior partner, Josiah Wedgwood. An immediate rapport seems to have been established between the two, and Greatbatch made a friend for life, who in later years was both generous and understanding. About 1760 Greatbatch opened his own business in Lower Lane, Fenton. He was both a potter and a pottery merchant. In 1764 he moved a few hundred metres to the north, to the then village of Lane Delph.

Greatbatch's speciality was teapots, many of which he had transfer printed from plates engraved by Thomas Radford. A high proportion carry pictures in the theme of the parable of the prodigal son (Plates 97 and 98). Some of these prints bear a publisher's imprint 'William Greatbatch', which has given rise to the erroneous belief that he was an engraver as well as a potter. A fine example of a print carrying his name is '*Aurora*', which shows that permissive goddess driving home between dawn and sunrise in her chariot drawn by winged horses. This is often found on teapots (Plate 99). Some pieces have prints with the imprint 'Published as the Act directs Jan'y 4 1778 by W. Greatbatch, Lane Delf Staffordshire'. It would be manifestly absurd for the engraver to claim responsibility for the publication, and remain silent over the engraving. The omission of 'Engraved and published etc., etc.' would have been consummate *mauvaise honte*.

Greatbatch incurred bad debts to such a degree that they resulted in his bankruptcy early in 1782, and he was again gazetted insolvent in 1789.

[3] Illustrated by Donald Towner in *English Creamcoloured Earthenware*, London, 1957, plate 95A.

98 *'The Prodigal Son in Misery'*: on a TEAPOT of creamware, made or merchanted by
WILLIAM GREATBATCH. 140 mm (5.5 in) high
Outline print engraved by Thomas Radford and printed in burnt umber and
polychrome over-enamelled. 1775–80. *See pages 99, 172*
Royal Pavilion, Art Gallery and Museum, Brighton

99 *'Aurora'*: on a TEAPOT of creamware, made or merchanted by WILLIAM GREAT-
BATCH. 127 mm (5 in) high
Probably engraved by Thomas Radford and printed in black, and over-enamelled
in four colours. 1775–80. *See page 172*
Victoria and Albert Museum

THOMAS WOLFE, STOKE-ON-TRENT (fl. 1776 to 1818)

Both Shaw and Chaffers stated that Thomas Wolfe established his pottery in 1776. In 1790 he took as partner a man called Hamilton, who remained with him until 1811. This released him for other interests, and from 1790 until 1796 he was in partnership with William Ball, in a Liverpool factoring business, and from 1796 until 1800 he was part-proprietor with Miles Mason and John Lucock of the Islington China Works at Liverpool (see page 140).

It is related that he proudly claimed to have been of the same family as Major-General James Wolfe (1727–59) who died on the Plains of Abraham, while capturing Quebec in 1759. Benjamin West P.R.A. (1738–1820), an American Quaker, painted a picture, *The Death of Wolfe*, which was exhibited in the Royal Academy in 1771, and this inspired a number of engravers. There exists a jug, reputed to have been made by Wolfe, with a capably engraved on-glaze print in purple of this picture, based on a line engraving made in 1776 by William Woollett (1735–85) (Plate 100). Sadler and Green did a similar subject for Josiah Wedgwood, but the Wolfe engraving is in mirror image compared with Wedgwood's. There are no recorded on-glaze transfer-printed pieces bearing Thomas Wolfe's name. The print on the reverse of this jug is of interest; it shows a *Naval Sloop*, or frigate, with a quite impossible rig (Plate 101). The vessel has a fifteenth-century stern sprit, for use with lateen sails of that period, and the mizzen gaff carries at its peak a yard with a square sail. There are many other inaccuracies, and quite obviously the engraver was unfamiliar with the sea. This suggests that the printing was done inland, possibly in Staffordshire or South Yorkshire. It is of interest that the same nautical errors appear in the print on an unattributed beaker (Plate 152).

JOHN AYNSLEY, LANE END (fl. 1780 to 1809)

About 1780 John Aynsley is known to have started a business at Lane End, and to have marketed on-glaze transfer-printed wares as early as 1788. Whether he was a potter or a china merchant is not clear, but he was shown on the map of 1802 in *The Staffordshire Pottery Directory* as a potter. (He is not to be confused with John Aynsley and Sons, potters, who commenced business in 1864 at Longton.) William Turner illustrated a plate transfer-printed and colour-enamelled, showing Masonic insignia and marked 'J. Aynsley'.[4] A rather crude example of on-glaze transfer printing, which is also colour-enamelled, is a print '*Here's to a Maid of Bashful Fifteen*', on a mug (Plate 102). This also has the imprint as publisher of John Aynsley. A much finer print in the Liverpool style, which suggests that he may have used more

[4] Op. cit., Fig. A.29.

100 *Death of General Wolfe*: on JUG of creamware. Transfer-printed probably in Staffordshire or South Yorkshire, for THOMAS WOLFE of STOKE-ON-TRENT. 152 mm (6 in) high
Printed in purple, with crimson fancy-diamond enamel border. Based on an engraving by William Woollett, after Benjamin West. 1790–1800. *See page 174*
Victoria and Albert Museum

101 *Naval Sloop*: printed in purple on reverse of JUG in Plate 100. (Similar errors of rigging can be seen in the print on the beaker in Plate 152.) 1790–1800. *See pages 174, 226*
Victoria and Albert Museum

than one transfer printer, is entitled '*Prudence Brings Esteem*', and is found on plates (Plate 103). This is marked 'J. Aynsley, Lane End', and is almost certainly the work of Joseph Johnson.

JACOB WARBURTON (1741 to 1826)

The Warburton family were potters of repute in the seventeenth century, and at the end of the first quarter of the eighteenth Joseph Warburton (1694–1752) was operating a pottery in the village of Hot Lane, about two kilometres (one and a quarter miles) south-east of the centre of Burslem. He married Ann Daniel, who after his death, and with the help of their son Thomas, ran the works until 1789. Their second son Jacob had opened his own pottery at Cobridge, about two kilometres further south, but on his mother's death he also took control of the Hot Lane pottery. The mother and both sons were individual members of the Staffordshire potters' price-ring formed on 4 February 1770. Jacob was a very able business man, much respected, and was one of the founder members of the New Hall China Manufactory. Around 1809 he retired, and was succeeded by his sons, Peter and Francis.

An example of Jacob Warburton's creamware is a large tankard with a picture *Keep that Chin Up!* (Plate 104). It shows a stern young woman receiving musketry drill from a sergeant of the Militia, with on the right a drummer, who has lost a hand, and on the left a monkey with a flute. The imprint 'J. Warburton' is at the bottom, beneath the drummer. This is a publisher's imprint, showing that he had paid for the copper plate, and the engraving and transfer printing are almost certainly the work of a free-lance engraver and printer. The style and execution strongly suggest that it is from the hand of Thomas Rothwell, and if this be so it was executed immediately after he left the Swansea Pottery, on his way to London, in 1794. If it is not his work it could have been done by any of the five black-printers at Hanley and its suburb Shelton. These were Thomas Fletcher, Thomas Baddeley, George Brammer, John Robinson and Francis Morris. The vigorous style, and the competent etching, engraving and transfer printing have resulted in a print which is a telling satire on the revival of the Volunteer forces in 1794 (after their disbandment in 1783), when for the first time companies independent of the Militia were permitted to be formed.

As far as is known no other marked pieces of Jacob Warburton's manufacture are recorded.

LEEDS POTTERY (c. 1750 to 1878)

Exactly when and by whom the Leeds Pottery was started is unknown. The factory was situated in Jack Lane, a turning off the Dewsbury Road, a

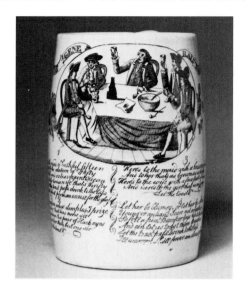

102 '*Here's to a maid of bashful fifteen*': on MUG of creamware by JOHN AYNSLEY of
Lane End
Printed in black and polychrome over-enamelled. Imprint 'J. Aynsley Lane End'.
1800–9. *See page 174*
Victoria and Albert Museum

103 '*Prudence brings Esteem*': on PLATE of creamware, by JOHN AYNSLEY of Lane End.
245 mm (9.6 in) diameter
Printed in black, and polychrome enamelled. Imprint 'J. Aynsley Lane End'.
Enamelled sprigs on condiments-rim. 1800–9. *See page 176*
Victoria and Albert Museum

kilometre (about half a mile) south of the River Aire and about one and a half kilometres (a mile) from Leeds city centre. In 1754 it was being run by Joshua Green of Middleton and his brother, John Green (d. 1805), a practical potter of Hunslet.[5] On the introduction of fresh capital in 1775 the trading name became Humble, Hartley, Greens and Company. One of the partners, William Hartley, became an increasingly powerful influence in the pottery's affairs, and in 1781 the firm was reconstructed, and became known as Hartley, Greens and Company. After Hartley's death in 1819 the concern went bankrupt, and was bought by Samuel Wainwright. It continued under a succession of names until 1878.

It had been generally accepted for nearly a century that, like Josiah Wedgwood, the firm sent its wares to Liverpool for transfer printing. This was a theory that was corroborated by the remarkable similarity of style and subject of Liverpool printing and many prints found on Leeds creamware. Joseph and Frank Kidson accepted without question that the factory, to begin with, did not do its own printing, but added: 'As time got on, however, and as the secret of the new decoration spread, Leeds would save the carriage and risk of breakage by doing their own printing at their own pottery.'[6] Some facts reported by Llewellynn Jewitt are responsible for a change of belief on this subject, but it is very doubtful whether any rethinking is justified. He quoted that in 1791 the stock of printing plates amounted to £204.[7] This had erroneously been assumed to indicate that the pottery must have done its own printing.

As is proved by the number of copper plates bearing the pottery's imprints many were the firm's property, and it would have been perfectly proper for their value to have been included in stock-in-trade, but this is not indicative in any way that the printing was carried out at Leeds. The plates may have been on the pottery premises, or every bit as easily in the workshops of free-lance transfer printers. The value of these copper plates seems, even for those days, a very inadequate one, and an alternative, and completely different, explanation could be that the amount referred to the value of the line-engraved copper plates used for the production of the firm's elaborate catalogues of designs, one of which contained no fewer than seventy-one plates, comprising two hundred and sixty-nine engraved patterns.

Whether in fact on-glaze printing was done at Leeds at all cannot yet be determined, but certainly it is most unlikely that any took place before the last decade of the eighteenth century. Some authorities are of opinion that no transfer printing occurred there until as late as 1815, and if this be true then it is certain that on-glaze printing never took place at the pottery.

It may have been the case that the firm was for many years the customer of

[5] Per letter of 20 March 1854 from Thomas Wilson of Leeds to Sir Henry de la Bèche, director of Jermyn Street Museum.
[6] Historical Notes on the Leeds Old Pottery, 1892, p. 69.
[7] Op. cit., Vol. 1, p. 470.

104 *Keep that Chin Up!*: on TANKARD of creamware, by JACOB WARBURTON. 154 mm
(6 in) high
Printed in jet black, with potter's imprint 'J. Warburton'. A satire on the revival
of the Volunteer forces, independent of the Militia. 1794–5. *See page 176*

105 *Liverpool Birds (Peafowl)*: on Queen's-pattern PLATE of cane-colour creamware,
by LEEDS POTTERY. 246 mm (9.7 in) diameter
Printed in deep Venetian red. The three border-vignettes printed from a single
engraving. 1760–5. *See page 180*

Sadler and Green, and later of Richard Abbey and Joseph Johnson. Lest it be thought that similar arguments to those advanced against Bow porcelain's having been transfer-printed in Birmingham apply to the products of Leeds having been printed in Liverpool, it must be pointed out, firstly, that the pieces were of creamware and not of porcelain; secondly, that the distance from Leeds to Liverpool, although a little further than from Burslem to Liverpool, is half that from Bow to Birmingham; and lastly, unlike Birmingham, Liverpool was an established centre for the manufacture of both porcelain and earthenware, as well as being the location of famous ceramic transfer printers.

Unfortunately Leeds creamware varied very much in colour, and it is not so easily dated as that of Wedgwood. Generally speaking it is more crazed, and for some years it was rather more yellowish, and sometimes more greenish than that from Staffordshire. An ivory colour was only achieved by about 1775, five years later than by Wedgwood.

Favourite early subjects on Leeds creamware plates were several versions of the *Liverpool Birds*. Illustrated is a very early plate showing the *Peafowl* pattern (Plate 105). This piece has a slightly sandy body, and is of overall cane colour, with the print in deep Venetian red. The uncrazed glaze is primrose, inclined to be slightly greenish, and unlike most plates of the period it has a very small footrim, with shallow furrows each side. The three vignettes round the edge are transferred from a single engraving.

It is interesting that a feather-edged plate of a slightly later period, carrying a similar pattern, is of a very much paler manilla colour (Plate 106). The uneven pale-olive glaze is finely crazed, and the printing is in ivory black. The central design is from a different engraved plate, while the surrounding prints are six varied subjects of the same genus. This forms an interesting comparison with the similar design on Wedgwood's Queen's Ware (Plate 71). There are small differences of detail consistent with different engravers being employed, and with the possible policy of Sadler and Green of introducing slight variations of design for work for individual customers. The vignettes round the condiments-rims are of similar design, but in each case they are anticlockwise when compared with the other. Even more striking is the similarity in the design and engraving style of the prints at twenty past and twenty to the hour on the Leeds plate, to the bird vignettes on the body of the Wedgwood comfiture dish (Plate 74). It is impossible to believe that these small engravings are from different hands.

Enlarged detail of the print on the feather-edged plate referred to above is shown (Plate 46). From examination of this it is possible to see in places the same disregard in the engraving of the underlying etching which characterizes so much of Sadler and Green's work (Plates 44 and 45).

Another early feather-edged plate bears a transfer-printed heraldic achievement, with the crest and motto top and bottom on the condiments-rim (Plate 107). The body is pale cream in colour, the pale-olive glaze is finely crazed, and the printing is in ivory black. It is interesting that the moulded

106 *Liverpool Birds (Peafowl)*: on PLATE of pale manilla-colour creamware, with
feathered edge (22 feathers) by LEEDS POTTERY. 236 mm (9.3 in) diameter
Lightly printed in ivory black. Impressed 'O' on back arch of rim. 1770–5. *See
pages 144, 180*

107 *Heraldic Achievement*: on PLATE of pale creamware, with feathered edge (23
feathers) by LEEDS POTTERY. 248 mm (9.7 in) diameter
With crest and motto on condiments-rim, printed in ivory black. 1775–80. *See
page 180*

feathers on Leeds ware have seven or nine barbs, with the second largest barb separated to the foot from the first. Wedgwood feathers invariably have seven barbs, with the second tending to join the first down two-thirds of its length.[8] It will also be found that on circular plates the Leeds feathers are appreciably smaller than those on Wedgwood, averaging 33 mm (1.3 in) from quill-end to quill-end, while on Wedgwood they average 31 mm (1.2 in). A coffee pot of the same period, 1775–80, shows allegorical subjects on both sides (Plate 108). These prints are from plates carrying the publisher's imprint 'Leeds Pottery'.

Unlike Wedgwood, the Leeds factory produced a quantity of colour-washed and enamelled on-glaze printing, and an attractive example is an ivory-coloured tankard which has the picture *Hare Coursing* washed over in a transparent rose-du-Barry enamel (Plate 109). A distinctive feature of this particular engraving is that in places, instead of cross-hatching, a most unusual technique was employed—comprising long lines in one direction, with in the other short lines stepped in relation to those between adjacent lines, so that the whole resembles the bonding of a brick wall. This is very noticeable on the jackets of both riders.

There exists a large early nineteenth-century creamware jug which carries the arms of the City of Leeds, the inscription 'Success to the Leeds Manufactory', and in script the initials 'J.B.' and 'S.B.' (Plate 110). This is transfer-printed with *The Vicar and Moses*, which is enamelled in five colours. The initials are thought to refer to John Barwick and his wife. Barwick was a practising surgeon in Leeds who put money into the concern in 1775, so the jug could commemorate the silver jubilee of his association with the pottery. The jug could have been a gift from the pottery, but the toast is such that it could equally, if not more, appropriately have been presented by an outside firm of transfer printers. The style of the engraving strongly suggests that it is from the same hand as that responsible for the Toby Philpot design signed 'R. Abbey' on Herculaneum creamware (Plate 128). Other prints such as *John Wesley* (1703–91) and *Love and Obedience* which have imprints 'Leeds Pottery' look very much as if they are the work of Richard Abbey.

A very large jug of Leeds origin shows on one side '*The Tar for All Weathers*' with a verse (Plate 111):

> After thus we at Sea had miscarry'd
> Another guess way sat the wind,
> For to England I came & got marry'd
> To a lass that was lovely and kind
>
> But whether for joy or vexation,
> We know not for what we were born
> Perhaps I may find a kind station,
> Perhaps I may touch at Cape Horn.

[8] Brought to notice by Donald Towner in 'The Melbourne Pottery', *E.C.C. Transactions*, Vol. 8, Part 1, 1971, p. 21.

108 *Allegorical Subject*: on COFFEE-POT of creamware, by LEEDS POTTERY. 228 mm
(9 in) high
Finely engraved and printed in black. Imprint 'Leeds Pottery'. 1790–1800. *See
page 182*
Victoria and Albert Museum

109 *Hare Coursing*: on TANKARD of ivory-coloured creamware, with slightly flared
base, by LEEDS POTTERY. 120 mm (4.7 in) high
The whole picture washed with thin rose-du-Barry enamel. Black enamel border.
1775–80. *See page 182*

110 *The Vicar and Moses*: on large JUG of creamware, by LEEDS POTTERY. 229 mm
(9 in) high
Printed in black and over-enamelled in five colours. Carries the City of Leeds
achievement, and the initials 'J.B.' and 'S.B.' (thought to be those of John
Barwick, shareholder, and his wife). Inscribed 'Success to the Leeds
Manufactory', and heightened with gilding. 1800–10. *See page 182*
Yorkshire Museum

On the reverse is *East Indiaman Shortening Sail*, flying from the ensign staff a
pre-1801 union flag (Plate 112). There can be no doubt at all that the
engravings are the work of Richard Abbey. The style is unmistakably his, and
the technique of the Tar picture should be compared with that of *Youthful
Lovers* (Plate 56). The overall colour is pale reseda, and the finely crazed glaze
is of pale grass-green. For some unexplained reason a proportion of the firm's
notoriously variable glaze became this colour at the commencement of the
nineteenth century, and continued so for at least two decades. Of a little later is
a bulbous jug of overall ivory colour, but the same pale grass-green glaze,
which bears on one side the *Society of Oddfellows Arms*, and on the reverse
Oddfellows' Apophthegms (Plate 113). The prints, as in the previous example,
are jet black. The jug has a copper-lustre band and line-border, and decoration.
      Pearlware is unquestionably difficult to attribute, but a hexagonal plate of
overall pale grey-cream colour is very probably of Leeds origin (Colour

111 'The TAR for all WEATHERS': on large PITCHER of baluster-shape and pale
     reseda-colour creamware, by LEEDS POTTERY. 309 mm (12.1 in) high
     Engraved by Richard Abbey, and printed in jet black. 1795–1801. See page 182
112 East Indiaman Shortening Sail: on reverse of PITCHER in Plate 111
     1795–1801. See page 184

Plate F). It bears a *Liverpool Birds* pattern printed in raw-umber colour, and is over-enamelled in five bright attractive colours. These same enamels have been used for the hand-painted border of alternate husk-festoons and swags. The glaze is uncrazed on the face, but finely crazed at the back where thick, and shows itself to be a pale grey-turquoise tint. From the early 1770s much Leeds creamware had been attractively enamelled, but this was mostly done by an outside decorating firm in Briggate, Leeds. From 1760, or earlier, this free-lance concern was run by David Rhodes and Jasper Robinson, but in March 1763, for some reason, Robinson ceased to be a partner. However, he remained an employee, and the trading name was changed to D. Rhodes and Company. One of the firm's customers was Josiah Wedgwood, and five years later Rhodes left Leeds to work for him in London. Robinson then, it seems, became the sole proprietor of the Leeds business, which he continued to run until 1779. At that date a Leonard Hobson bought the venture, which he ran for a further twenty years. On the plate illustrated it is manifestly obvious that the outline print was purposely executed with the intention of the transferred impressions being hand enamelled. Without the advantage of comparison of two identical plates, it might be thought that the outline had been hand pencilled, but in fact it is mostly etched with a very little engraving added.

Underglaze printing appears to have commenced at the factory at the turn of the nineteenth century, and it is probable that decoration by the on-glaze method of the factory's wares then very quickly ceased.

MELBOURNE POTTERY, DERBYSHIRE (c. 1770 to 1785)

A great deal is now known about the Melbourne Pottery thanks to Donald Towner.[9] This was situated a little over one kilometre (three-quarters of a mile) south of a village of the same name in Derbyshire, itself some eleven kilometres (seven miles) south of Derby. The site is now covered by the Staunton Harold Reservoir, on the right-hand side of the B 587 road coming from Melbourne to Ashby-de-la-Zouch. Towner has proved that the pottery was in existence in 1776, by the discovery of an advertisement for staff, in that year, in a local newspaper.[10] It is probable that the life of the pottery was short, and that it operated at the most for the fifteen years from 1770 to 1785.

Nothing is known of the owners, but it is now possible to identify an engraver who worked there. There is in the Liverpool City Museum a teapot, the characteristics of which prove it to be of Melbourne origin (Plate 114). It bears a signed print of Thomas Rothwell. The subject is *Minerva* in jet black, from a heavily engraved plate in typical Rothwell style. Although from a different printing plate the same subject, obviously by the same hand, appears on a plate with a fancy moulded, black-enamelled border (Plate 115). The

[9] Ibid., p. 18 et seq.
[10] *Derby Mercury*, 8 March 1776.

113 *Society of Oddfellows Arms*: on bulbous JUG of ivory-colour creamware, by LEEDS
POTTERY. 120 mm (4.7 in) high (With *Oddfellows' Apophthegms* on reverse.)
Printed in jet black, with copper-lustre line-border and decoration. 1810–15. *See
pages 184, 201*

114 *Minerva*: on a TEAPOT of creamware, with plaited handle, by MELBOURNE
POTTERY. 140 mm (5.5 in) high
Engraved by Thomas Rothwell and printed from a worn plate in jet black. With
surrounding rococo cartouche, and dead game hanging at each side. Beneath a
ribbon, with 'Let Wisdom Unite Us'. Imprint 'T. Rothwell Sculpt'. 1775–80. *See
page 186*
Merseyside County Museums

overall colour of this piece is pale reseda, and the pimply uncrazed glaze is of very pale eau-de-Nil. In other words although of greenish colour, neither the overall appearance nor the glaze are as green as the wares of the neighbouring Derby Pot Works. On the base of the plate there is a workman's mark in the shape of an impressed ogee, or pinched, heart.

A feather-edged plate has on it the design *La Pêcheuse Chinoise* (Plate 116). It is most interesting to compare this with the similar picture on the Derby creamware plate (Plate 41). Both appear to have been derived from the same source as a print in mirror image, on a delft tile, by Sadler and Green. Who copied whom is impossible to say. Differences in style and detail preclude the possibility of the Derby and Melbourne engravings being by the same hand, and it is possible that the former is the work of Thomas Radford, and that from Melbourne is from the hand of Thomas Rothwell. These men are often confused, but the style of Radford stems from Worcester, by reason of Holdship's influence, while Rothwell was Liverpool trained. Unlike Cock Pit Hill wares, Melbourne pieces are found with transfer prints of a version of *Liverpool Birds* (Plate 117). This is a further link with Rothwell, who would have been very familiar with these designs in his earlier days. It has recently been suggested that Cock Pit Hill, Derby, teapots exist with transfer prints by Thomas Rothwell, because they bear the imprint 'T.R.S.' This theory is quite unacceptable, for it is against reason that any engraver would work at a factory with, or subsequent to, an engraver with the same initials, and use an imprint which did not distinguish him. Any such imprint can only refer to Thomas Radford. Many characteristics of Melbourne Pottery creamware are similar to those of the wares of its neighbouring pottery, Cock Pit Hill, and the question immediately arises as to whether such pieces are of Melbourne origin. Should this be so then all incongruities vanish.

SWANSEA POTTERY (1765 to 1870)

In 1765 a small pottery was built at Swansea, on a fairly extensive site on the waterfront of the estuary of the River Tawe, between the Strand and where now stands the North Dock. In 1789 it was being run by John Coles (c. 1762–99), a Quaker, with another of the same faith, George Haynes (c. 1745–1830). In 1790 the works were enlarged and became known as the Cambrian Pottery. In that year Haynes engaged Thomas Rothwell, late of Sadler and Green, of the Melbourne Pottery, and of Henry Palmer of Hanley, who was then working for the publishing trade in Birmingham. Rothwell stayed at the Cambrian Pottery for about four years. By 1794 he was again engraving for book publishers, this time in London, and some eight years later he returned to Birmingham, where he died in 1807.

The Cambrian Pottery commenced to transfer print both on glaze and under glaze at much about the same time, but the former was confined to creamware.

115 *Minerva*: on moulded shell-pattern PLATE of pale reseda-colour creamware, by
MELBOURNE POTTERY. 252 mm (9.9 in) diameter
Engraved by Thomas Rothwell, and printed in jet black. Border picked out in
black enamel. Impressed ogee heart on base. 1775–80. *See page 186*

116 *La Pêcheuse Chinoise*: on PLATE of creamware with feathered edges (25 feathers),
by MELBOURNE POTTERY. 245 mm (9.6 in) diameter
Printed in black. Two nicks in footrim. 1765–70. Cf. Plate 41. *See pages 114, 188*
Donald Towner Esquire

117 *Liverpool Birds*: on hexagonal PLATE of creamware, with moulded diamond border, by MELBOURNE POTTERY. 238 mm (9.3 in) diameter.
The four border-vignettes transferred from only two engravings. Printed in red. 1770–80. *See pages 114, 188*
Derby City Museum and Art Gallery

This is of overall ivory colour, but the bisque is decidedly sandy, and of nothing like such fine texture as that of Wedgwood or Leeds ware. The glaze is quite colourless, sometimes orange-peel texture, and usually crazed. The crazing is in places lineal, like that of Derby, but often stained light brown in the crazing, like a modern pie-dish that has been used a few times for baking.

A coffee pot with a kettle spout, much more crudely potted than was usual for that date, is certainly of Swansea make (Plate 118). In addition to the normal characteristics of shape, body and glaze, the steam vent was drilled through the knop of the lid, and the swarf inside, made by the bit breaking through the underside of the paste, has been left, over-glazed and fired, resulting in a sharp jagged edge to the hole, distinctive of Swansea wares, among others. This pot has the old stalwarts, *Tea Party No. 1* and, on the other side, *The Shepherd* (Plate 119). They are from heavily engraved plates, and are typical of the work of Thomas Rothwell. The patterns, it will be remembered, had been appearing on porcelain and pottery for more than thirty years by the time of the manufacture of this coffee pot, but seldom had such large engravings been used. They form very good and clear examples of Thomas Rothwell's style of engraving.

An export piece made for the North American market is a plate with a print, *United States Man-of-War*, printed in jet black, with rather original decoration

118 *Tea Party No. 1*: on COFFEE POT with kettle spout, of ivory-colour creamware, by
SWANSEA POTTERY
Heavily engraved by Thomas Rothwell and printed in jet black. 1790–2. *See pages
114, 190*

119 *The Shepherd*: on reverse of COFFEE POT shown in Plate 118
Engraved by Thomas Rothwell and printed in jet black. 1790–2. *See pages 114,
190*

of the condiments-rim, composed of vignettes of nautical emblems and flowers (Plate 120). The rigging of the vessel is quite impracticable, and one would suppose that the engraver had little knowledge of nautical matters. It is however very much in Rothwell's style, and if from his hand it leaves one mildly surprised that, having originally come from Liverpool, he should have forgotten details of a ship's rigging, but perhaps it is expecting too much for an artist to remember, over nearly thirty years, such minutiae. It will be noted that the United States flag is intended to represent the original, before the number of both stars and stripes was increased in 1792 to fifteen.

Another piece of creamware of Swansea manufacture is a large jug of what is known as Liverpool shape. This is very much more heavily potted than similar jugs from Herculaneum and Leeds potteries, and the porous body and colourless glaze are characteristic of the Welsh factory. Nevertheless, the paste is not quite so sandy as that of the previous, rather earlier, examples. Provenance was the initial clue to the attribution of this piece, just as it was for the foregoing plate, both having been discovered in a small South Wales village, near Carmarthen. The jug carries a crowded design of *Masonic Emblems* (Plate 121). Under the spout are dividers and square, and on the reverse side of the jug there are more masonic emblems surrounding a verse *Masonic Secrets*. The piece would appear to date from between 1800 and 1805, and the printing differs from that on earlier creamware from Swansea by being lightly engraved and printed in ivory black, in contrast to Rothwell's heavily engraved, jet-black prints. It no doubt served its purpose for fraternal libations, but it is essentially a functional vessel, hardly qualifying as artistic or decorative in any way. It forms a poor comparison with its brother from the Garrison Pottery, Sunderland, which is a pleasing ornament in its own right (Colour Plate H).

The factory also produced that much collected, and rather scarce, yellow-glazed ware, and striking results were obtained by printing over this in jet black. The jug illustrated, however, has a print of the *Prince of Wales's Feathers* in red, and the copper plate used for this is known to have also been employed for underglaze printing in blue (Plate 122). A coffee pot so decorated can be compared side by side with an on-glaze printed jug in the National Museum of Wales.

HERCULANEUM POTTERY, LIVERPOOL (1796 to 1840)

Samuel Worthington, who was a Welsh-born merchant from Bangor, settled and had extensive business interests in Liverpool. In December 1796 he opened a pottery near to the village of Toxteth, about three kilometres (two miles) south of the centre of Liverpool, where by the side of the Mersey estuary there was an eighteenth-century precursory trading-estate.[11]

[11] *Gore's General Advertiser*, 15 December 1796.

G. *'The Farmers Arms'*: on HARVEST JUG of pearlware, by the HERCULANEUM POTTERY.
223 mm (8.8 in) high
Probably engraved by Richard Abbey, and printed in deep violet. Inscribed 'J.
Etchells July, 17, 1811'. Floral border enamelled in pale cobalt-blue, pale olive-
green and rose pink. 1811. *See page 196*

H. *Masonic Insignia*: on large ivory-colour JUG of creamware, by the GARRISON
POTTERY, BISHOPSWEARMOUTH. 183 mm (7.2 in) high
Printed in burnt umber, and over-enamelled in deep violet-brown, grass green,
deep orange, pale saxe-blue and copper lustre. Enamelled decoration and large
fouled anchor under spout in similar colours. 1810–15. *See pages 192, 210*

120 *United States Man-of-War*: on Royal-pattern PLATE of ivory-colour creamware,
     by SWANSEA POTTERY. 257 mm (10.1 in) diameter
     Printed in jet black, with sea and cannon washed in very pale biscuit-colour
     (probably over-fired green). 1790–4. *See page 192*
121 *Masonic Emblems*: on large baluster-shape JUG of ivory-colour creamware, by
     SWANSEA POTTERY. 230 mm (9 in) high. (On reverse more symbols, and the verse:
                         The World is in Pain
                          Our secrets to gain
                     But let them wonder & gaze on
                        For they ne'er can divine
                         The WORD nor the SIGN
                      Of a Free & Accepted Mason)
     Lightly engraved and printed in ivory black. 1800–5. *See page 192*

Just as with the Leeds Pottery, there are dilemmas as to whether or not on-glaze transfer printing was carried out at the Herculaneum Pottery itself. But in the case of Herculaneum the evidence is stronger, by reason of documentary and other support, and it is uncertain whether the pottery ever had an on-glaze transfer-printing department. It is indisputable that Richard Abbey's engraving and Joseph Johnson's printing are found on creamware and earthenware from the pottery. Johnson's imprint on Herculaneum wares usually has 'Liverpool' after it, which is proof positive that he still had his own business, and was not on the staff of the pottery. The print, *The Upright Man*, already mentioned, which has the imprint 'R. Abbey sculpt. Jph. Johnson Liverpool' suggests that Abbey may have been at one time on the staff of Johnson, but certainly not on that of the Herculaneum company.[12]

The pottery had an underglaze-printing department some time prior to 1809, but the fire insurance schedule of 1816, although it covers a printing department and plant, makes no mention of an engraving department.[13] Richard Abbey died in 1819, and in board minutes of 1822 reference is made to efforts to buy two sets of printing plates in Staffordshire.[14]

Although pearlware and earthenware were in full production at most potteries when the Herculaneum factory opened, it nevertheless produced large quantities of creamware, and continued so to do, certainly for the export market, until 1815. The overall colour is ivory, but the glaze is reseda and often finely crazed. In common with nearly all the potteries and porcelain factories that had earlier been in Liverpool, Herculaneum inherited the singular defect of making wares with pitted and dirty bases.

Nautical subjects were popular and varied, and ranged from portraits of admirals and sea captains, square-rigged vessels under sail and naval engagements, to sailors and their sweethearts; although *The Sailor's Farewell* and associated prints were never produced as prolifically as on Tyneside and Wearside. A considerable export trade was maintained to North America, and illustrated is a fine creamware jug with nearly a score of separate prints (Plate 123). The habit of covering a single piece with a profusion of small pictures was frequently practised at Liverpool. This economy custom presumably arose after the factory had commissioned a considerable quantity of engraved plates for earlier use, because quite often these grouped prints can be found used singly on small earlier pieces. In marked contrast is a very early cylindrical tea canister with on back and front jet-black transfers from a single copper plate of *L'Amour* (Plate 124). The engraving is almost certainly by Richard Abbey, and similar prints are found on Herculaneum pearlware. An interesting feature is that the footrim is bevelled both on inside and outside, resulting in a fulcrum section which makes only a circular-line contact with

[12]See p. 126.
[13] Liverpool Public Record Office, *Herculaneum Pottery, Records of the Committee, 1806–22*, H380 M.D47 KF295, 2 April 1816.
[14] Ibid., 5 March 1822.

122 *Prince of Wales's Feathers*: on bulbous, yellow-glazed JUG, by SWANSEA POTTERY.
146 mm (5.7 in) high
Printed in red. 1790–1800. *See page 192*
Amgueddfa Genedlaethol Cymru, Caerdydd (National Museum of Wales, Cardiff)

123 *American Motley*: on large barrel-shaped JUG of creamware, by HERCULANEUM
POTTERY. 381 mm (15 in) high
Multiple transfers in black. 1805–10. *See page 194*
The Philadelphia Museum of Art: Bequest of R. Wistar Harvey

whatever the piece stands on. There is a workman's nick on this footrim.

Pearlware from the factory has a sandy body, and bases are usually pitted and rough, while the glaze is a distinctive saxe-blue generally crazed. Prints in Abbey's unmistakable style are plentiful on pearlware jugs and mugs, of which the pottery had an abundant output during the first fifteen years of its existence. Mostly these pictures have either a nautical or agricultural connotation, and the most common of the latter are *The Farmer's Arms*, *Harvest Home* and *The Farmyard*. All of these over the years were subject to variation of detail, and probably modifications were introduced so that different customers did not market wares with identical pictures.

The Farmer's Arms was a pseudo-heraldic device engraved time and again, and normally found opposed to *Harvest Home*, or *The Farmyard*, which are very often confused. Both have, as it were, similar backdrops showing a farmhouse, rick and a distant harvest-wagon in a field. *The Farmyard* has in the middle distance farm-workers about their labours, a stationary plough and a large tree on the right-hand side (Plate 125). *Harvest Home* instead has a group of farm-hands dancing in the middle distance to the music of a fiddler, with in the foreground a cow, or perhaps two. There is never a tree on the right. The pictures were in use from about 1797 until 1815, and earlier dating of pieces carrying these prints is suspect. Illustrated is a handsome pearlware Herculaneum jug with a version of '*The Farmer's Arms*' printed in deep violet (Colour Plate G). On the reverse is '*Harvest Home*' (Plate 126). The collar of the jug has polychrome-enamelled floral decoration in typical Herculaneum style, and under the spout is a dedication in large enamel script to 'J. Etchells, July, 17, 1811'. Mock arms were also designed for carpenters, masons, plaisterers, bricklayers, joiners, bakers, cordwainers and watch-toolmakers. How the College of Arms, in those more heraldically Draconian times, viewed these amateur efforts is unrecorded.

A bulbous jug of a little later date has a pattern which became extremely popular—and still is. This is *Bird in a Magnolia Tree*, which is printed in grey-brown and over-enamelled in five colours. The jug has copper-lustre decoration and a band border (Plate 127). Another polychrome-enamelled transfer print of interest, this time on a mug, is '*Toby Fillpot*' (sic), which has the imprint 'R. Abbey' (Plate 128). The engraving is based on a mezzotint by Robert Dighton (1752–1814), who had the questionable distinction of being caught in 1806 abstracting etchings from the British Museum.

KNOTTINGLY POTTERY, WEST YORKSHIRE (1792 to date)
(*After 1804 known as the Ferrybridge Pottery*)

On the River Aire downstream from Leeds, and some twenty-two kilometres (thirteen and a half miles) south-east of that city, was the village of Ferrybridge. This is four kilometres (two and a half miles) from Pontefract,

124 *L'Amour*: on a cylindrical TEA CANISTER of ivory-colour creamware, by
HERCULANEUM POTTERY. 90 mm (3.5 in) high. (Similar print from the same
copper plate on other side.)
Printed in jet black. Fulcrum footrim, and base dirtied by powdered vitreous
pigment. 1796–1800. *See pages 70, 194, 232*
125 *The Farmyard*: on bulbous JUG of creamware, by HERCULANEUM POTTERY.
184 mm (7.2 in) high. (*The Farmer's Arms* on reverse.)
Printed in puce by Joseph Johnson. Dedicated to Robert Roberts. Cf. the
background with that on Plate 126. 1805–15. *See page 196*
Merseyside County Museums

126 '*Harvest Home*': on HARVEST JUG of pearlware, by HERCULANEUM POTTERY. The other side of the jug shown in Colour Plate G
Probably engraved by Richard Abbey, and printed in deep violet. 1811. *See page 196*

127 *Bird in a Magnolia Tree*: on bulbous JUG of pearlware, with moulded acanthus-leaf spout, by HERCULANEUM POTTERY. 121 mm (4.7 in) high
Printed on each side in grey-brown, from a single plate, and over-enamelled in Venetian red, deep cyclamen, canary yellow, grass green and grey-ultramarine. Border and decoration in copper lustre. Sandy base. 1810–20. *See page 196*

128 *'Toby Fillpot'*: on TANKARD of creamware, by HERCULANEUM POTTERY. 118 mm (4.6 in) high
Engraved by Richard Abbey, after a mezzotint by Robert Dighton, and printed in deep brown-black, and polychrome over-enamelled. Imprint 'R. Abbey'. 1780–90. *See pages 126, 182, 196. Merseyside County Museums*

and half that distance from Knottingly. Between Ferrybridge and Knottingly, but nearer to the former village, a pottery was started in 1792 by William Tomlinson with four partners. Tomlinson was a potter from Staffordshire, and in the early 1770s had been a partner of young Josiah Spode I. In 1796 Ralph Wedgwood (1766–1837) of Burslem was admitted to the partnership, which included a Selby shipowner called Foster. The trading name was Tomlinson, Foster, Wedgwood and Company, but the wares were frequently marked 'Wedgwood & Co.', to profit by the reputation of that famous name. Ralph was Josiah Wedgwood's cousin-german, but his stay at Knottingly was of short duration and he left in 1801, when the style of the firm reverted to Tomlinson and Company.

Reference has already been made to a Knottingly Pottery jug with a transfer picture, '*Colonel Tarleton*', with the imprint of 'J. Johnson Liverpool' as printer and 'Wedgwood a Co.' as publisher (Plate 129). There seems little doubt that the engraver was Richard Abbey. Other transfer prints in typically Abbey style are found on Knottingly wares, and an example is *The Carousal* on a large tankard (Plate 130). It seems most probable that all on-glaze transfer printing on the factory's products was the work of Joseph Johnson from plates engraved by Richard Abbey.

SWINTON POTTERY, SOUTH YORKSHIRE (1745 to 1842)
(*After 1826 known as the Rockingham Pottery*)

It is believed that the pottery at Swinton was commenced in 1745 by Edward Butler. The site was on the estate of that prominent Whig, Charles Watson-Wentworth, second Marquis of Rockingham (1730–82), who became prime minister in March of the year in which he died. Swinton is in South Yorkshire, seven kilometres (four and a quarter miles) north-east of Rotherham, on the road to Doncaster via Mexborough, and two kilometres (one and a quarter miles) short of the latter village.

During the first fifty years of its existence it was run by a variety of proprietors and partners, including William Malpass, John and William Brameld (d. 1813) and Thomas Bingley. In 1787 four men from the Leeds Pottery, John and Ebenezer Green, William Hartley and George Hanson became partners. The title of the firm from 1778 had been Thomas Bingley and Company, but this was now changed to Greens, Bingley and Company. Possibly because of financial difficulties at Leeds, in 1806 all the partners with interests in that concern withdrew from the Swinton firm, leaving only John and William Brameld, and the trading name became Brameld and Company. Because of successive rescue operations, in 1825 the pottery came under the control of William Wentworth, second Earl Fitzwilliam (1784–1833), the nephew and heir of the second Marquis of Rockingham. The following year it was renamed the Rockingham pottery.

129 *'Colonel Tarleton'*: on JUG of creamware, by KNOTTINGLY POTTERY. 182 mm
(7.1 in) high
Probably engraved by Richard Abbey, after a painting by Sir Joshua Reynolds,
and printed in jet black. Imprints 'J. Johnson Liverpool' and 'Wedgwood & Co.'
1796–1801. *See pages 124, 200*
Merseyside County Museums

Until 1826 the works produced a variety of creamware, pearlware and
earthenware; after that date it concentrated on bone china. Illustrated is a
small pearlware mug, probably from the factory, with the *Society of Oddfellows
Arms* printed in jet black and over-enamelled in four colours (Plate 131).
Compared with the contemporary rendering of the same design on Leeds ware
the engraving is extremely crude (Plate 113). The inside of the footrim of this
mug is a quadrant in section, an unusual feature found sometimes on Swinton
products.

130 *The Carousal*: on large TANKARD of creamware, by FERRYBRIDGE POTTERY.
124 mm (4.9 in) high
Printed in black. Impressed 'Wedgwood & Co.'. 1796–1801. *See page 200*
Yorkshire Museum

131 *Society of Oddfellows Arms*: on MUG of pearlware, probably by FERRYBRIDGE
POTTERY. 80 mm (3.1 in) high
Printed in jet black, and over-enamelled in grass green, Venetian red, lemon and
salmon pink. Distinctive quadrant section footrim. 1810–15. *See page 201*

132 *Wearmouth Bridge*: on TANKARD of creamware, by LOW FORD POTTERY. 137 mm
(5.4 in) high
Printed in burnt umber, with river washed in green. Imprint 'The Olde Sanders
Low Ford Pottery'. Made before the completion of the bridge, and therefore with
many inaccuracies. 1792–6. *See page 204*
G. F. Arnold Esquire

133 *'God Speed the Plough'*: on MUG of creamware, by LOW FORD POTTERY. 116 mm
(4.5 in) high
Printed in deep brown-black, and over-enamelled in king's blue, vermilion and
emerald tint, with jet-black border. Imprint 'I. Dawson & Co. Low Ford'.
1796–1800. *See page 206*

NORTH HYLTON POTTERY, TYNE AND WEAR (1762 to 1845)

The first sizeable pottery to be opened on Wearside for the manufacture of creamware and earthenware was started in 1762 by William Maling, for the benefit of his sons, Christopher Thompson (1741–1810) and John (1746–1823). It was situated at North Hylton, on the left bank of the River Wear, four kilometres (two and a half miles) west of Sunderland.

There are no existing pieces of eighteenth-century transfer-printed North Hylton ware, and none recorded of any period that are printed on-glaze, and the factory would not qualify for consideration here except for one puzzling fact. The notebooks of the famous wood-engraver, Thomas Bewick (1753–1828) of Beilby and Bewick of Newcastle-upon-Tyne show that in June 1775 a copper plate was supplied to the 'Hilton Pottery', and another in July 1776, for half a guinea. In February 1777 yet a third, of the *Masons Arms*, was sold to the pottery for two guineas, and in the following March a fourth of the same subject for one and a half guineas. In the same month it was charged five shillings for a fifth plate of a hunting scene, and half-a-crown for the repair of a plate. In June 1778 a sixth plate comprising three Masonic designs was supplied for one and a half guineas.

The precise use to which these plates were put can only be the subject of speculation, and it is puzzling why the purchases should have ceased after only six had been bought. The doubt exists whether like some Staffordshire potters, those at North Hylton made abortive attempts to transfer print, and these uninstructed efforts failed through lack of knowledge and experience.

LOW FORD POTTERY, SOUTH HYLTON (c. 1795 to 1864)

A few hundred metres from the North Hylton Pottery on the opposite, or right, bank of the River Wear there was in the eighteenth century a village called Low Ford, now known as South Hylton. Here was situated a pottery run by a man called Sanders, of whom unfortunately nothing is known. In 1796 a half interest in the pottery was advertised in the local newspaper.[15] Three years later the business was purchased by John Dawson (1760–1848), who had been trained as a potter at the North Hylton works.

There exists a creamware tankard carrying a print of the *Wearmouth Bridge*, that most famous of all bridges to be found on pottery, but it is inaccurate in important detail (Plate 132). The imprint reads 'The Olde Sanders Low Ford Pottery', and in a cartouche is the title: 'An EAST View of the Iron Bridge erecting Over the Wear near Sunderland by R. Burden Esqr. M.P. Height 100, span 236 ft.' The bridge, composed of a single cast-iron span of seventy-two metres (two hundred and thirty-seven feet), was opened on 9 August 1796, and

[15] *Newcastle Chronicle*, 1 July 1796.

134 *Peace and Plenty*: on TANKARD of ivory-colour creamware, with moulded foot, by
      LOW FORD POTTERY. 137 mm (5.4 in) high
      Printed in deep brown-black, and over-enamelled in grass green, tobacco, grey-
      ultramarine, stone and vermilion. Imprints 'Dawson & Co. Low Ford' and at
      bottom right 'W.C.' Probably a Peace of Amiens celebration piece. 1802–3. *See
      page 206*

135 *East Indiaman Cleared for Action*: on baluster-shape JUG of creamware, by LOW
      FORD POTTERY. 147 mm (5.8 in) high
      Printed in jet black. 1800–4. *See page 206*

at the time was the largest span in the world. The tense of the verb in the title, as well as the errors, shows that the piece dates from between 1792 when the building commenced, and 1796 when the bridge was opened. As erected the deck of the bridge was of pedimental shape, whereas in the print it is flat, which is perhaps the biggest mistake of detail. Only after reconstruction in 1859 by Robert Stevenson (1803–59), son of George, was the deck made level.

Another example of on-glaze printing, dating from between 1796 and 1800, is a mug with a lightly etched and engraved print in deep brown-black, '*God Speed the Plough*' (Plate 133). It is rather a naive effort with the imprint 'I. Dawson & Co. Low Ford', and is washed over in three thin enamels. These early products of the factory had a very porous bisque, and the glaze is usually finely crazed, which often results in their being very stained.

Of a few years later is a tankard with the design *Peace and Plenty*, which shows an East Indiaman from the port beam in full sail, and enclosed in a central panel with a husk border (Plate 134). It is flanked by figures of Peace and Plenty, and beneath in a rectangular panel is the rhyme: 'May Peace with Plenty on Our Nation smile & Trade and Commerce bless the British Isle.' The imprint is 'Dawson & Co. Low Ford' with the engraver's initials 'W. C.' The whole is polychrome enamelled, and it was probably made in celebration of the Treaty of Amiens in 1802. This piece proves that considerable progress had taken place in enamelling and firing techniques.

Another example from the factory from between 1800 and 1804 is a jug with a print showing *East Indiaman Cleared for Action* (Plate 135). The vessel is becalmed, with open gun-ports, and is viewed from the port quarter. On the reverse is the popular pattern, '*Come Box the Compass*', with the extraordinary engraving mistake that eighty degrees west-by-south is entirely missing (Plate 136).

All early Low Ford engravings appear to have come from the same hand, with a minimum use of stipple, and a total lack of cross-hatching. The preliminary etching is of the lightest, the over-engraving carefully super-imposed, and the colour washes thin and transparent. From a very amateurish start there is a progressive improvement in quality of engraving, but the standard reached was never very high. The engraver 'W. C.' remains unknown, but as his initials are also found on transfer prints on wares from the Garrison pottery the strong probability is that he had a local free-lance business.

WEAR POTTERY, SOUTHWICK, SUNDERLAND (1789 to 1882)

Established by John Brunton in 1789, the Wear Pottery was situated adjacent to Scott's Pottery, on the left bank of the River Wear, at Low Southwick, one kilometre (three-quarters of a mile) north-east of the centre of Sunderland. In 1803 it was taken over by Samuel Moore (1775–1844) and Peter Austin (1770–

136 *'Come Box the Compass'*: on reverse of JUG shown in Plate 135
Note: 80° west by south is missing. 1800–4. *See page 206*

137 *'HOPE'*: on PLATE with guttered edge, of ivory-colour creamware, by THE WEAR
POTTERY, SOUTHWICK. 251 mm (9.9 in) diameter
The printing over-fired, resulting in a French-grey print, over-enamelled in
primrose, Venetian red, pale cobalt-blue and aquamarine. The intended green-
enamel border burnt and powdered. 1803–10. *See page 208*

1863), who traded as S. Moore and Company. The firm was so known until the final closure of the pottery seventy-nine years later. Being close to the famous Sunderland Bridge, the pottery is often depicted in transfer prints of east views beneath the bridge on the left, and in west views in the foreground on the right.

It is improbable that any creamware was produced prior to the 1803 take-over, and it seems that considerable firing difficulties were experienced, so much so that two of the identifying characteristics of the early wares are over- and under-firing. A plate marked 'Moore & Co' exists, which clearly shows the over-firing of the enamel band round the border.[16] Another example which has been subjected to too great a temperature in the firing-on kiln shows a version of '*HOPE*' over-enamelled in three colours (Plate 137). It is of very smooth white body, and clear glaze—which distinguish much of the nineteenth-century wares of the Sunderland potters. However, the printing has turned a French grey, except where protected by the enamelling, and the colours of the latter have lost their true values. The border intended to be green, has powdered leaving a patchy, greenish grey at the bottom, fading to a pale yellow at the top of the plate, which was perhaps too close to the side of the muffle or sagger. The engraving is a very good one, and it is sad that the piece has been marred by lack of technical ability.

THE GARRISON POTTERY, BISHOPSWEARMOUTH, TYNE AND WEAR (c. 1755 to 1865)

At the mouth of the River Wear, on the right bank of the estuary, is situated that district of Sunderland known as Bishopswearmouth. Here was a barracks, and hard by a pottery known as the Garrison Pottery. As early as 1753 a pottery existed here, for in that year there appeared an advertisement for the sale of a share in 'A pot house in Sunderland . . . situate nigh the Pier'.[17] In 1807 John Phillips, one-time manager and partner of the North Hylton Pottery, leased the Garrison Pottery, but six years later is was in the hands of Robert Dixon (1779–1844), whose descendants were associated with it until its closure in 1865.

The creamware made at this factory is of ivory colour and extremely fine in texture. At the beginning of the nineteenth century there was no finer quality made. The glaze is very pale eau-de-Nil and usually uncrazed. Illustrated is a large mug showing *The Wear Bridge* printed in deep brown-black and over-enamelled in four colours (Plate 138). It was engraved by the same 'W. C.' responsible for plates used on Dawson and Company's wares, and his initials are on the copper plate as an imprint. The publishers imprint is 'Dixon & Co.

---

[16]Geoffrey Godden, *Illustrated Encyclopaedia of British Pottery and Porcelain*, London, 1966, Pl. 428.
[17]*Newcastle Journal*, 23 June 1753.

138 *The Wear Bridge*: on TANKARD of ivory-colour creamware, by THE GARRISON
POTTERY, SUNDERLAND. 120 mm (4.7 in) high. (On the reverse the rhyme:
A little House with Freedom;
And at the end a little Friend
With little cause to need him.)
Printed in deep brown-black, over-enamelled in grass green, deep violet-brown,
deep orange, pale saxe-blue, dull yellow-ochre and copper lustre. Imprints
'DIXON & CO. SUNDERLAND 1813' and 'W.C.' 1813. *See page 208*

139 *'Toss the Grog Boys'*: on large JUG of creamware, by THE GARRISON POTTERY.
Reverse of that on Colour Plate H
1810–15. *See page 210*

140 *Treaty of Amiens*: on TANKARD of creamware, by BRISTOL POTTERY. 118 mm (4.6 in) high
Printed in Vandyke brown, and polychrome over-enamelled. Imprint 'Bristol Pottery'. 1802. *See page 211*
Bristol City Museum and Art Gallery

Sunderland 1813'. A fine large jug dates from the same period, and this carries prints in burnt umber; on one side *Masonic Insignia*, and on the other two sailors with large flags and the song '*Toss the Grog Boys*' (Colour Plate H and Plate 139). It has a large fouled anchor enamelled under the spout. Both the last pieces are hand decorated round the prints in brown and green enamels and copper lustre.

From about 1825 transfer printing at the Garrison Pottery, in common with that of other potteries in the North East, was confined to underglaze. This of course applied to later editions—and there were many—of the Wear Bridge, and this printing was nearly always in jet black.

BRISTOL POTTERY (1683 to c. 1906)

The Temple Pottery, Bristol was started in 1683 by Edward Ward at the southern corner of Water Lane with Temple Backs, on the south side of the main channel of the River Avon—now called the floating harbour. At the turn of the nineteenth century it was being run by William Taylor, Henry Carter and Josiah Ring II (1774–1813). There exists a number of specimens of transfer-printed creamware made at the factory. These are mostly cylindrical tankards and usually have the same printed design, a commemorative print of the *Treaty of Amiens, 1802* (Plate 140). The fact that this is a solitary recorded example of transfer printing on-glaze on Bristol ware suggests very strongly that it is the work of a free-lance transfer printer—probably in Staffordshire, which could be reached comparatively easily by river transport up the River Severn.

Chapter 8

ABERRATIONS AND VAGARIES

There exist a comparatively few pieces of earthenware and porcelain that, although transfer printed, did not originate from any of the factories known either to have carried out, or commissioned, the process. The rarity of these odd-men-out suggests that they were experimental pieces not made on a commercial scale, or alternatively job lots purchased on the closure of a factory and decorated by others. With all on-glaze printing it is important to remember firstly that the printing does not need to be done at, or on the instructions of, the makers of the ceramics, and secondly there is no time limit, and it can be carried out at any time after manufacture of the pieces.

CHELSEA PORCELAIN WORKS (c. 1745 to 1769)

It is believed that the pottery a hundred metres (about a hundred yards) from Cheyne Walk, at the corner of Lawrence Street and Justice Walk, Chelsea was commenced about 1745. On 5 February 1770 the factory was acquired by William Duesbury of Derby, who re-opened it after its closure the previous year by Nicholas Sprimont (1716–71). In 1784 Duesbury in his turn closed the works, and moved the plant and some of the men to Derby. In the same year the buildings were entirely demolished.

The plant at the time of the sale in 1770, and at earlier abortive sales in 1764 and 1769, was described in considerable detail in the auction particulars; however, no mention was made of any printing presses, equipment or plates. There is no evidence to suggest that transfer printing was ever carried out at the factory, which concentrated upon high-quality figures and hand-painted wares. There are but three recorded pieces of porcelain that are claimed to be of Chelsea origin, and transfer-printed. Two of these carry the raised anchor mark, which is thought to have been last used by the factory in 1752—before the invention of transfer printing. Provided that the unmarked piece is indeed of Chelsea make, then it is probable that all three were amongst wares purchased in the white at one of the auctions of the factory's contents between 1764 and 1769. If in fact the pieces are transfer-printed, and not carefully pencilled, then they were so decorated elsewhere, quite possibly at Worcester in the 1770s, in the circumstances suggested below as being plausible for transfer-printed Chinese porcelain.

CHINESE PORCELAIN

In a rather similar character to transfer-printed Chelsea porcelain is like-decorated Chinese porcelain. Experts still differ as to whether these hard-paste pieces are from the orient, or not, but it is of little moment from the transfer-printing point of view, for it is clear that they did not originate from any factory known to have used the process. There is some evidence from shards excavated from near the Worcester factory site, that experiment was carried out transfer printing competitor's wares and hard-paste porcelain. The reasons for this are unknown, but they could be many.

At this stage the author would like to offer a theory, the basis of which is entirely circumstantial, but one that would explain the existence of many of these stray prints, which almost invariably bear the imprint of Robert Hancock, or are in his unmistakable style. Thomas Turner, apprenticed engraver to Hancock at Worcester in 1765, is believed to have left at the expiry of his indentures in 1772, and set up as a wholesale china-merchant, and perhaps decorator, in Worcester. The account books of James Giles of Kentish Town, then a village five kilometres (three miles) north-west of London, a china wholesaler and decorator, who also had a warehouse in Cockspur Street, between Pall Mall and Charing Cross, show that Turner ran this business until 24 June 1775.[1] This date fits perfectly with the presumed date, 1 July 1775, of the partnership of Turner with Ambrose Gallimore, the owner of the Salopian China Works at Caughley, whose daughter, Dorothy, he married.

Turning now to Robert Hancock, he definitely quarrelled with his partners at Worcester, and the firm was dissolved on 31 October 1774.[2] The next reliable evidence of his whereabouts was an advertisement in a Birmingham paper of 3 July 1775, confirming the severance of his connections with Worcester, and stating that 'he is now engaged in the Salopian China Manufactory on such terms as enable him . . .'.[3]

[1] Geoffrey Godden, *Caughley and Worcester Porcelains, 1775–1800*, London, 1969, p. 78.
[2] W. H. Binns, *A Century of Potting in the City of Worcester*, 1865, p. 83.
[3] *Aris's Birmingham Gazette*, 3 July 1775.

What more probable than that Hancock, for the eight months November 1774 to June 1775 inclusive, was working with Turner in his merchanting business in Worcester, and if this be so that he occupied himself in decorating on-glaze transfer-printed wares, purchased in the white from various sources. The Worcester Porcelain Company had ceased to print on-glaze several years earlier, and Turner would have known very little of the process. In fact his printing at Caughley for the next quarter century was in underglaze blue, with the possible exception of some 'bat' printing in the last few years of the century. His merchanted wares must have been purchased glazed, so could only have been printed over-glaze. It would have been natural for Hancock to decorate some of this by using his old engravings, made specifically for on-glaze printing. If at the end of 1774 Hancock did join Turner, the arrangement in Worcester must have been known to be of a temporary nature, which would not have warranted a new staff of engravers and printers, and no doubt Hancock could attend to the latter, if not engaged in fresh engraving. This would account for the use of old copper plates with mostly forgotten patterns. Illustrated is a hard-paste saucer dish with a most unusual version of *Tea Party No. 2* (Plate 141). In the foreground is a group of musical instruments and a cat. This has the imprint 'R. Hancock fecit. 1757', but under the circumstances the date is probably of no significance other than being the date of the engraving.

If this hypothesis is correct, then much is explained. In addition to the small amount of Chinese porcelain with Hancock prints, the equally small number of pieces from the Castle Green Pottery, Bristol, referred to below, with Hancock designs were almost certainly printed under similar circumstances. The postulate is a very tempting one, and it must be re-emphasized that at the moment it is conjectural, with the Bristol pieces providing the strongest circumstantial evidence.

CASTLE GREEN POTTERY, BRISTOL (c. 1764 to 1778)

The genesis of the porcelain factory at Bristol goes back to William Cookworthy (1705–80). In 1768 he opened a small factory at Cockside, Plymouth, to make hard-paste porcelain from china clay and stone that he had found at St. Stephen in Cornwall. One of his partners was Richard Champion (1743–91), a much younger man, who in the same year started a pottery at 15 Castle Green in Bristol. This was situated two-thirds of the way down the hill between the east side of that part of Castle Green now known as Tower Street, and Lower Castle Street. In 1771 the Cockside factory was shut, and Cookworthy and Champion were in partnership producing hard-paste porcelain at the Castle Green Pottery. In 1774 Cookworthy sold his interest to Champion, who ran it until his bankruptcy in 1778. The patents and licences

141 *Tea Party No. 2*: on large SAUCER of hard-paste Chinese porcelain. 152 mm (6 in)
diameter
An unusual version, including the footman, and in the foreground musical
instruments and a cat, engraved by Robert Hancock. Printed in deep brown-
black, polychrome over-enamelled and gilded. Imprint 'R. Hancock fecit 1757'.
Possibly used in this instance in 1774–5. *See page 214*
Sotheby Parke Bernet and Company Limited

were then sold to the consortium of Staffordshire potters known as the New
Hall China Manufactory.

Some on-glaze transfer printing is known on Bristol hard-paste porcelain,
but it is most improbable that it was done at the factory. It is the general belief
that pieces so decorated date from the Champion and Company period of 1774
to 1778, that is, immediately before the closure. Many of the few remaining
specimens show evidence of incomplete firing-on of the printing, resulting in
faulty fusion and bare patches. This suggests that the transfer printer was
inexperienced with the glaze of high-temperature ware.

An interesting example is a print, *La Terre*, on a bulbous creamer, with three ball-and-claw feet (Plate 142). The transfer has been taken from a copper plate first etched, and then most carefully over-engraved, which is unquestionably the work of Robert Hancock. Very rare pieces of early Worcester and Bow exist decorated with this design. Hancock copied one of the engravings, *The Four Elements*, by P. A. A. Aveline (1710–60), after François Boucher. Another from the same series, *Le Feu*, is also found on Bow and Worcester pieces.

Reference was made above, under Chinese Porcelain, to the strong probability that these Bristol hard-paste pieces were transfer-printed by Robert Hancock, after he left the Worcester Porcelain Company in October 1774, and before he joined the Caughley concern in July 1775. This period fits perfectly the supposed date of manufacture of the few extant pieces of transfer-printed Bristol porcelain, and explains the hitherto extraordinary and perplexing anomaly of Bristol under-glaze blue-printed pieces pre-dating those printed on-glaze. It was a cheap, quick, and above all very safe journey for porcelain, by barge, via the Rivers Avon and Severn, from Bristol to Worcester, less than eighty kilometres (fifty miles). If this work was done at Worcester, as has been explained, it would have been perfectly natural that old designs, on copper plates no longer in current use should have been employed, and quite understandable that some transfers should have been below standard, due to unfamiliarity with the Bristol glaze. The latter feature rules out any possible alternative of Hancock having spent a few months at Bristol, unlikely for many other reasons, because there he would have been instructed and helped in the firing-on process.

The design on the next illustration, *The Quarrelling Tits*, on a Bristol bowl, immediately strikes one as having a most pronounced Hancock style in subject and technique (Plate 143). It has been printed from a plate prepared for a monochrome picture, but nevertheless has been polychrome over-enamelled, in the ill-contrived manner of much Worcester transfer printing.

LONGTON HALL, STAFFORDSHIRE (c. 1750 to 1760)

Although a few transfer-printed pieces attributed to Longton Hall exist, there is no evidence that the process was ever carried out there, or that wares were ever printed on instructions from the factory. Situated one kilometre (three-quarters of a mile) south-west of Lane End, The Hall was the most southerly in the Staffordshire complex of potteries. It was started sometime about 1750 by William Littler, William Nicklin and William Jenkinson. By 1760, in spite of a fresh infusion of capital, it was forced to close, and in September of that year the entire stock of ninety thousand pieces was sold by auction. William Duesbury of Derby is reputed to have been a buyer on a large scale, and other purchasers were almost certainly some of the Liverpool potters and merchants, including Sadler and Green.

There is no doubt that glazed stock in the white, awaiting decoration at the

142 *La Terre*: on CREAMER of hard-paste porcelain, with three ball-and-claw feet, by
     CASTLE GREEN POTTERY, BRISTOL. 125 mm (4.9 in) high
     Etched and engraved by Robert Hancock, after an engraving by P. A. A. Aveline,
     after François Boucher. Printed, probably at Worcester, in deep brown-black.
     1771–5. *See page 216*
     City of Bristol Museum and Art Gallery (piece on loan)
143 *Quarrelling Tits*: on BOWL of hard-paste porcelain, by CASTLE GREEN POTTERY,
     BRISTOL. 70 mm (2.7 in) high
     Printed, probably at Worcester, in raw umber, and thinly polychrome over-
     enamelled. 1771–5. *See page 216*
     City of Bristol Museum and Art Gallery (piece on loan)

time of the closure, was printed later by Sadler and Green, but whether on their own account, or on behalf of their merchant customers, is unclear. Existing examples include a baluster-shaped mug with a print, *The Arms of the Order of Foresters*, which has the imprint 'Sadler Liverpool'. Another piece is a similarly shaped mug with a transfer print of a head and shoulders portrait of *Queen Charlotte*, with crown above (Plate 144). This has the imprint 'J. Sadler Liverpl.', and is obviously a royal marriage or coronation memento. It is important as the queen was not married to George III until 8 September 1761, which was twelve months after the closure of the factory. It is probable that the engraving was by Thomas Billinge, for a similar line-engraving on paper, by him, was published at about the same time, when he is known to have been working for Sadler and Green.

Because these Longton Hall pieces are confined to bankrupt stock, it is natural that they should be amongst the rarest of all transfer-printed ceramics. Another slightly larger baluster-shaped mug has a three-quarters length portrait of *William Pitt*, first Earl of Chatham (1708–78) (Plate 144). This is based on a mezzotint by Richard Houston (1721?–75), a pupil of John Brooks, after a painting by William Hoare (1707?–92), a founder member of the Royal Academy. The mug is inscribed: 'The Right Honble Wm Pitt Esqr. One of His Majesty's principal Secretaries of State, And One of His most Honble Privy Council.' It probably dates from before his resignation as prime minister on 5 October 1761. Sadler and Green are known to have used this printing plate on an enamel plaque.[4] Mention has already been made of another piece, a teapot with metal spout, carrying the print *The Courted Shepherdess*, which some authorities believe was made at Longton Hall (Plate 62, and see page 132).

J. WARBURTON, NEWCASTLE-UPON-TYNE

There exists an unusual creamware teapot thay may well now be unique. This carries a version of *The Liverpool Birds* that seems very probably to have been the work of Sadler and Green, and the publishing imprint is 'J. Warburton N. C. Tyne' (Plate 145). This poses a problem of identity, for there were two contemporary J. Warburtons at Newcastle-upon-Tyne. A John Warburton in the 1740s opened a pottery at Carr Hill on the then Durham side of the River Tyne, and about two and a half kilometres (one and a half miles) south of the city. He is known to have made earthenware, and to have had a warehouse at Quayside, Newcastle-upon-Tyne.

The second was a Joseph Warburton of the South Shore Pot House, also on the Durham side of the river, and like that of John in what is now the town of Gateshead. From advertisements he inserted in the local paper he is known to

[4] E. Stanley Price, op. cit., pl. 16.

144 *Queen Charlotte*: on MUG of porcelain, by LONGTON HALL. 121 mm (4.7 in) high
   Engraved by Thomas Billing and printed in black by Sadler and Green, a year
   after the closure of the factory. Imprint 'J. Sadler Liverpl.'. 1761. And *William
   Pitt*: on a MUG of porcelain by LONGTON HALL. 153 mm (6 in) high
   Based on an engraving by Richard Houston, and printed in black by Sadler and
   Green. 1761–2. *See page 218*
   Sotheby Parke Bernet and Company Limited
145 *Liverpool Birds*: on a TEAPOT of creamware by JOHN (or JOSEPH) WARBURTON,
   NEWCASTLE-UPON-TYNE. 110 mm (4.3 in) high
   Printed in deep grey-brown. Imprint 'J. Warburton N.C.Tyne'. 1760–9. *See page
   218*
   Royal Pavilion, Art Gallery and Museum, Brighton

have operated there between 1757 and 1769.[5] He was both a manufacturer and a merchant.

It is impossible to be certain which of these two J. Warburtons was responsible for having the teapot transfer printed, but Joseph, because he had wider connections, is the more probable.

SALT-GLAZED WARES

By the time that transfer printing was developed the manufacture of salt-glazed tableware was in a rapid decline. Mostly its manufacture had ceased by 1760, although it lingered on for a time at some factories, as for example at Leeds. It is unfortunate that there are no recorded examples of transfer-printed salt-glazed wares that can be positively attributed to a particular factory. As for the printing, it seems certain that this can only be the work of Sadler and Green. The other transfer printers in Liverpool and Staffordshire had not started until salt glazing of tablewares had come to an end. Specimens that have survived are amongst the most attractive of eighteenth-century transfer printing.

Illustrated is a scalloped-edged plate with a charming print, *Le Marchand d'Oiseaux* (Plate 146). This is copied from an engraving by J. Daullé after François Boucher (1703–70), and is printed in Venetian red. Another example shows *Dido and Aeneas Sheltering from the Storm* (Plate 147). It is a copy in mirror image of an engraving by G. Scotin, of a painting by Hubert François Gravelot (1699–1773), the one-time pupil of François Boucher. There is little hope that it will ever be known for certain where such examples were manufactured. Liverpool is a very natural supposition, and much more probable in those very early days than Staffordshire.

It has been suggested, in the author's opinion without any real grounds, that some salt-glazed plates were printed at Battersea, but the arguments against porcelain having been printed there apply equally forcefully to salt-glazed stonewares. There is, however, record of a print having being found on a piece of salt-glazed stoneware, thought to have been taken from a printing-plate used for the decoration of enamels.

DELFTWARE VESSELS AND TABLEWARE

Transfer printing was done on delftware other than tiles, but it is even harder to come by today than similarly decorated salt-glazed stoneware. All of it probably originated in Liverpool, where in the middle of the eighteenth century there were at least ten potteries manufacturing delftware. Similar difficulties attend the attribution of delftware as they do salt-glazed ware, and

---

[5] *Newcastle Journal*, 12 November 1757 and 4 March 1769.

146 *Le Marchand d'Oiseaux*: on PLATE of salt-glazed stoneware, with scalloped, indented and diaper-moulded condiments-rim. 230 mm (9 in) diameter
Engraved from another by J. Daullé, after François Boucher, and printed in Venetian red. 1756–60. *See page 220*
Stoke-on-Trent Museum

147 *Dido and Aeneas Sheltering from the Storm*: on PLATE of salt-glazed stoneware, with indented and diaper-moulded condiments-rim. 185 mm (7.3 in) diameter
Engraved in mirror image from an engraving by G. Scotin, after François Gravelot. Printed from worn plate in lilac colour. 1756–60. *See page 220*
Stoke-on-Trent Museum

again for the same reasons all that is transfer-printed was probably done by Sadler and Green. Illustrated is a plate with a popular print of the period, *The Tythe Pig*, about which there are no doubts as to the printer, for it has the imprint 'Sadler, Liverp' (Plate 148). The design is based on an engraving by Louis Peter Boitard.

An extremely rare transfer print on a delftware plate is a head and shoulders portrait of Admiral Edward Boscawen (1711–61), based on an engraving by Simon Ravenet, after a portrait by Sir Joshua Reynolds (Plate 149). Boscawen was made an Admiral of the Blue three years before he died, and as the plate does not appear to be a posthumous, commemorative one it must date from between 1758 and 1761.

CONTINENTAL FACTORIES

Although on-glaze transfer printing was primarily an English form of ceramic decoration, the process was also used in France in the closing years of the eighteenth century, and it is thought that a limited amount was carried out in Sweden and Switzerland. In the first quarter of the nineteenth century production on the continent seems to have been confined to one or two factories in France and Germany—and then it was underglaze. Continental transfer printing has been little studied, and information is scarce.

It is recorded that the process was used on glazed wares made at Rörstrand (1726–1926), on the mainland, two kilometres (one and a half miles) north-west of the centre of Stockholm, as well as on glazed pieces from Marieberg (1758–1788), on the island of Kungsholm, two kilometres west of the city centre. In the eighteenth century the first named factory made faience and creamware, while Marieberg made faience, creamware and porcelain. Transfer-printed decoration in black is stated to exist on faience from both factories. Transfer printing in black was also practised on the faience and creamware produced at the Swiss factory of Zürich (1763–c.1890).

Considerably more is known of the French use of the process, which it seems was probably introduced to that country by two Englishmen. On-glaze transfer printing was certainly carried out on creamware made at Creil, forty-eight kilometres (thirty miles) north of Paris, on the River Oise, in the department of Oise. Here a very good-quality creamware was made from about 1794. In the early years of the nineteenth century the pottery was taken over by Clark, Shaw et Cie, of Montereau. This is in the department of Seine et Marne, at the confluence of the rivers Aube and Yonne, sixty-two kilometres (thirty-eight and a half miles) south-east of Paris. This latter concern had been opened in 1774, as its name suggests, by two Englishmen, William Clark and George Shaw, who were two of a number of potters who emigrated to France in the eighteenth century to found potteries.

Illustrated is a plate made at Creil, with an on-glaze transfer print showing

148 *The Tythe Pig*: on a PLATE of delftware, LIVERPOOL. 205 mm (8 in) diameter
Printed in deep brown-black by Sadler and Green. Imprint 'Sadler Liverpool'.
1756–60. *See page 222*

149 '*Admiral Boscawen*': on a PLATE of delftware, LIVERPOOL. 222 mm (8.7 in)
diameter
Engraved after another by Simon Ravenet, published in 1757, after Sir Joshua
Reynolds P.R.A. Printed in deep brown-black. 1758–61. *See page 222*
Merseyside County Museums

Magius upbraiding his cowardly troops (Plate 150). It portrays an incident in 218 BC, in the second Punic war, and is entitled '*Magius Reproche Aux Campaniens Leur Lacheté. An de Rome 536*'. The talented etching with a little over-engraving is printed in Payne's grey, as is the grapevine border, which was etched to fit this eact size of plate without a break. The overall colour of the very smooth body is ivory, and the uncrazed glaze is quite colourless. The plate is back-marked 'Creil', impressed from five separate letter-punches. The printing was carried out by Stone, Coquerel et Le Gros of Paris, who in a printed mark on the back describe the process as patented, and themselves as decorators of porcelain and earthenware. The probable date of the piece is between 1794 and 1796, because in a very short space of time the factory was doing its own similar grey transfer printing, but underglaze. Later pieces carried quite magnificent etchings, by the same hand, of early French history. Naturally on these there are no transfer printers' back-marks, and the impressed factory mark, 'CREIL', is made from a single punch.

REPRODUCTIONS AND FAKES

The collector of on-glaze transfer-printed wares is fortunate, as so far the market is comparatively free from fakes. This is due to the fact that the cost of commissioning an etched and engraved copper plate from a competent artist, to print one or two fakes, is such as to bring their price nearly up to today's value of an original. If a quantity of impressions is taken from a reproduction plate, this would defeat the whole object, by reducing the rarity value, as well as immediately inviting suspicion.

The only twentieth-century copies of eighteenth-century transfer prints known to the author are those of the New Chelsea Porcelain Company (Plates 28 and 29). These were most honestly produced, having clear marks as well as new imprints to the engravings. However in the hands of the faker all these marks, without too much difficulty, can be removed, and imitation eighteenth-century marks added. The differences of body and glaze are then the only protection for a prospective purchaser. Unexpectedness, and consequent excitement on the part of the collector, coupled with those well-tried strategies of the fraudulent, dust and poor light, can contribute to a foolhardy purchase.

Potentially the greatest dangers lie in the reuse of eighteenth-century printing plates, but by good fortune these all seem to be in the keeping of responsible persons and organizations, who can be relied upon to take adequate precautions should their re-employment ever arise.

150 '*Magius Reproche aux Campaniens leur Lacheté*' : on PLATE of off-white creamware by CREIL POTTERY. 246 mm (9.7 in) diameter
Finely etched and printed in Payne's grey by Stone, Coquerel et Le Gros. The perfectly fitted printed border has no joins. Impressed 'Creil' from separate letter-punches, and printed Stone, Coquerel et Le Gros badge. 1794–6. *See page 224*

UNATTRIBUTED PIECES

Ten free-lance transfer printers in Staffordshire and Liverpool have been listed. Apart from those factories already considered, any of the scores of remaining potters in Staffordshire, Derbyshire, Lancashire, Yorkshire and the North East were free to use the services of these specialist decorators, and no doubt many did so. It is therefore inevitable that there are a great many pieces which today it is impossible to attribute with any certainty. Although such pieces can be vexatious, ceramics would be a much less interesting subject if all specimens were marked.

An unattributed example, which carries prints from plates by an engraver unfamiliar with the sea, is a small creamware beaker of overall pale-reseda colour, with pale grass-green finely crazed glaze. It has a thick vertical footrim, and the base is pitted with black foreign matter. The main print, *'Poor Jack'*, has under it the rhyme 'The sweet little Cherub that sits up aloft, Will look out a good birth for POOR JACK' (Plate 151). It is passably well etched and engraved, but no British ship would ever fly the Union flag, which incidently is pre-1801, from the mizzen-topmast-head. On the opposite side of the beaker is *East Indiaman Before the Wind*, which is rigged in a manner of no ship which has ever sailed the seven seas (Plate 152). The mizzen gaff carries at its peak a yard from which a square sail is set, which seems to be controlled from an inconceivable spar projecting at the stern. The rigging of this ship should be compared with that of a similar, but correctly rigged, East Indiaman shown on a Liverpool transfer print (Plate 79), as well as the print of a *Naval Sloop*, with exactly the same errors of rigging, on the Thomas Wolfe jug (Plate 101). It is possible that this piece is of south Yorkshire origin, perhaps from the Castleford Pottery, which was founded in 1786, five kilometres (three miles) north of Pontefract.

Another piece with a print from a plate by an engraver unfamiliar with the sea is a 'Liverpool'-shape jug, which has on one side the familiar *Frigate on the Starboard Tack*. In this case if the pennant and ensign are correctly shown, the ship is sailing impossibly close to the wind (Plate 153). On the other side is an unusual picture *'Sweet Poll of Plymouth'* (Plate 154). The verse reads:

> Our Anchor weigh'd for sea we stood
> > The Land we left behind
> Her Tears then swell'd the briny flood
> > Her sighs increased the Wind
> And have they torn my Love
> > And is he gone she cried?
> My Polly sweetest flower of all
> > She languished droop'd and died.

This is not the usual *Sailor's Farewell* theme, but is a copy of one of the engravings by Thomas Stothard, R.A. (1755–1834), illustrating a poem about the press gang. Sweet Poll's young lover was one of the hundreds that 'were torn from pleasures and occupations, and places of amusement were not privileged. The theatres were thrown into riotous confusion as the performances were cleared of the physically fit, and the way to the water's edge was a prolonged free fight, the press gang cleaving their course through the seething mass, with their bleeding victims bound by the wrists.'[6] The glaze is lime colour, giving an overall very pale-lime tint to the piece. In fact the body and glaze are identical in appearance to those of the Derby Pot Works; the

---

[6] Whitfield, *Plymouth and Devonport: In Times of War and Peace*, 1900, p. 222.

151 *'POOR JACK'*: on BEAKER of pale reseda-colour creamware, unattributed, but possibly SOUTH YORKSHIRE. 96 mm (3.8 in) high
Printed in ivory black. Dirty pitted base. 1795–1800. *See page 226*

152 *East Indiaman before the Wind*: on reverse of BEAKER in Plate 151
Engraved by someone without maritime experience, as much of the rig is quite impossible. 1795–1800. Cf. *Naval Sloop*, Plate 101. *See pages 174, 226*

153 *Frigate on the Starboard Tack*: on baluster-shape JUG of very pale lime-colour
creamware, unattributed. 186 mm (7.3 in) high
Printed in jet black. 1775–85. *See page 226*

154 '*SWEET POLL OF PLYMOUTH*': on reverse of JUG shown in Plate 153
Printed in jet black. 1775–85. *See page 226*

155 *The Shepherd*: on a flattened-oval TEA CANISTER, with fluted corners and serpentine top, of pale creamware, unattributed. 105 mm (4.1 in) high
Simple engraving printed in ivory black. 1785–95. *See page 231*

156 *Tea Party No. 1* (in mirror image): on other side of TEA CANISTER shown in Plate 155
Printed in ivory black. 1785–95. *See page 231*

157 *Rendezvous à la Mode et Pastorales*: on TANKARD of pearlware, with flared base, unattributed. 120 mm (4.7 in) high
Printed in Vandyke brown, and carelessly over-enamelled in Brunswick green, primrose, deep crimson and chestnut. Pale peacock-blue glaze, uncrazed, and with fulcrum footrim. 1780–5. *See page 232*

glaze however is uncrazed. The shape of jug was in manufacture from about 1775, or earlier, and the potting is not all that good—a Derby failing—so it is possible, but in the author's opinion improbable, that it is a late piece of Derby creamware.

The next example, a silver-shape tea canister, offers even fewer clues, except that the engraving of the prints on it could be by two different hands. It is probably of the period 1785 to 1795, and could be from Staffordshire. On one side is *The Shepherd* in a very direct and unusual style (Plate 155). He is minding only two sheep, instead of the more usual three, and is sitting beneath a single tree with a thick trunk, in place of the customary two thin trees. On the reverse is *Tea Party No. 1* (Plate 156). The overall colour of the piece is pale cream, the printing in ivory black, and the finely crazed glaze is a most unusual pale grey-turquoise, more usually associated with pearlware. The copper plates used were entirely engraved, and the absence of any etching suggests that the engraver could have been a pupil of Thomas Rothwell.

The last example illustrated is a puzzling piece in the extreme. It is a

cylindrical pearlware tankard, with slightly flared base, and the uncrazed glaze
is pale peacock-blue in colour. It carries a large wrap-round print of two
courting couples, *Rendezvous à la Mode et Pastorales*, which is printed in
Vandyke brown from a beautifully engraved copper plate (Plate 157). The
impression is only light, and the whole picture has been carelessly enamelled-
over in four colours. It would seem to date from the 1780s. The simple grooved
strap-handle is little help in attribution, and the only unusual feature is that the
piece has a similar fulcrum footrim to that described earlier on a Herculaneum
tea canister (Plate 124). Unfortunately both the date and the colour of the glaze
preclude the possibility of its having originated at that pottery. Any thought of
its having come from an earlier Liverpool factory is dispelled by the style and
lightness of the engraving, which suggests that it might have emanated from
the Battersea, Bow, Worcester school.

On-glaze transfer printing progressively died from 1770 onwards, and by
1815 had almost vanished. There was however an Indian summer for a
specialized branch: from about 1792 for about thirty-five years a fashion
prevailed for fine stipple-printing on-glaze, known rather imprecisely as 'bat
printing'. This was a form of decoration used by scores of earthenware and
porcelain manufacturers, and is a subject on its own. Line-etched and engraved
plates were almost, but not quite, entirely confined to underglaze transfer
printing. The exception, which occurs to this day, is outline printing for over-
glaze enamelling. This is because the firing-on of the print can take place at the
same time as the firing of the enamels, thereby avoiding the additional expense of
a separate firing.

At the most on-glaze transfer printing had lasted a total of seventy-five
years, and it was not until the factory-produced, dry, lithographic transfer was
invented, in the last quarter of the nineteenth century, that printed decoration
once more was applied over the glaze.

POSTSCRIPT

The discovery of unrecorded Robert Hancock designs is always of interest but alas, as time passes, is becoming more and more infrequent. While the present volume was with the printers, just such a piece of good fortune occurred. A Worcester sparrow's beak jug was discovered with a previously unknown print, *The Aquatic Folly*, printed in deep amethyst (Plate 158). This transfer has been over-enamelled in a very similar manner to the saucer-dish in Colour Plate B. The enamels are from the same palette, except that coerulean blue has been added, and dark-drab and grey-salmon-pink omitted. The engraving, as in the case of the saucer-dish, is completely shaded, and was intended for monochrome use. Aesthetically, it would have been more pleasing uncoloured. For the purpose of record the opposite side carries an extremely rare transfer, *The Bather*, similarly printed and over-enamelled (Plate 159).

158 *The Aquatic Folly*, previously unrecorded design by Robert Hancock: on
CREAMER with sparrow's beak spout, of steatitic porcelain by WORCESTER
PORCELAIN COMPANY. 110 mm (4.3 in) high
From etched and engraved plate, intended for monochrome decoration,
transferred in deep amethyst, and heavily over-enamelled in terracotta, primrose,
verdigris, plum, tawny, grey-ultramarine and coerulean blues. Heightened in
gold, with gold edge to spout and inverted panache on handle. 1760–65. *See page*
233

159 *The Bather:* on opposite side of CREAMER in Plate 158
Printed and enamelled in the same colours. 1760–5. *See page 233*

GLOSSARY OF COLOUR TERMS USED

Note: Broad definitions, such as blue, brown, red, etc., are used generally, and have no reference to precise hues.

	Munsell		British Standards
Creamware, Surface Colours			
Biscuit	5 YR	8/4	2 – 030/2660
Pale biscuit	8.75 YR	8/2	08 B 17/4800
Off-white	10 YR	9.25/1	08 B 15/4800
Cane	2.5 Y	9/3	367/381C
Parchment	2.5 Y	9.25/1	
Pale cream	5 Y	9/2	10 C 31/4800
Pale manilla	5 Y	9.25/4	4 – 052/2660
Ivory	5 Y	9.25/1	10 B 15/4800
Pale reseda	10 Y	9/1	
Very pale lime	2.5 GY	9/1	
Creamware, Glazes			
Pale straw	5 Y	8.5/4	
Pale canary	5 Y	9/8	
Buttercup	6.25 Y	8.5/13	10 E 53/4800
Primrose	7.5 Y	9/4	
Pale olive	10 Y	8/4	
Reseda	10 Y	8/2	
Pale reseda	10 Y	9/1	
Pale lime	2.5 GY	8/2	12 B 17/4800
Lime tinted	2.5 GY	9/1	
French grey	5 GY	8/1	

	Munsell		British Standards
Creamware, Glazes *continued*			
Pale eau-de-Nil	5 GY	9/1	12 B 15/4800
Pale grass-green	7.5 GY	7/4	
Pearlware, Glazes			
Grey-peacock	5 BG	6/4	
Pale grey-turquoise	5 BG	6.5/2	
Turquoise tint	5 BG	8/2	
Pale saxe-blue	7.5 BG	6/2	7 – 077/2660
Ice blue	5 B	8/4	7 – 082/2660
Earthenware, Glazes —as under Blue			
Black and Grey			
Jet black			
Ivory black	N	1	642/381C
Silver grey	N	9	9 – 093/2660
Graphite grey	10 B	3/1	671/381C
Deep Payne's grey	7.5 B	2/1	18 B 29/4800
Payne's grey	7.5 B	2.5/2	633/381C
Lead	2.5 G	3/1	635/381C
French grey	5 GY	6/1.5	630/381C
Dark drab	7.5 Y	2/2	437/381C
Ash-grey	5 Y	4/0.5	10 A 11/4800
Deep brown-black	8.75 YR	2/2	08 B 29/4800
Deep grey-brown	5 YR	1/2	
Grey-brown	5 YR	3/1	436/381C
Buff and Cream			
Biscuit	5 YR	8/4	2 – 030/2660
Deep stone	10 YR	7/4	
Pale stone	10 YR	8/2	3 – 035/2660
Stone	10 YR	9/3	
Beige	1.25 Y	7.5/4	
Marjoram	2.5 Y	6/4	
Naples yellow	2.5 Y	8/4	
Pale beige	2.5 Y	8/3	
Deep cream	2.5 Y	8.5/8	353/381C
Cane	2.5 Y	9/3	367/381C
Putty	4 Y	9/2	

	Munsell		British Standards

Orange and Yellow

Deep orange	2.5 YR	5/16	
Orange	2.5 YR	6/14	557/381C
Salmon	2.5 YR	7/6	447/381C
Deep chrome	6.25 YR	6/14	368/381C
Ochre	10 YR	6.5/8	359/381C
Naples yellow	10 YR	7/6	08 C 35/4800
Pale chrome	10 YR	7.5/12	356/381C
Pale ochre	2.5 Y	7/6	
Lemon	2.5 Y	8/12	355/381C
Deep cream	2.5 Y	8.5/8	353/381C
Raw umber	5 Y	3/4	10 C 39/4800
Biscuit	5 Y	6/6	
Stone	5 Y	8.5/4	10 C 33/4800
Canary	5 Y	9/14	309/381C
Buttercup	6.25 Y	8.5/13	10 E 53/4800
Primrose	7.5 Y	9/8	310/381C
Mimosa	7.5 Y	9.5/10	

Brown

Deep violet-brown	7.5 R	2/4	449/381C
Deep rust	7.5 R	2.5/6	473/381C
Red oxide	10 R	2.5/6	446/381C
Terracotta	10 R	4/8	444/381C
Chestnut	2.5 YR	5/8	
Pale sienna	2.5 YR	5/5	2 – 032/2660
Vandyke brown	5 YR	1/6	
Burnt umber	5 YR	2/4	412/381C
Tobacco	5 YR	3.5/6	489/381C
Golden brown	5 YR	4/8	414/381C
Tawny	7.5 YR	3/6	411/381C
Yellow-ochre	7.5 YR	4.5/6	410/381C
Dull yellow-ochre	7.5 YR	5.5/6	360/381C
Dark oak	10 YR	2.5/4	499/381C

Red

Carmine	2.5 R	5/12	
Deep crimson	5 R	2.5/12	540/381C
Alizarin crimson	5 R	3.5/16	538/381C

	Munsell			*British Standards*
Red *continued*				
Rose madder	5	R	4/8	
Grey salmon-pink	5	R	7/4	
Maroon	7.5	R	1/4	541/381C
Deep alizarin-crimson	7.5	R	3/10	04 D 45/4800
Cadmium red	7.5	R	4.5/16	537/381C
Rust red	7.5	R	5/8	1 – 023/2660
Cardinal red	8.75	R	5/17	593/381C
Deep Venetian-red	10	R	2/5	448/381C
Venetian red	10	R	3/8	445/381C
Vermilion	10	R	5/16	592/381C
Shrimp	10	R	8/2	04 B 17/4800
Salmon	2.5	YR	7/6	447/381C

Pink and Violet				
Purple	10	PB	3/8	22 D 45/4800
Deep lavender	10	PB	5/6	22 C 37/4800
Deep grey-violet	5	P	3/3	0 – 014/2660
Deep amethyst	5	P	4/8	
Pale grey-violet	5	P	4/6	
Grey-violet	5	P	4/4	
Pale violet	5	P	6.5/6	797/AMD.467
Deep violet	7.5	P	3/7	796/381C
Grey-lilac	7.5	P	4/4	
Violet	7.5	P	5/7	
Lilac	7.5	P	6/6	
Deep red-violet	10	P	3/8	
Crimson-violet	2.5	RP	6/7	
Mars violet	5	RP	2/4	
Plum	5	RP	3/6	
Magenta	5	RP	4/12	
Deep cyclamen	5	RP	5/10	
Lavender	5	RP	6/2	
Grey-cyclamen	5	RP	7/6	
Puce	7.5	RP	3/6	02 C 39/4800
Bright cyclamen	7.5	RP	3/12	
Deep rose	7.5	RP	4/10	
Red-violet	7.5	RP	4/7	
Bright puce	7.5	RP	5/8	
Rose-du-Barry	7.5	RP	5/6	02 C 37/4800
Deep puce	10	RP	3/8	8 – 092/2660
Rose pink	10	RP	5/8	8 – 091/2660

	Munsell		*British Standards*
Blue			
Pale turquoise	5 BG	7/4	102/381C
Pale grey-turquoise	5 BG	6·5/2	
Turquoise tint	5 BG	8/2	
Peacock	5 B	3.5/4	103/381C
Coerulean	7.5 B	6/6	7 – 084/2660
Prussian blue	2.5 PB	3/7	109/381C
Mandarin blue	2.5 PB	4/10	107/381C
Saxe	2.5 PB	5/6	
Paris blue	5 PB	2/4	
Pale cobalt	7.5 PB	3.5/12	166/381C
Bright cobalt	7.5 PB	4/16	
King's blue	5 PB	4.5/10	175/381C
Sky blue	5 PB	7/6	
Midnight blue	7.5 PB	1/4	106/381C
Ultramarine	7.5 PB	2/14	
Oxford-blue	7.5 PB	2/6	105/381C
Grey-ultramarine	7.5 PB	2.5/10	108/381C
Royal blue	7.5 PB	2.5/8	110/381C
Powder blue	7.5 PB	5/10	
Indigo	8.75 PB	3/8	
Green			
Bronze green	2.5 GY	3/4	223/381C
Grass	7.5 GY	4.5/8	218/381C
Pale olive	7.5 GY	7/4	216/381C
Leaf	7.5 GY	7/6	
Apple	7.5 GY	8/8	
Deep grey-green	10 GY	3/2	5 – 061/2660
Pale Brunswick-green	10 GY	3.5/6	225/381C
Grey-green	10 GY	5/2	
Eau-de-Nil	10 GY	9/2	6 – 069/2660
Terre verte	2.5 G	3/5	267/381C
Pale emerald	2.5 G	6.5/8	14 E 51/4800
Deep Brunswick-green	5 G	2/2	
Grey-emerald	5 G	4.5/7	228/381C
Emerald	5 G	5/10	14 E 53/4800
Verdigris	5 G	5.5/6	280/381C
Viridian	5 BG	5/8	
Aquamarine	5 BG	7/4	111/381C

BIBLIOGRAPHY

This is as comprehensive a bibliography as has been found possible, but some articles listed are only of indirect relevance.

PRINTING

Alfred Whitman, *The Print-Collector's Handbook*, London, 1901
Processes and Schools of Engraving, Trustees of British Museum, 1923
David Bland, *A History of Book Illustration*, London, 1958
S. W. Hayter, *About Prints*, London, 1962
Michael Twyman, *Printing 1770–1970*, London, 1970
Anthony Gross, *Etching, Engraving and Intaglio Printing*, London, 1970
Bryan Allen, *Print Collecting*, London, 1970

TRANSFER PRINTING

John Hodgkin, 'Transfer Printing on Pottery. Part I—John Sadler, the Inventor', *The Burlington Magazine*, London, December, 1904
John Hodgkin, 'Transfer Printing on Pottery. Part II—A Catalogue of Liverpool Tiles', *The Burlington Magazine*, London, January, 1905
William Turner, *Transfer Printing on Enamels, Porcelain and Pottery*, London, 1907
J. A. G. Watson, 'Liverpool Delft Transfer Tiles', *The Connoisseur*, London, November, 1924
J. A. G. Watson, 'A Rare Liverpool Transfer Tile', *The Connoisseur*, London, January, 1925
J. A. G. Watson, 'Some of the Less Known Liverpool Transfer Tiles', *The Connoisseur*, London, May, 1927

Bernard Rackham, 'Porcelain as a Sidelight on Battersea Enamels', *English Porcelain Circle Transactions*, V.4, London, 1932

Aubrey J. Toppin, 'Notes on Janssen, and the Artists of the Battersea Factory', *English Porcelain Circle Transactions*, V.4, London, 1932

Aubrey J. Toppin, 'Robert Hancock and his Sons', *English Ceramic Circle Transactions*, V.1, part 2, London, 1934

Newman Neild, 'Early Polychrome Transfer on Porcelain', *English Ceramic Circle Transactions*, V.1, part 3, London, 1935

W. H. Hughes, 'Authorship of some Designs on Porcelain and Enamels and Robert Hancock's Connection with Battersea and Bow', *English Ceramic Circle Transactions*, V.1, part 3, London, 1935

Aubrey J. Toppin, 'The Will of Henry Delamain, The Dublin Potter', *English Ceramic Circle Transactions*, V. 2, part 8, London, 1942

W. B. Honey, 'Limerick Delftware', *English Ceramic Circle Transactions*, V.2, part 8, London, 1942

Cyril Cook, *The Life and Work of Robert Hancock*, London, 1943

Aubrey J. Toppin, 'Battersea: Ceramic and Kindred Associations', *English Ceramic Circle Transactions*, V. 2, part 9, London, 1946

E. Stanley Price, *John Sadler, a Liverpool Pottery Printer*, private, 1948

Aubrey J. Toppin, 'The Origins of some Ceramic Designs', *English Ceramic Circle Transactions*, V.2, part 10, London, 1948

Cyril Cook, 'The Art of Robert Hancock', *English Ceramic Circle Transactions*, V.3, part 1, London, 1951

Geoffrey Godden, 'Derby Pot Works, Cockpit Hill', *English Ceramic Circle Transactions*, V.3, part 4, London, 1955

Cyril Cook, 'Ravenet and his Work at Battersea', *English Ceramic Circle Transactions*, V.3, part 4, London, 1955

Cyril Cook, *Supplement to the Life and Work of Robert Hancock*, private, 1955

G. W. Capell, 'Some Transfer-Printed Pieces,' *English Ceramic Circle Transactions*, V. 3, part 5, London, 1955

Geoffrey Godden, 'Chinese Porcelain, Transfer-printed in England', *English Ceramic Circle Transactions*, V.4, part 2, London, 1957

Bernard Watney, 'The Origins of some Transfer-Prints on two Derby Mugs decorated by Richard Holdship', *English Ceramic Circle Transactions*, V.5, part 5, London, 1964

Bernard Watney, 'Engravings as the Origin of Designs and Decorations for English Eighteenth-century Ceramics', *The Burlington Magazine*, London, August, 1966

Bernard Watney and R. J. Charleston, 'Petitions for Patents concerning Porcelain, Glass and Enamels with special reference to Birmingham . . .', *English Ceramic Circle Transactions*, V.6, part 2, London, 1966

E. N. Stretton, 'Thomas Rothwell, Engraver and Copper-plate Printer, 1740–1807, *English Ceramic Circle Transactions*, V.6, part 3, London, 1967

J. Howell, 'Transfer-printing on Lowestoft Porcelain', *English Ceramic Circle Transactions*, V.7, part 3, London, 1970

Eric Benton, 'John Brooks in Birmingham', *English Ceramic Circle Transactions*, V.7, part 3, London, 1970

Roberto Bondi, 'La Decorazione a Riporto Nella Produzione Primitiva di Doccia', *Faenza*, V.57, Florence, 1971

Bernard Watney, 'Origins of Designs for English Ceramics of the Eighteenth Century', *The Burlington Magazine*, London, December, 1972

Bernard Watney, 'Notes on Bow Transfer-printing', *English Ceramic Circle Transactions*, V.8, part 2, London, 1972

Anthony Ray, 'Liverpool Printed Tiles' (with a fully illustrated catalogue), *English Ceramic Circle Transactions*, V.9, part 1, London, 1973

Anthony Ray, 'Liverpool Printed Tiles—some further Notes', *English Ceramic Circle Transactions*, V.9, part 2, London, 1974

Bernard Watney, 'The Origins of some Ceramic Designs', *English Ceramic Circle Transactions*, V.9, part 3, London, 1975

E. Norman Stretton, 'Liverpool Engravers and Their Sources,' *The Connoisseur*, London, August, 1976

Catalogue of Transfer-Printed English Ceramics, and Printed and Painted Enamels (property of the late Sir William Mullens), Sotheby Parke Bernet and Company, London, 22 February, 1977

Emmeline Leary and Peter Walton, *Transfer-printed Worcester Porcelain at the Manchester City Art Gallery*, Manchester, 1977

Mrs D. W. Bridges, 'Sadler Tiles in Colonial America', *English Ceramic Circle Transactions*, V.10, part 3, London, 1978

GENERAL

Simeon Shaw, *History of the Staffordshire Potteries*, Hanley, 1829

Hugh Owen, *Two Centuries of Ceramic Art in Bristol*, London, 1873

William Chaffers, *Marks and Monograms on European and Oriental Pottery and Porcelain*, London, 1874

Llewellynn Jewitt, *The Ceramic Art of Great Britain*, London, 1878

L. M. Solon, *The Art of the Old English Potter*, London, 1885

William Burton, *Porcelain, Its Art and Manufacture*, London, 1906

G. Woolliscroft Rhead and Frederick Alfred Rhead, *Staffordshire Pots and Potters*, London, 1906

Oxley Grabham, *Yorkshire Potteries, Pots and Potters*, York, 1916

W. J. Pountney, *Old Bristol Potteries*, Bristol, 1920

J. Arnold Fleming, *Scottish Pottery*, Glasgow, 1923

M. S. D. Westropp, *Irish Pottery and Porcelain*, Dublin, 1935

The Potteries of Sunderland and District, ed. J. T. Shaw, Sunderland, 1951

Donald C. Towner, *English Cream Coloured Earthenware*, London, 1957

Geoffrey A. Godden, *Encyclopaedia of British Pottery and Porcelain Marks*, London, 1964

Arnold A. Mountford, *Staffordshire Salt Glazed Stoneware*, London, 1971

R. S. Bell, *Tyneside Pottery*, London, 1971

John Thomas, *The Rise of the Staffordshire Potteries*, Bath, 1971

F. H. Garner and Michael Archer, *English Delftware*, London, 1972

Anthony Ray, *English Delftware Tiles*, London, 1974

Donald C. Towner, *Creamware*, London, 1978

Geoffrey Godden, *Guide to English Porcelain*, London, 1978

Transactions of the English Porcelain Circle, Vols. 1 to 4, London, 1928–32.

Transactions of the English Ceramic Circle, Vols. 1 to 10, London 1933–80

Encyclopaedia Britannica

Dictionary of National Biography

TECHNICAL

Paul Rado, *The Technology of Pottery*, Oxford, 1969

INDIVIDUAL POTTERIES AND FACTORIES

Over the last century and a half, many scores of books have been written about specific factories and their products. These are essential for the study of particular potteries and ceramic pieces. The reader is recommended to obtain the last one or two published on a certain factory, when usually a comprehensive bibliography will be found relative to the particular works and its wares.

INDEX